OTHERWORLD

BOOK 1 OF THE INSPECTOR DALTON FILES

ADAIR HART

Editing by Miranda Miller of Editing Realm
Cover by Tom Edwards
Interior design by Colleen Sheehan
Proofreading by Alexa

Published by Quantum Edge Publishing
ISBN: 978-1-7327422-5-3

www.AdairHart.com

To get updates on new books and other notifications, sign up for my mailing list at

www.AdairHart.com/MailingList.aspx

OTHERWORLD

CHAPTER
ONE

Chasing a demigod through the sewers of New York City was not how Inspector Dalton Kingston expected to spend his Saturday. Azua was hard to track and adept at keeping herself concealed. Unfortunately for her, Dalton had been assigned to bring her in for murder. All it took was him getting in range to use his cosmic senses to detect her, then it was a matter of apprehending her.

Evot, Dalton's embedded AI, controlled two servbots, small disk-shaped objects, with a surrounding nanoswarm that morphed into various shapes. She flew in crow form through the sewer, and he appreciated the real-time visual feed he saw in his augmented reality interface, or ARI. She had retrieved the sewer layout and was hot on Azua's tail.

He grimaced as he hustled through the round brick tunnels. The ground slanted on the sides, and a trickle of brown liquid ran down the middle. He did not need to lower his helmet to verify that it probably smelled rancid. It was dark, and rats and roaches scurried as he ran.

His nanotech provided him with a thin layer of nanobots that he controlled. At the moment, he had formed them into an advanced armored suit known as Scoutspectre mode. His helmet allowed him to see in low to no light and provided additional information on the inside faceplate.

The sewers were dangerous. He traveled in the domain of Beezlo, the wererat king. Thankfully, Dalton had not seen any signs of wererat patrols. The Earth Ward, his employer, had good relations with Beezlo, but Dalton did not think Beezlo would care for an unauthorized intrusion into his territory even if it was an Earth Ward inspector. Wererats did not like humans, evolved or otherwise.

Dalton focused his cosmic senses which caused everything around him to slow. He sensed Azua much more clearly now. Between that and Evot's visual feeds, he would catch up to Azua shortly. He had concerns about her moving toward a known wererat checkpoint. It would be heavily guarded, and they would not hesitate to shoot him or her. Her plan remained a mystery, but perhaps she did not know the sewers or what lived in it.

"Azua has entered the checkpoint tunnel," said Evot over comms. "The wererats have ordered her to stop and put her hands up."

"Okay," said Dalton. "I'm almost there."

When he arrived at the end of the hallway, he surveyed the scene. Azua faced the wererats with her hands up, but she peeked back at him for a moment. She wore black clothing, and her bright-purple hat was hard to miss. Her tan skin was also difficult to see due to the orange bandanna across the lower half of her face. Her black combat boots glistened under the checkpoint's spotlights.

At the other end of the corridor stood steel bars, a small guard post behind them. Several wererats pointed machine guns forward.

Dalton suspected they sensed what Azua was. She was a mix of human and Outsider, a class of dimensional beings that crossed over to Earth at some point. Although Outsiders in the past were worshiped as gods, like Odin and Zeus, they sometimes mated with humans and created demigods. Azua was the daughter of Serqet, the Egyptian goddess of scorpions.

One of the wererats stepped out with his gun aimed at her. "I'm Pachua, overguard for this checkpoint. Who are you?"

"I'm Azua, and I'm being hunted by a slayer!"

Pachua aimed at Dalton. "Are you a slayer?"

Dalton raised his hands. "Your senses should tell you I'm not. I'm Inspector Dalton Kingston, Earth Ward. Azua is wanted for several crimes."

"Identification."

Dalton lowered his hands.

"Slowly…" said Pachua.

"I understand," said Dalton. He retrieved his badge wallet and held it out.

Pachua nodded at one of the wererats behind him.

The wererat used a device to shoot a beam at the badge wallet. "It's valid."

"Then this is easy," said Pachua. He walked back behind the bars and closed them.

"What? You're gonna leave me to him?" asked Azua.

Pachua shrugged. "We have a treaty with the Earth Ward. We *don't* have a treaty with you, though. We could shoot you in the leg to make it easier."

She glared at them.

"All yours, Inspector," said Pachua.

Azua faced Dalton. "Why can't you leave me alone?"

Dalton sighed. "Because you killed eight humans, carved them up, then sold them. Your spicy human rinds were in high demand. I wasn't even looking for you specifically. I just followed where the facts led me, and they ended with you."

"Why do you care so much about humans? They're beneath us."

"I'm an evolved human. Your father was human, but you definitely take after your mother."

Azua scowled. "My father was weak. He got what all humans deserve. They're just food."

"No, they're much more than that. Besides, you're half human yourself and it seems a cannibal," said Dalton. He raised a finger. "Your crimes were particularly heinous. You killed a family of three in their remote cabin. They tried to enjoy a short vacation. Instead, you tortured them, and you killed the boy's parents in front of him before cutting off parts of him. That can't stand, and the Earth Ward won't allow it to."

Azua shook her head. "You could let me go. I'll promise to keep my hands clean."

"That's not how this works. You can plead your case to the Earth Ward."

"You know what? I'm not afraid of you," she said. Bone stingers emerged from her wrists. "You say you're human? Oh, sorry, evolved human. Fine. Then die like one."

She charged forward.

Dalton formed his nanoshield on his left forearm. In one continuous motion, he used his right hand to grab his multipurpose handle, or MH, and extended it to form a stun baton.

She jabbed at him.

He blocked and swung out with his baton.

She rolled to the side and jumped away.

Her speed surprised him.

"That all you got?" she asked.

Dalton rushed her.

Azua jumped over him, then pierced his back with one of her stingers.

He grimaced. Thankfully, his super cells would handle the paralyzing poison she injected, but the fight raged inside him. He focused and spun around, bashing her into the wall. With gritted teeth, he dashed forward and stunned her.

She stopped moving.

Dalton scrunched his face and leaned against the wall. Her jump-and-stab-from-behind maneuver had caught him by surprise. It would have been a very different outcome if he did not have his super cells. Apparently, she was not aware of that.

Instead of attacking him, she should have run. That would have given her a chance, but he had his retractable stun gun, or RSG, he used with his right hand. It formed on demand and created a blocky, rectangular structure that wrapped around his fingers. It had a button on top and a small extension in the front.

His stun baton had been set on medium, which used two charges. Light used one, and heavy, three. With one hundred charges on his baton, he had more than enough to deal with Azua.

Evot flew in as two crows and merged into one before morphing into her human form. "You're hurt."

"I'll live. It's her damn poison."

"You said she wouldn't hit you."

Dalton frowned. "Well, I didn't plan on her jumping over me. Plus, she's much faster than her Earth Ward profile suggested."

Evot glanced at Azua. "Not faster than you."

"I know. All right, can you carry her?"

"Of course. The nearest exit topside is half a mile away. We should wait until your super cells have purged the poison. The amount she injected in you would have paralyzed a human for two hours. I calculate with your super cells, you will not be paralyzed, but you will suffer reduced ability for thirty minutes."

Dalton nodded. "That's why you're doing the carrying."

Evot scooped up Azua.

Dalton took a moment to catch his breath. He studied Pachua and his guards. They talked among themselves while pointing. Dalton suspected they were curious as to what was going on. Unfortunately for them, he did not want to be in the sewers any longer than necessary.

When he woke up the next day, Dalton stretched his aching body. Azua had been handed off to the local Earth Ward response team, and he still hurt from the poison she had injected. Although his super cells removed most of it, a portion lingered in his system. It was not hard to see how Azua abducted humans. One shot of her poison, and they would be paralyzed and vulnerable. He grimaced as he sat up. Evot was nowhere in sight.

"Evot?"

She bounded into the room in her gray cat form and jumped onto the bed. "I'm here. Are you feeling better?"

Dalton stretched his arms as he swung his legs to the side. "Well, I'm not dead, so that's a good sign."

She hopped into his lap and laid a paw on his chest. "I will not allow that."

"Thanks," he said, chuckling.

"Of course," she said. She jumped down as he stood.

Dalton got his morning ritual in. He loved the fact he could brush his teeth and shower without worry of where his next meal came from or what might attack him. It had been six months since he arrived to this Earth, and he enjoyed every minute of it. His original Earth had turned into an irradiated wasteland with mutants, so he much preferred this one.

He moved to the balcony of his apartment and gazed below. Data labels from his ARI popped out around people hustling about. It was roughly 7:00 a.m., and the sun smiled at him. The fresh air and sounds of nearby traffic were consistent with what he had come to expect.

His eyes narrowed as he focused on a few people. Daedroulds. It amazed him that they walked in full view of the clueless humans moving around. He suspected most humans would barricade themselves in their houses if they truly understood what existed around them. On the other hand, some would come gunning for nonhumans.

In his first case, he had run into the Faith Militia and their slayers. Their goal was nothing short of the extermination of nonhumans. They had shot him, but thanks to his nanosuit, he survived. On the nonhuman side, he met Hammer, a powerful werebear enforcer, and his werewolf gang. Thankfully, Dalton was able to close the case with only one casualty, but it provided a glimpse into what he would face on this Earth.

Evot jumped up on a nearby table. "Did you want some coffee?"

"Sounds good."

She morphed into her humanoid shell and exited the balcony.

Dalton loved having her around. She had been upgraded to a full AI before he arrived to this Earth, and she continued to learn to work with organics, as she called them. Her acclimation process remained ongoing, and her friendly and warm personality sometimes got her into trouble. As she found out the hard way, not all organics could be trusted.

She returned in her silver one-piece, formfitting suit. Her red hair and pale skin accentuated her green eyes. Although she normally had metallic skin and glowing yellow eyes, most humans would run at the sight of that. She had taken some time to choose a more pleasing appearance and even updated her cat and crow form to make them appear friendlier.

He was protective of her, and she had been his constant companion as an enhanced virtual intelligence for over seventy years. He would help her with whatever she needed in her new life as an AI.

"Did you not want your coffee?" asked Evot.

Dalton cleared his throat and accepted the cup. "Thank you."

"Of course," she said. She peered over the railing. "You like this city."

Dalton smiled. "Yeah, I do. Dr. Snowden and Emily live around here. Plus, the regional Earth Ward command hub is here."

Dalton enjoyed Columbus, Ohio, and he owed everything to Evaran, the space- and time- traveling cosmic being who saved him and brought him here. Dalton referred to his cosmic sensory ability as Evaran-sense since it mirrored Evaran's ability. Dr. Albert Snowden and his niece, Emily, were Evaran's traveling companions, as was V, an artificial intelligence with some cosmic energy who was also Evot's mentor. Dalton possessed a sliver of cosmic energy, the strongest of all exotic ones, thanks to Evaran's ship, the *Torvatta*. Reality was more bizarre than even Dalton had expected.

Evot nodded. "I like hanging out with Evaran and 'the gang,' as they call themselves." She studied Dalton. "You're in pain."

He sighed. "A little. There's still a trace of Azua's poison in me."

"I understand. It should leave your system today."

"Let's hope so."

"I have an observation," she said.

Dalton gestured at her. "Shoot."

"Your cases would be easier with a team. When you traveled with Evaran and the gang, you assisted in taking down the Tenagrin Hegemony, an alien empire that spanned over a thousand systems. That was possible due to teamwork. In your time here, some cases were tougher than expected. I can only help so much, and I do not possess combat abilities. You should form your own gang."

He rubbed his chin. "I've thought about it."

"What about Brad Washington?"

Dalton eyed her. Brad possessed Wildborn energy, which created one-off mutations of humans. His ability manifested in a way that allowed him to talk to technology. An image of Brad with his dark skin and casual wear popped up in Dalton's mind and made him smile.

"You miss talking to him," he said.

She smiled. "He was fun to be around."

He laughed. "So that's your ulterior motive?"

"No, but if you did pick a team, he is one of the more qualified people to join."

Dalton sighed. "I know. These cases aren't getting any easier. My fear is one of your servbots could get smashed, and we've come close to that a few times."

"You're referring to that nasty dwarf who tried to smash me in cat form."

"Yeah, that encounter did cross my mind."

She faced him. "I have a list of qualified people you should vet. They complement the deficiencies exposed on these cases."

"Deficiencies?"

Evot nodded. "I ran several simulations and calculated that you would function better with a team and you possess natural leadership abilities."

She was right. He would be better with a team. Azua might have been taken down much easier and faster, not to mention safer. He wished he could poach some ancient vampires, such as Mikhail, Lord Vygon, and Lord Noskov, who all welcomed him to Earth and provided a safe place to stay until he got on his feet. They were busy with their own vampire stuff, although he knew they would be there for him if he really needed assistance.

"All right. Send me the list, and I'll review it," he said.

"Of course."

He sipped his coffee. In order to have a team, he would need to get some things in place. He also needed to figure out what would have helped in the past, based on the various cases already completed. While most were not as difficult as his first one, some had been challenging even for someone with his abilities.

The Earth Ward possessed advanced stun weapons he did not use since he had his own, but having someone along with them would be beneficial. Evot was right that Brad would be an immense help as well. Although she usually handled all technological issues, he also used her in the field.

The other issue was how many people he should recruit. Brad was probably a given, assuming he would accept. Personality was important, and he easily fit in and then some. Dalton had worked on teams before where cohesion failed due to toxic personalities. That would need to be factored in. Availability was another concern. Even if Dalton found the right group, they might already be committed elsewhere.

He rubbed his temples. This would take some time, and as always, it took a blunt observation from Evot for him to take action. He had come to rely on her assessments since he knew she did it with good intentions. Outside of her, he was alone. Although he visited friends from time to time, he did not expect them to drop what they were doing to go out in the field. If he had a time-traveling ship like the *Torvatta*, where he could drop people off a minute after picking them up, then maybe, but he did not have anything like that.

A servbot jumped out of his upper left arm and formed a crow.

Dalton wrinkled his brow. "Going somewhere?"

Evot's human form nodded. "I will fly around and perform my morning scan of the building exterior while my human form assists you with your team selection."

"All right," said Dalton.

Evot's crow form took off.

He envied her being able to fly around. As a Scoutspectre on a former Earth, which was essentially a space inspector, he had access to advanced technology that approximated flying. He could not use tech like that on Earth unless he wanted to cause a disruption. Thankfully, he was allowed to use what he already possessed and what the Earth Ward had available, but that was it.

He nodded. "Let's get to work forming a team, then."

CHAPTER
TWO

B rad Washington ran his hands over his shaved head. He enjoyed working for the Earth Ward. With his ability to talk to technology, he had been busy the last six months.

He loved the travel aspect of his new job. He used to be hunted for being a Wildborn, but now that he registered as an Earth Ward employee, that issue disappeared. If he had known that two years ago when he crossed over from his cyberpunk parallel Earth, he would have done it sooner.

The outside part of the cafe in Orlando, Florida, bustled with activity. His current job for the local Earth Ward center had been completed, and he decided to relax. It was 1:30 p.m., and he had desired to eat lunch somewhere public. He got a kick out of being able to do that without an extermination android after him.

The primitive technology on this Earth was no match for him. On his former cyberpunk Earth, ruthless security AIs and exterminator androids were common. Although this Earth was a few hundred years from that, he had no doubt they would reach it at some point. Hopefully, they put in some safeguards before then.

Another thing he loved about his job was the company credit card. He normally would not get the deluxe grilled ham and cheese sandwich if he had to pay. He appreciated that this Earth's human population still engaged in social interactions in the real world. Virtual simulations were the norm from his Earth, and the only time humans gathered was when they raged against the AIs.

The casual dress code was a bonus. He wore his black shoes, jeans, and band shirt, and no one cared if you did your job. Although he could talk to technology, the Earth Ward contracted him for simple things, such as figuring out data center attacks or scouring external networks for information. The small size of the Earth Ward technology department seemed strange, given how many things they worked with.

He focused on two guys at different tables. Brad had wanted to enjoy his sandwich in peace and perhaps check out everyone's phones and laptops. However, the two men had no noise filter when they talked.

One looked like he lived in the gym, and an attractive woman sat next to him. He berated her and anyone else who looked over. The other guy talked loudly on his phone as if everyone needed to hear his conversation. The one thing they had in common, besides being disruptive, was their rudeness to the staff.

The guy on the phone went to the bathroom and came back. A quick check on his phone showed that he had taken a dick pic and prepared to send it to someone, perhaps his girlfriend.

Brad smiled. He got the phone number of the gym guy, then made the phone guy send the dick pic to him. Although Brad usually avoided interfering like this, he was done with their nonsense.

The gym guy checked his phone and stood. "What the hell is this?" He tapped at his screen.

The phone guy wrinkled his brow as his cell phone rang.

The men stared at each other.

"Is this your number?" asked the gym guy, shoving his phone forward.

"Uh, yeah…" said the other man.

"What's up, dude?" said the gym guy, puffing out his chest and extending his hands to the side.

Brad laughed as they got into it. Two assholes fighting each other made his day. The sly grins of the staff indicated they enjoyed the show.

One of the female staff stopped by Brad's table. "Need a refill?"

"Yeah, actually. I'll need more for the show."

She smiled. "Those two guys come here every day and stir up trouble. Wonder what they're fighting about?"

Brad shrugged. "No idea, but they deserve each other."

She nodded and took off.

Brad's eyes narrowed at an incoming text message from Dalton. Brad had not seen Dalton or Evot in a while, and they worked in a different department. The message stated that Dalton had someone waiting at the local Earth Ward center to pick Brad up and take him to a meeting if he had time. His curiosity flared up. Nothing was simple with Dalton, and he was by far the most powerful person Brad knew outside of Evaran.

Brad first met Dalton six months ago. Orbit Industries put out a kill contract on Brad, and Dalton not only took them down, but he disabled Hammer, a prominent werebear enforcer, and his werewolf gang. Not to mention that he also defeated an elite Blood Pact unit. It probably helped that Evot was around.

Brad wondered about the meeting topic. He focused and texted back that he had finished his current job and could meet whenever. He smiled when Dalton messaged that Jake Melkins would fly him out. Brad liked Jake, and they had become fast friends, although they did not interact often due to their jobs.

It would be good to reunite with all of them. Perhaps they needed him for a case. He wished he could work with them, as most of his work was solo. Although he got to meet a lot of interesting people, it was not as exciting as he thought it would be. He signaled the server for his check. It was time to see what was going on.

Valerie Simmons rested on her couch in a motel in Austin, Texas. It was 3:00 p.m., and she enjoyed what she called a lazy day. She only had one appointment today, and after that, she would have money to enjoy the rest of the night.

She was a Zikarian, a non-Daedrould vampire, and the only one of her kind in the world. Most vampires possessed an exotic energy called Daedrould, but her species came from another dimension long ago.

She sighed as she recalled arriving on this Earth back in AD 1906. Her group thought they had found paradise with so many humans, then the nonhuman world introduced itself. Encounters were not friendly, and now in AD 2013, she remained the last one of her kind alive. In order to turn someone, three Zikarians were needed, so she had no plans for anything of that nature.

She had mastered the art of assassination, but due to a promise, she stopped that and relied on odd contracts here and there to make money. Cash flow remained tight, but she salivated at the opportunity arriving in thirty minutes. She had broken into the house of the client's ex-wife and copied a hard drive, and the former husband was coming over. The easy job paid a thousand dollars. She even did it in broad daylight while the woman was at work and her kids were in school. Valerie also made a point to sip some wine in the woman's kitchen before leaving. It was a small bonus to her.

The actual copy did not take long, and she had a specialized device that took two hard drives and then copied one to the other. Although the client would be able to boot it up, he would still need to log in. She assumed he had thought of that before asking for her services.

Valerie enjoyed hitting different cities, and sometimes she took on other types of contracts. She liked the roughing-up ones. Most didn't expect a thin, pale woman with black hair and blue eyes to saunter up and kick the crap out of them. She would have thought her jeans, black boots, gray shirt, and tactical jacket would have given them some idea, but most ended up on the ground.

She had thought briefly about joining the movie industry. It cracked her up how humanity perceived vampires. Some myths were accurate, but most were plain wrong. There were also many different types of vampires, each with their own strengths and weaknesses.

She loved garlic and sunlight, but a stake through the heart would kill anyone, including her. She did not sleep in a coffin, but she did drink blood. Hundreds of years ago, vampires resorted to unscrupulous means to obtain blood, but in this era, it was just a swipe away on a phone app. There were even bite bars for the adventurous.

She had learned quickly to navigate the various nonhuman factions. There was definitely a pecking order, with ancient vampires and the Ollikrin nation at the top. She had also encountered many of the more unusual factions, like faeries, dwarves, witches, and mambos.

Outsiders, who crossed over from another dimension like she did, made her wary. Werebears and tree shifters sat at the top there. Outside of that, elementals remained dangerous. There were even demons, such as the Kaz Lodat. They possessed no exotic energy, and she did not know where they came from.

Then there were humans with Wildborn energy, which caused one-off abilities. They scared her, as they usually did not know they were Wildborn. When their powers manifested, they could easily cause a lot of damage.

Some possessed benign abilities, like being able to regenerate or move slightly faster, while others turned bones to mush or, even worse, affected others with their mind. She gave them a wide berth whenever possible, even if their blood generally tasted better. She focused back on the upcoming meeting and decided to get up and freshen up her place.

Thirty minutes later, two knocks sounded on her door.

Valerie hustled over and opened it. She nodded at Chris. He wore a way-too-small blue business suit that did not complement his pudgy build. He looked like he had stepped right out of a corporate office. His fair-skinned face and slicked-back brown hair completed the office look. He was wisened, a term nonhumans gave to humans who knew about the nonhuman world. She verified the area was clear.

"You're on time," said Valerie.

Chris nodded. "Were you expecting me not to be? For what you're doing?"

She smiled. "Come in."

He complied and sat on her couch.

She went to her bedroom and got the hard drive, then came back and sat with it in her hands. "You have the money, I hope."

"One thousand dollars like we agreed," said Chris. He laid some bills on the table.

Valerie counted the money and then handed him the drive. "Here you go."

"Thank you, thank you, thank you!"

She grinned. "I usually don't ask what something is for… but why did you want that?"

Chris sighed. "My messy divorce. She got child support even though *she* cheated on me with a drug dealer. I hired a private investigator, and he mentioned she might be more involved in that area than is known."

"I coulda searched the house for clues."

He shook his head. "I wouldn't be able to prove anything you found without implicating myself. However…she spent a lot of time on the computer before we broke up. I put a key logger on there, which has been collecting her keystrokes for a while. But recently, it wasn't able to send for some reason, but there are logs. I thought I would get the computer in the settlement. That didn't happen." He held up the drive. "I got the next best thing, though, and it's current."

"Better hope she didn't format," said Valerie.

"Nah. She's not tech savvy. I'm just glad you got it."

"I'm damn good at what I do," she said.

"Yeah," said Chris. He licked his lips. "Before I go…I heard that you do bite jobs."

Bite jobs were essentially giving someone, man or woman, an orgasm in exchange for drawing life-nourishing blood. She did do them for the right people. The temporary client's joy was nothing compared to a week's worth of power, at least in her eyes.

"I do, and I'm guessing you're asking."

Chris nodded.

"I'm declining for these reasons. First, your blood is bad. Yes, I can sense it from here. You should visit a doctor as soon as possible. Second, I already have a full list of clients."

He shrugged. "Worth a shot. I mean, you're gorgeous. Maybe we skip the bite part?"

She did not want to tell him the third reason was that she avoided certain personalities and situations, like this one. Some clients became obsessive, and that usually did not work out well. She preferred married men or women since they kept things quiet. Lonely people invited trouble, although she did exceptions for certain personality types.

"No, I'm not interested."

"It's only a few minutes. I just…I really need it," said Chris.

She stood. "You know I'm a vampire and that I'm much faster and stronger than you. I could kill you where you sit within two seconds."

He jumped up and backed away. "Sorry, sorry. I…I know I overstepped."

"Our business is concluded. Leave."

He dashed out the door.

Valerie sighed. Chris was a red flag. She would not underestimate him, though. He had vengeance in his heart, and she needed to move on. The last thing she wanted was to get entangled in his fragile emotional state, something humans tended to succumb to far too often.

Her phone buzzed.

She picked it up and saw a text from Dalton Kingston. Her heartbeat accelerated. The last time she saw him, he saved her from certain death. She promised him she would never kill slayers, humans who hunted nonhumans, and she had kept her word. The message said he was having a meeting and he wanted her there. Someone would pick her up at the local Earth Ward center. Her curiosity got the better of her, and she replied that she would be there.

Valerie enjoyed collecting a grand, but the appointment left a bad taste in her mouth. She focused on Dalton. He mentioned a meeting but did not give details. That was probably on purpose, maybe a security thing. She flipped through the hundred-dollar bills. That would cover her for a few days, but if she was going to meet Dalton, he was paying for dinner.

CHAPTER
THREE

Todd Armani huffed as he split a log in his backyard. He had wanted to get the trailer filled with wood for a while, and it was a nice day out. Rick Westmoreland, his bud, was driving over to watch some movies, and although he lived two hours away, he made the trip once a month. Todd enjoyed whatever time he got with Rick, as he was one of the few to ever stop by. Todd was almost done with the log splitting, then it was time to get the grill out.

He took a moment to survey the back of his rural house in Salem, Indiana, sometimes referred to as Kentuckiana due to the closeness of Kentucky. It sat tucked away in a forest, with a winding driveway to get to it. He enjoyed the privacy. Most did not know he had a stocked bunker and a small underground network on the property. His nearest neighbor lived half a mile away, just the way he liked it.

Although he had grown up in the area, a third of the nearby small town blacklisted him. He used to be a slayer and worked with the Faith Militia in killing nonhumans.

An event six months ago changed all that, and now he kept to himself. The only friends he had were others who had quit slaying. Unfortunately, the Faith Militia had people in various positions of power. He wondered why they had not tried to take him out.

Todd split the next log. His fingers ached, and he decided he had enough wood. A pickup pulled up to the house. The sputtering indicated it was Rick and his beaten-down truck. Todd had offered to help fix it, but Rick took pride in having something last as long as it had. Based on the noise, it might not have much longer.

Todd put away his axe and circled around to the front. The truck's hood was up, and Rick peered at something. He wore camouflage pants, black boots, and a tight black shirt. His red beard was well-trimmed, and his shaved head showed some stubble.

What amazed Todd about Rick was his toughness. He had been known as Executioner, the legendary slayer, and he wore a custom outfit with dual blades, pistols, and an assortment of gadgets. After he departed the Faith Militia, he became the head of a group that welcomed those who had also left. That was hard to do, especially since slayers were often recruited in churches and served in law enforcement.

Rick had been one of the first people Todd reached out to after quitting slaying, and he had been nothing but supportive. It also helped that Rick could call a dozen guys to defend someone, and if he showed up as Executioner, slayers ran.

"You need a new truck," said Todd.

Rick grinned as he stepped back and closed the hood. "Nah. She's just being cranky."

"Yeah, I heard her being that your whole drive up here."

They laughed and slapped hands.

"How you been, brother?" asked Rick.

Todd nodded. "All right. Still feel like I'm adjusting to a new life."

Rick nodded. "I hear ya. How's contract work?"

"Bad," said Todd, laughing. "I did a bouncer gig for a few nights. Paid decent."

"A bit different than the old days."

Todd shrugged. "It's work. As long as I can cover the house and the land, I'm good."

He did not want to disclose his financial troubles. Work remained hard to come by, and anything decent meant a trip to Louisville. Even then, the gigs were usually security related, which often did not pay well. He was between contracts, and it ate at him that this would be the first month where he only worked one gig. And that barely covered the gas for the month, much less food.

"Up for some burgers?" he asked.

Rick walked around to the passenger side and pulled out a case of beer. "Yeah, and I got the beer."

"Mmm, warm beer."

They laughed and went to the back of the house. After stocking the fridge and getting some burgers and hot dogs on the grill, they sat in lawn chairs and relaxed.

Rick lit up a cigar and puffed a few times. "Ahh. I love it out here. It's so isolated. Any trouble?"

"Some," said Todd. "Wolfer passed by a few weeks ago. I gave it a few warning shots."

"A werewolf out here? Slayers must be losing control if that's happening."

Todd sighed. "Or more are leaving like me and you did."

"That'd be nice," said Rick, taking a swig of his beer. "We're getting bigger every day. You should move up near me. We're building a small compound and keeping the area clear of Faith Militia."

"The cult of Rick, or should I say, Executioner. The only requirement to join is you have to own an old, shitty truck."

"Fuck you," said Rick, laughing.

The smell of the grilled meat and the fun of having Rick over made everything seem okay. Todd could forget about his problems and focus on the moment. He looked forward to spending the day watching movies and drinking beer in nice weather.

His phone buzzed.

He ignored it at first, but it buzzed again. Whoever it was, they were persistent. He took a quick peek. His heartbeat shot up. Dalton Kingston asked to meet and stated someone would pick him up at his house if he agreed to come by and listen to a contract proposal.

Todd's pulse raced. He saw what Dalton did to eight slayers. Although he did not kill them, he all but obliterated them. He even took down Hammer, one of the Faith Militia's top targets. Dalton also wore some type of advanced suit that Todd had a hard time believing was real.

"Who is it?" asked Rick.

Todd sighed. "You remember when I quit slaying?"

"Yeah, the trailer park incident. Earth Ward, right?" asked Rick.

Todd nodded. "Well, the guy who laid up eight slayers? He wants to meet and discuss a contract."

Rick sat up. "He also took down Hammer, right?"

"Yep."

"When does he want to meet?"

"Now. He has someone who will stop by if I agree to meet."

Rick looked around. "He has someone coming out here?"

"That's what he said."

"Do I need to suit up?"

Todd ran a hand over his mouth. "Nah, I think we're okay. Dalton is one of the good guys, although he looks like a robot at times. This guy has some advanced tech. It sounds like he has work…"

Rick sighed. "I'm guessing no movies today."

"I hate to bail."

Rick shook his head. "Nah, man. If you can get work, and it pays well, you need to take it."

"Look at you, all wise and stuff," said Todd. He exhaled. "If you want to crash here, you're welcome to. No sense wasting all the beer and food. Just don't pass out naked."

Rick laughed.

Todd replied back to Dalton that he was interested, and Dalton said to pack a bag, then go to a nearby field. "All right. Looks like it's on. I got fifteen minutes to get my shit and meet whoever over there." He pointed.

"In a field?"

"That's what he said."

Rick rubbed his chin. "You sure this isn't a trap of some type?"

"We'll find out, but he isn't that type of person."

Todd hustled inside and grabbed his go bag, which contained clothing, cleaning items, and other miscellaneous things for a short trip. It was not a true bug-out bag, although he had that if he needed it. There were several bags, depending on how long he expected to be out. He made sure he had his handgun and knife. He probably did not need them, but it did not hurt to have them. After switching to his former slayer outfit, he exited the house.

Rick accompanied Todd to the field.

Todd's eyes widened when a ship of some type appeared. A young man stood next to it and waved Todd over.

"What the...?" said Rick. "The Earth Ward has this type of tech?"

Todd shrugged. "Apparently so. All right. I'mma go see what all this is about. I'll be back soon hopefully. If I'm not back by tomorrow, then I probably took the contract. Lock up if you do stay." He tossed Rick a house key.

"Be safe, brother," said Rick. He slapped hands with Todd.

Todd did a final look around and then headed to the ship.

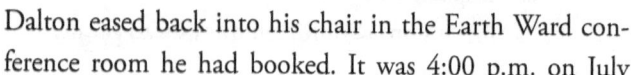

Dalton eased back into his chair in the Earth Ward conference room he had booked. It was 4:00 p.m. on July

16, 2013, and he looked forward to meeting the team he had selected. Jake Melkins, a close friend, had retrieved everyone over the last three days. Brad had been picked up on the fourteenth, Valerie the fifteenth, and Todd earlier today. Each of them was in an individual room, waiting, and he had kept them separate up to this point.

Now it was time to bring them together, throw out a team pitch, and see how they reacted. Evot sat next to him in her human form. She had been a chatterbox as she ran simulations and made predictions. Dalton wanted to get on with the new case he had on his plate, and he did not want to do it solo again.

"Evot, inform our guests to come to this room," he said.

"Of course," she said. A moment later, she nodded. "It is done."

Dalton exhaled and rolled his head. He was used to either joining a team or having Scoutspectres promoted to his. This was new for him. He had completed his research on the three coming and understood their strengths and weaknesses as well as their current status. If they did not agree to join up, then he would have to proceed solo.

Brad Washington was the first to arrive. He wore his usual black shoes, pants, and shirt, which had a music band on the front. His shaved head had stubble on it, but his face was smooth.

"Dalton! Evot," he said as he strode forward.

Dalton extended a hand, and they shook.

Brad hugged Evot. "It's been a while."

"Six months," she said.

"Damn, that has been a while." Brad gestured at Dalton. "I've been tracking your cases. You're tearing things up."

Evot tilted her head. "He hasn't torn anything up."

Brad laughed.

Dalton grinned. "Those were easier cases than the one we did long ago." He motioned for Brad to sit.

"I hear ya," said Brad as he took his seat. "So what's up?"

"I'll get to it here shortly. There's two more coming."

Brad drew his head back. "Really? This'll be interesting."

Valerie Simmons was the next to arrive. She wore jeans, black boots, a gray shirt, and a tactical jacket. Her pale skin was a sharp contrast to Brad's.

"Hey," she said, surveying the room.

Dalton and Evot shook hands with her.

Brad stood and extended a hand. "Brad Washington."

Valerie smiled as she returned the handshake. "The Wildborn from the trailer park."

"Yeah…how'd you know? Oh…you're the Outsider I sensed there!"

"That's me," she said as she took her seat. "This meeting has my curiosity."

"Yeah, me too."

The others sat.

Dalton nodded. "I understand, and we have one more coming. After that, I'll begin." His eyes narrowed. "Is everything okay? I sense your exotic energy is in flux. Hopefully not due to this meeting."

Valerie shrugged. "Just had to deal with an asshole yesterday is all." She shook a hand at him. "Don't worry. I didn't kill him."

"All right," said Dalton.

Todd Armani arrived. He wore black-and-gray camou-flage cargo pants along with a formfitting black shirt that had a camouflage pattern on the arms. A zipper went up from near the middle of the shirt to a neck cover collar. His black hiking boots and general aesthetic were that of slayers Dalton had run into before.

"Hey," said Todd, extending a hand toward Dalton.

Dalton returned the handshake. "I'm glad you came. Please sit, and we can begin."

Valerie eyed Todd. "I remember you."

"The trailer park incident, right?" asked Todd.

She nodded.

"For the sake of this meeting, let's put that to the side."

She shrugged. "No worries here…at least not yet."

Dalton sighed. He did not expect everyone would get along right off the bat, and there was some history between Todd and Valerie.

"All right, as you all know, I invited each of you here to talk about a proposal. However, before I begin, I wanted to introduce everyone," said Dalton. He gestured at them in sequence. "Brad Washington is a Wildborn who can talk to technology. Valerie Simmons is a Zikarian, a non-Daedrould vampire, and Todd Armani is an ex-slayer human. I'm Inspector Dalton Kingston, Earth Ward, and with me is Evot."

She smiled and waved.

"Now, I selected each of you with Evot's help, so I'm going to cut right to the point. I'm forming a team to handle Earth Ward cases. I tend to get the hardest ones out there, and going at it alone is hard. I wanted to extend an invitation to each of you to join my team."

"You took down Hammer and his werethugs. If it's hard for you, it would be insane for us," said Brad.

"I understand. Evot, get them the contracts."

She picked up three envelopes from behind him and distributed them.

"Go ahead and check that out," said Dalton.

He studied them as they each pulled out a packet of information. Their faces told him a lot. Todd's eyes looked like they were going to pop out of his head, while Valerie drew her head back slightly. Brad was all smiles as he read his.

Todd focused on Dalton. "Let me get this straight. We join your team, complete contracts, and split the pay three ways on the contract?"

"That's right," said Dalton.

"You're not taking a cut?"

Dalton shrugged. "I'm covered by the ancient vampires. They handle any funds I require. That's all I need financially."

"You're dedicated."

"I like to think so," said Dalton.

Valerie ran her finger over something in her packet and raised her head. "The Earth Ward would cover all our expenses?"

"Yep," said Dalton.

"And provide us with whatever gear we need?"

Dalton smiled. "Yes."

Todd shook a hand out. "Wait a minute. You mean I'd have access to the Earth Ward armory?"

"Definitely," said Dalton.

"This looks a lot more exciting than what I've been doing," said Brad. He glanced at Dalton. "I appreciate you hooking me up with the initial entry into the Earth Ward, but it's been…routine. I'm all in for tackling something challenging, unless it's me throwing down with some werebears."

Dalton grinned. "I knew I liked you."

They shared a laugh.

He scrutinized Valerie and Todd. They flipped through pages and studied everything with intent. Dalton understood it was a massive change in their lives if they joined his team, but everything in him said this was the right group.

"What questions do you two have?" he asked.

Valerie glanced around the table. "What types of cases are we talking about here?"

Although Dalton could use a small projector cube to display holographic information, he wanted to showcase Evot's abilities. He glanced at her. "Show them."

She extended her hand, palm forward.

A holographic projection shot up of a bar with motor-cycles out front.

Todd slid back in his chair. "What the hell?"

"I'm an artificial intelligence," said Evot. "I can morph into various forms."

"No shit?"

"None that I'm aware of."

Brad laughed.

Todd eyed Valerie and Brad. "That's not strange to either of you?"

Brad shrugged. "I came from a cyberpunk world far more advanced than this."

"What?"

Valerie grinned. "I'm over a hundred years old, and I've seen how fast the nonhuman world has advanced. Same with humanity. No surprise to me."

Todd ran a hand over his mouth and moved his chair back to the table. "Okay...so an AI, a Wildborn, and a hundred-plus-year-old vampire. I already know Dalton has that power armor thing going on."

"Does this bother you?" asked Evot.

"I guess...no. It doesn't. It just caught me off-guard is all."

Evot nodded.

Brad scrutinized the projection. "What're we looking at here?"

"My current case," said Dalton. "I just got it. Pays fifty grand and involves meeting with the Tanner Pack in Waverly, Ohio, a city in the southern part of the state."

Valerie scrunched her face. "The Tanner Pack is a were-gang known for its brutality."

Todd's eyes narrowed. "Yeah, and Waverly has a strong Faith Militia presence, although they're...different. Also, not a lot of wisened there." He gestured at Brad. "They wouldn't like me or you."

"Why?" asked Brad.

"I'm second generation Persian-American and have light-tan skin. Yours is darker. That's not very welcome in those parts."

Brad shook his head. "Well, that sucks." His eyes glowed blue for a moment indicating he was talking to something technological. "That's odd. This case is ongoing there, so it's already started."

Dalton chuckled.

Everyone focused on him.

"I haven't even looked at the case in any great detail, and yet, in less than a minute of showing you it, you all provided details," he said. "Todd, as a wisened and ex-slayer, knows the human world, particularly where it intersects with the nonhuman one. He's far more knowledgeable than most wisened in general. He's also trained in combat with a focus on weapons."

Dalton motioned at Valerie. "You know the nonhuman world, and due to your past, you have a lot of knowledge about power players beyond raw data. You're also well versed in hand-to-hand combat and social engineering."

"Don't I know it," she said, smiling.

Dalton gestured at Brad. "And he's a walking computer. How about you all do this case with me, and if you're good with it, then you can sign the contracts. I'll still honor the split three ways, with all expenses paid."

Todd cocked his head. "Would I still be able to hit the armory?"

"Yeah, and I've got a few things there already for each of you."

Valerie's eyes narrowed. "You assumed we would say yes."

"I was hopeful," said Dalton. "What have you got to lose for a trial run?"

"Our lives if the case turns crazy."

"All cases have a risk. That's why the Earth Ward uses a contract-based system. The payment is geared to the case's difficulty."

Valerie nodded. "Well, I could use fifteen grand or so."

"Same here," said Todd. "Sure beats minimum wage as a bouncer and a temp one at that. Count me in for the trial."

Dalton smiled big. "Great. As Brad mentioned, the case is already live, and I am taking it over. We need to fly to upstate New York to pick up the contract and get additional details, but first, since it's about dinnertime…"

Evot exited the room and then returned with two pizza boxes.

"Hell yeah," said Brad.

Dalton gestured at the pizzas. "Let's eat before we go."

CHAPTER
FOUR

The flight out to the Earth Ward headquarters did not take long. Valerie had already met Jake Melkins, the young man who had picked her up and who seemed to be good friends with Brad. He had sat up front with Jake, while she, Dalton, and Todd resided in the back. The ship reminded her of the interior of a sport utility vehicle except for the wall between the front and back with a door to go between.

Dalton had been informative as he answered questions. She was somewhat uneasy about Todd. He changed since they first met during Dalton's initial solo case on Earth. Valerie did not dwell on the past other than to learn from it. Those who understood her personality said she was cold, but Zikarians possessed a different emotional range than humans or other nonhumans. It was not that she did not care, but she did not receive the same chemical signals during certain emotions.

Brad would be an interesting person to work with. She suspected his confidence was due to his high intelligence. His friendly personality endeared him to others, and he favored blunt truthfulness. The ability to talk to technology fascinated her, and she wondered how Brad worked with Evot.

Valerie liked Evot. Like Brad, she was blunt, maybe due to her being an AI. Valerie suspected Brad and Evot would mesh well.

"We're landing now," said Jake over ship comms.

Valerie peeked out her window and studied the sprawling city in upstate New York. The city's layout intrigued her. In the center resided a massive circular area with a park. Each quadrant off of it contained a specific focus. The Earth Ward headquarters sat in the northeast area. It had a massive campus-like design with no hint of a residential area. The Wild Haven Institute occupied the northwest quadrant. A number of residential areas integrated with its big campus.

The southern quadrants created a town that essentially supported the northern ones. The southwest area focused on nonhumans and the southeast one on wisened. The main roads between each quadrant were packed with businesses and also served as a mixing point between areas. The area as a whole was kept off the radar, and the humans who lived there not only had to be wisened, but they had to qualify skill-wise to do so.

Valerie had thought about moving there at one point, but her rocky relationship with the Earth Ward and their recent installation of a headquarters made her reconsider. This might be an opportunity to get in right with the Earth Ward, and she suspected they would have her take some classes at the Wild Haven Institute. Whatever happened, she trusted Dalton. He was honorable, not a trait she found to be common among others.

The ship landed.

Valerie disembarked with the team into an underground landing area. Apparently, there was a large opening that allowed ships to enter. Easier to keep satellites from spying. The Earth Ward possessed advanced technology to help obscure the area along with control of most major media outlets via the Imperium, a powerful global corporation formed by Outsiders who used to be called gods. Odin ran a tight ship, and he could tell any narrative he wanted.

Their immediate surroundings reminded Valerie of a parking garage except for the massive pillars and other small ships. There were some ground vehicles, but she suspected they came in from a different entry point.

Dalton pointed at a terminal entrance. "For those new to this place, we're going there."

Valerie followed him. Evot used her human form, which did not surprise Valerie. Brad talked to Evot, while Todd kept to himself. He was probably surveying everything, similar to her.

Todd fell back to walk alongside her. "Hey."

She eyed him. "Hey."

"I just wanted to say for the sake of this case, maybe we start fresh?"

Valerie shrugged. "There's no need to worry if I'm upset about our previous encounter. You didn't kill my sister, so I have no fight with you."

"Yeah, but I *was* a slayer at the time."

"But you aren't now. That's what's important. I don't know how you will react to all this, so there's that uncertainty, but I'm willing to try this out."

Todd nodded. "I…that works for me."

Valerie smiled. "Besides, if you want to get in my good graces, help me finish this case and get my split."

"Sounds good. I could really use the cash."

"Same here."

Although Todd did not mention it, she suspected he probably thought this might become a stable source of revenue. She did not need much money, but she preferred to have more of it than not. A few cases with Dalton would set her up for the year. More cases would be stockpiling for a rainy day. She understood the opportunity being afforded to her. Dalton was powerful, and his role allowed him access to the high-paying jobs.

The group entered the terminal and walked into a large concourse.

Valerie sensed other nonhumans around her. The perplexed stares indicated they did not know what she was—not an uncommon reaction. Most vampires were Daedrould and easy to detect. Those looking at her would have no idea she was a Zikarian. Brad got some looks, but almost everyone they passed stared at Dalton. He had some prestige built up.

The large concourse split ended in a hub area with hallways running out on all sides. Apparently, Dalton knew the area well, for he showed no hesitation as he veered off to the left. The smaller hallway they entered had various offices and hallways on the sides.

The Earth Ward uniforms intrigued Valerie. Some wore casual clothing she would expect at a mall, but most wore a uniform that consisted of black pants, a colored shirt with an officer collar, and a light jacket. The shirt's color probably indicated something, and the jackets had patches on them. Dalton wore a gray shirt, with a golden emblem on his black jacket. Perhaps that combination indicated inspectors.

After ten minutes, they reached a foyer area with a large counter. Several Earth Ward personnel stood behind it.

Dalton approached and talked with one of the receptionists, Valerie assumed, and after a moment, they took off to the left.

"Place is a maze," said Brad.

"Yeah, it is," said Valerie.

Todd looked around. "I don't suppose they have a layout of this place to give us."

"They do," said Dalton. "You'll get all that after this meeting. The focus is to talk to the issuer of the contract, then we'll gear up and get anything you might want, such as a layout."

"Sounds good, chief."

Dalton and Todd acted like old friends. She thought Todd might be scared of Dalton after the trailer park incident, but she did not sense fear in Todd. If anything, he was calm, not something she expected from a human in a new situation. Perhaps that was one reason Dalton chose him. She also sensed Todd's blood, and it was better than average.

They arrived outside the office of Case Manager Dakris five minutes later.

Dakris was definitely a Helian name. Helians were an advanced Outsider group that came to Earth thousands of years ago and ran everything until the Earth Ward took their place a few years back. The Helians did not go quietly, and from what Valerie understood, they hated the Earth Ward but were allowed to work for them as part of the transition.

It seemed strange to have to fly out all this way to meet with Dakris, especially with someone like Brad or Evot around. Something about this case must be unique enough to warrant the trip, and Valerie's curiosity had been piqued. It could also be that Dakris wanted to meet Dalton.

Dalton faced them. "So you're aware, Dakris doesn't know I've added you all to my group. There shouldn't be an issue, but if there is, let me handle the talking."

"Works for me," said Todd.

"Yeah, no problem here," said Brad.

Valerie shrugged. "I would have nothing to say anyhow."

Dalton took a breath and then knocked on the door.

Dalton entered the room with the others. He immediately recognized Dakris, who was seated in his blue Earth Ward outfit. His black hair, fair skin, and athletic build were common for Helian males.

The woman sitting on a couch to his right caught Dalton's eye. She wore an Earth Ward outfit, and her patch indicated she was a director. More importantly, she was human. That probably did not sit well with Dakris.

She stood and extended a hand. "Director Kathy Siko-wicz. You can just call me Kathy."

Dalton returned the handshake. "Inspector Dalton Kingston." He pointed at each person in his group. "With me are Brad Washington, Valerie Simmons, Todd Armani, and Evot. They're my team for this case."

Dakris nodded at everyone. "I wasn't aware you had a team."

"Last minute thing," said Dalton.

"Is he allowed to do that?" asked Dakris, glancing at Kathy.

She shrugged. "In our department, not without approval. However, the Inspector Department is different."

Dakris smirked. "Right. Special."

Dalton sensed Dakris did not like the team concept or maybe even Dalton's presence.

Kathy gestured at some chairs and couches around the room. "Please sit. Don't mind me. This case is of particular importance to the Earth Ward, and I'm here to lend any assistance."

The group sat.

Dalton eyed Dakris. "So what's going on? I thought this case was already being handled. Something bad must've happened if Kathy is here."

Dakris sighed. "There's been complications. The special agent we sent out was hurt."

"Who'd you send and to where?"

"We sent Special Agent Maria Guerrara to the Warehouse, a bar in Waverly, Ohio. She was beaten to within an inch of her life, and she's in critical care now."

Dalton rubbed his chin. "Who attacked her?"

Dakris grimaced. "The Tanner Pack runs that place. They're a weregang, and she was a Raskarian vampire. Some things never change. Savages."

Valerie scrunched her brow. "You sent a Raskarian vampire to a weregang hangout?"

"I thought she could handle it."

"Apparently not," said Valerie.

Kathy raised a finger. "Let me clarify the situation a bit. The Tanner Pack does not recognize Earth Ward authority. However, they were open to it recently when several of their group ended up getting murdered and they had no idea who did it." She cleared her throat. "They asked for you to come out and investigate, and in exchange, they would open talks with us. Dakris sent Agent Guerrara instead."

"I see," said Dalton. "Why wasn't I contacted in the first place? Not only was I requested by name, but agents aren't inspectors."

"Special agents have detective training. Contrary to what you might believe, the world doesn't revolve around you," said Dakris.

Dalton bored a gaze through him. "Maybe not, but it sounds like you put someone in harm's way to stroke your ego."

"Damn," said Brad, chuckling.

Dakris glared at Dalton. "Yes…I made a mistake. However, we try to use internal resources before external ones."

Dalton glanced at Kathy. "So the real reason she's here is revealed. Also, inspectors are internal resources; we just have a different organizational and pay structure."

Kathy frowned. "Look…can we get past all the bravado? The case is still active, they still want you, and the case has been bumped up in priority. The Tanner Pack is big in Pike County, as is a local Faith Militia cell. Getting the Tanner Pack on our side is important." She studied Dalton. "Yes, you're an inspector, and I've followed the rise of that arm of our organization. It's still new, though, and we're adjusting to working with them."

"I understand," said Dalton. "Was there any specific reason Maria was attacked?"

"Probably have to fight someone to talk to the pack leader," said Todd.

Everyone stared at him.

He shrugged. "I'm an ex-slayer, and I'm aware of pack laws."

"An ex-slayer…great, but he's right," said Dakris. "Those barbarians believe in power. In order to talk to Jim Duggan, their pack leader, Maria fought Bog, a werecroc and also their champion."

Valerie shook her head. "No wonder she got messed up, then. Hopefully, there wasn't an ulterior motive in sending a Raskarian vampire to a guaranteed trip to the hospital. You're lucky she's alive."

Dakris eyed her. "Are you implying something?"

"I hope not."

Dalton motioned for her to stop. "All right. Let's focus back on the case. So we're going to go down there and investigate something for them, but before they'll accept our help, Bog needs taken down. Once we resolve whatever their issue is, they'll open dialogue with the Earth Ward. That about it?"

Kathy nodded. "You got it. From what I understand, you pick and choose your cases, you get a base salary, and you are also paid per case like a freelancer. I'm here to green-light whatever is necessary to have you on this one."

"No problem," said Dalton. "I've already requisitioned a vehicle, custom suits, and equipment for my team. The contract pays fifty thousand, and that can be sent to my account directly."

"You inspectors…" said Dakris. "Why can't you just work on a base salary like the rest of us?"

Dalton eased back into his chair. "This is how the ruling council set up the Inspector Department. We report directly to them and are, for the most part, freelancers. This loose structure allows us to be agile and gives us wide latitude when dealing with other departments…such as yours. There's no political games or red tape. Just the case and if we resolve it, the payment. It's an incentive for us to succeed. Don't solve cases, and, well, you may want another line of work. Only those who show results stick around. It's based on merit, not seniority."

"Feast or famine," said Dakris. He smirked. "Great way to run things."

Dalton studied him. "I understand the Helians had a dedicated special agent wing and had managers to deal with these types of cases. However, in the last six months, I've already resolved five that were in the Helians' backlog for the last twenty years. Other inspectors have done it as well. Clearly, the approach works."

"Okay, okay," said Kathy. "We're getting offtrack. Is there anything you need from our department to help you?"

Dalton's gaze swept across the group. "Any questions?"

They shook their heads.

"All right. Evot will get additional details from the system, and then we'll head out there."

Kathy stood and smiled. "Thank you. We do appreciate this. This would be a big win for the Earth Ward."

Dalton nodded. If he resolved the case, it would benefit Kathy's department. It highlighted the forward thinking of the ruling council in regard to inspectors. Various departments could have cases, and they had to make a pitch to inspectors to take them.

He had seen some cases that were personal or vindictive in nature. Having to justify the case usually weeded those out. The departments also had to price it accordingly. This case appeared legitimate, though. He was less concerned with money for himself, but he wanted to make sure his team was compensated.

"We'll handle it," he said as he rose and extended a hand toward Kathy.

She shook his hand. The others stood.

Dalton offered a handshake to Dakris.

"Good luck," he said, crossing his arms.

Dalton shrugged. "We'll be in contact."

After they exited the office, he heard Kathy tearing into Dakris. Their department had issues. She was probably worried Dalton would not take the case. He would have on principle alone, but he also enjoyed listening to the justifications for the case. It saddened him that an agent was hurt, but it was a boneheaded decision to send one there when they clearly had asked for him. But he understood Dakris's anger. Inspectors chose cases they deemed important, which took power away from a case manager who could assign them.

"That was more intense than I expected it to be," said Todd.

"You get used to it," said Dalton. "The main thing is we have a case, and hopefully, I have a team that will stick around. To that end, who wants to visit the armory?"

Todd grinned. "What're we waiting for?"

Todd reflected on the meeting as they walked to the armory. Dakris came off as bitter but resigned to the fact he had to reach out to Dalton. Kathy's presence intrigued Todd, but he had a better understanding now of how inspectors worked.

The freelancer aspect made sense, and he saw value in merit over seniority. From his slayer days, he had seen questionable decisions from senior members even though there were better ideas from newer members. The inspector structure cut all that out.

Dalton's ability to close cases made him a hot commodity, and his decision to take a case or not spoke volumes. The pay was not bad at all. It still boggled Todd's mind that Dalton handled the types of cases he did solo up to this point. It showed how tough he was.

Todd saw an opportunity to be on the ground floor of something not only worthwhile but lucrative as well. Maybe the Earth Ward was his future. It sure beat the menial jobs he did after leaving the Faith Militia.

"That was tense in there!" said Brad.

Dalton shook his head. "Dakris has always been a concern. I'm not sure why he still is where he is."

"Because he's Helian," said Valerie. "Going from running the world to reporting to a human is a disgrace."

Todd eyed her.

"From his perspective."

Evot studied Valerie. "You believe Dakris is disgruntled."

"Yeah, you could say that," said Valerie.

"Interesting."

Brad gestured at Dalton. "I take it most case introductions aren't like that?"

"No, not at all," said Dalton. "That's okay. We have what we needed, and I decided to take it on. If completed, you'll all be wealthier."

"Money's good…but I kinda like the idea of cracking challenging cases," said Brad.

"There are 461 unresolved cases in the Earth Ward case list," said Evot.

"Damn," said Todd. "That's a lot."

Dalton nodded. "Some of those are also from other departments where their agents couldn't handle them. As more inspectors come on board, hopefully that number decreases. However…that doesn't necessarily mean the cases will get resolved."

"Well, you've got a good track record for only being here for six months," said Brad.

"Let's add this one to that pile, then."

After twenty minutes, they reached a warehouse-sized room packed with steel structures that held pallets of equipment. Off to the side was a shooting range. Doorways ringed parts of the room, and a desk sat to the left of the entrance.

Dalton walked up to the desk.

A young, tan-skinned woman in an Earth Ward outfit smiled at him. "How can I help you?"

"Inspector Dalton Kingston, and with me is my team. I put in a custom order for some gear."

She interacted with a tablet-like device. "Ah. Follow me."

They followed her to a side room filled with cabinets.

"There you go. Will that be all?" she asked.

"I think we're good," said Dalton.

She took off.

Dalton approached a center table with the others in tow. "All right. I have some undersuits you can wear. Each one was crafted to your body specifications." He pointed at some nearby steel lockers. "You'll find your suit inside. Just check the label on the locker."

Todd sauntered over to his locker. He was not sure what to expect or even how an undersuit had been crafted to his body. Brad and Valerie rushed over to their lockers and pulled out black suits that reminded him of a scuba diver's outfit. Todd opened his locker and grabbed his suit. The first thing he noticed was the lightness. The second thing was the small holes spread throughout and the zippers in some parts.

"This is cool," said Brad. He glanced at Dalton. "Is this the graphene composite underarmor series AX-52?"

"The one and only," said Dalton.

Todd wrinkled his brow. A graphene composite would be tough, much tougher than Kevlar. The technology needed to produce something like this would be way beyond what humanity had, but for the Earth Ward, it was apparently not an issue.

"It's thin enough that it can be worn under your regular clothing and can stop most small arms fire," said Dalton.

"Sounds good to me," said Todd. "The Faith Militia has nothing like this outside of normal body armor."

Dalton nodded. "The suit can unzip in spots to allow for using the bathroom and the like."

"Won't it get hot with this on?" asked Valerie, fidgeting with hers.

Brad grinned. "You don't need to worry about that with these! The suits have micro vent holes and channels that help with sweat evaporation. Also, a network of fibers, powered by kinetic energy, funnels the heat away. That can be configured on your interface."

"Interface?" asked Todd. "Where—?"

Valerie stripped down. Dalton, Brad, and Todd looked away.

"What? Never seen a naked woman before?" she asked as she donned her new undersuit.

"Usually not in a room with other guys," said Todd.

Valerie laughed. "Humans. And Wildborn." She gestured at Evot. "She didn't look away."

Evot smiled. "I was observing."

"Well, you can look now," said Valerie, strutting around. "Now, about this interface…"

Dalton extended his left forearm. "Just swipe a finger across your left inner forearm."

She complied. A screen appeared that had a variety of options.

That was definitely not what Todd expected. Then again, he did not expect Valerie to get nude in front of everyone.

"How does that work with something covering it? Like a shirt?" asked Valerie.

Dalton nodded. "There is a transparent screen you can wrap around your outerwear. It will bind to the interaction screen and is easy to put on and off. Here." He went over to a table, picked up three wraparounds, and handed them out.

Todd fidgeted with his wrapround. "This is some pretty fancy stuff, and we get all this on our first case?"

Dalton smiled. "I find that in order to truly understand what someone is capable of, give them every advantage, and see what they do." He motioned at a large wall-mounted cabinet. "Everyone, over here."

They assembled around him.

He opened the cabinet.

Todd ran a hand over his mouth when he saw the mounted weapons. He was familiar with some of them from having fought Earth Ward in the past, although that was usually by accident. Earth Ward weapons were known for being nonlethal.

Dalton grabbed a metallic module that resembled a blue cylinder with a metal wrapper around most of the side. "You'll need this for the stun gun, version five, or SG-5." He handed the SG-5 over.

Todd's eyes widened as he realized how much power was in his hand. He had heard of the SG-5's usage in the field. It was about the size of a submachine gun, but it could extend some. There were retractable grips, one in the front and the other in the back, along with a short stock for stability. The overall design was futuristic with a sleek aesthetic and a slight curve on top.

"Its usage is fairly straightforward," said Dalton. "Configure, aim, fire. Each power cell has ten charges. There is also integration with goggles for long range, and you can control the stun effect."

Todd inspected his SG-5 at eye level. "Not too heavy, but I suppose this is something I can't carry around in public."

"Actually, you can," said Brad. "Earth Ward is allowed to."

Evot gestured at a backpack. "You can carry it in that along with additional power cells."

"Well, hot damn," said Todd.

Everyone laughed.

Dalton grabbed two weapons and handed them to Valerie. "These are stun pistols, version eight, or SP-8s. They use a modified power cell and have about six charges per cell."

Valerie flipped them around. "I like them. I guess I get additional charges too?"

"You do," said Evot. She grabbed a belt that had five charge holders. "You can use this."

Valerie slipped it on. "Nice. Now I just need some holsters and straps."

Brad grinned and pointed at some straps. "Looks like you can choose from a variety. I assume I get a SP-8."

"Yep," said Dalton. "Unless you want two. However…" He opened another cabinet.

Brad ran over.

Dalton gestured inside the cabinet. "This is a prototype hunter drone. Yes, it's a sphere with retractable tentacles, but it has a stun cannon port, basic kinetic shielding, and it's quite resilient. The drone also fits into a backpack and can be deployed wherever you are. With your ability, it will act as an extension of your body."

"I didn't even know these existed," said Brad.

Evot raised a finger. "It's experimental due to the brain-machine interface not working as intended."

Brad smiled. "Yeah, no problem with me."

"You're uniquely gifted to use it," said Dalton. "There is a range limitation, though."

"It's like Christmas in here!" said Brad. He focused on the drone.

It leapt out of the cabinet and landed on Brad's shoulder.

"Oh…I like!" he said.

Todd stepped back. The drone looked like a spider somewhat, except it had upward of ten retractable, spindly legs. The monocles with red highlights were probably visual sensors, and where there would be mandibles, a port with two small barrels pointed out. That was most likely the stun port.

The drone's color was the darkest black he had ever seen, and it made the drone difficult to fully see as it moved around. It would be able to meld into any shadow with ease. Brad's ability to control the drone impressed Todd, and he understood how effective something like that could be.

Dalton gestured at some stun batons. "You each get one of those." He glanced at Valerie. "Or two if you want."

She twirled her dual batons with ease. They were apparently no stranger to her.

"All right. There's a shooting range here for you all to test your gear out and, yes, even an obstacle course that a drone can play in," said Dalton.

Evot glanced at Brad. "Perhaps I can team up with your drone."

"Gizmo. His name is Gizmo."

"You named it," said Evot.

Brad nodded. "Gizmo has a rudimentary interface, definitely not on your level, but it works for me."

Evot nodded.

"Okay," said Dalton. "We'll stay the night here. Tomorrow we'll fly out to Chillicothe, and then we'll drive down to Waverly in a specialized SUV. Enjoy the rest of your night, and be ready to go tomorrow."

CHAPTER
FIVE

B rad stared out the window of the customized luxury SUV Dalton had secured. They had just arrived in Waverly. It was 9:00 a.m. and the day after they had received their gear. Brad loved Gizmo and had been playing around with him all last night. He also had taken some time to familiarize himself with his SP-8.

The SUV had black, bulletproof armor and appeared larger than a normal vehicle. The Earth Ward spared no expense in making sure personnel traveled in style and safety.

Inside were the usual two front seats occupied by Dalton on the driver's side and Brad on the other. Between them was a thick separator area that had holders and several compartments. The front was packed with all sorts of electronics, and the dashboard was essentially buttons, dials, and embedded screens. The passenger side had a pullout, which Brad had placed his laptop on. He grinned at Evot, who lay curled up on the dashboard. That seemed to be her favorite spot.

Valerie and Todd sat behind them in two chairs with a similar separator. The front chairs also had a screen in the rear and a table support that popped out from the back. That allowed for laptops or other utilities for those in the rear to use.

In the far back was a metallic cabinet that had several slide-out panels containing an assortment of gear and equipment. The cabinet was accessed when the back hatch was raised. The rear chairs could recline enough to form a comfortable sleeping position.

The other unusual feature that caught Brad's attention was the circular steel hatch door in the leg area between the front and back seats. The hatch door opened and allowed for things to be dropped outside. When parked, he could let Gizmo out that way, or when driving, they could drop mines.

"Heads up. We're almost there," said Dalton.

Todd peered out the window. "I wonder how deep the Faith Militia is here now. Last time I checked, they were everywhere in various positions."

"Hopefully not too deep," said Valerie.

He nodded. "Speaking of which…are we going to get official outfits at some point? I'm guessing we wouldn't need to put the forearm device on each time we change our shirt."

"If you plan to stick around after this case, you'll have one waiting for you," said Dalton.

"Fair enough."

They pulled in and parked outside the Pike County sheriff's office.

Dalton reached over to the visor in front of Brad and handed him a pair of sunglasses. "Once we're inside, see if you can connect to their network."

Brad studied the sunglasses. "All right." He stepped out and stretched along with the others. He pointed at some fields in the distance. "Definitely a small town. That's for sure."

"Oh yeah," said Todd.

Evot morphed into her human form and exited the SUV.

"Evot, I'll need you to keep a servbot here," said Dalton. "You'll still have a servbot on me and be able to see what's going on via our link. I'll need you to probe for any weaknesses over wireless and if you can, infiltrate their systems along with Brad. Also, if someone tries to hijack our ride, you can drive away."

She frowned. "Okay." She transformed into cat form and jumped back in.

Brad wondered how Evot handled emotions and what algorithms she used. A part of him wanted to hang with her. He hated seeing her frown, and the thought of an AI doing it was so much different than the AIs he had dealt with in the past. She probably disliked that she could not interact with her human shell.

"We won't be long," said Brad, scratching her behind the ears.

Her eyes sparkled as she made a toothy grin.

"So that's why we're really here," said Valerie with a smirk.

Dalton nodded. "They aren't going to freely give up any information they don't have to. Of course, they might not

be completely digital, but it doesn't hurt to take a peek."
He glanced at Brad and Evot. "It's not like they're going to
track anything back to us, right?"

"No way," said Brad, raising his head a bit.

"I will be stealthy, like my cat form," said Evot.

Dalton grinned. "That's what I like to hear."

After they locked the SUV, they entered the office.

Brad knew they probably appeared as unusual to everyone.

They approached the information desk.

"Can I help you?" asked a fair-skinned, lanky man with
a mustache and brown hair.

Dalton pulled out his badge wallet. "Inspector Dalton
Kingston, Earth Ward, and this is my team. This is a courtesy
visit for Sheriff Paul Jackson."

"Huh," said the man. "Wait here." He took off to the
back.

The mention of Earth Ward had caused some to stare.

A fair-skinned, pudgy man with a tight uniform walked
over. "Earth Ward, huh?" He gestured at Dalton, then the
others. "Nice outfit. I'm guessing the others are undercover.
Hard to identify they're Earth Ward."

Dalton smiled. "Maybe."

The man eyed Brad. "Why are you wearing sunglasses
in here?"

"Medical condition," said Brad.

"Uh-huh." The man pointed outside. "Nice ride out
there. B6?"

"Seven," said Todd.

Brad chuckled when the man's eyes widened. B6 was in reference to a standard that covered ballistic protection levels or armor levels. While B6 was used for protection against high-powered rifles, including armor-piercing, B7 was even stronger and could withstand sniper rifles. Apparently, that was something that happened often enough that the Earth Ward moved all their SUVs from B6 to B7. Brad was thankful for that.

"Derek!" said a tall man coming from the back.

"What?"

"Don't you have something to do?"

Derek sighed and took off.

The man walked around the counter and extended a hand. "Sheriff Paul Jackson."

Dalton shook his hand and introduced everyone.

"Why don't we go to my office?" asked Paul.

"Sounds good," said Dalton. "Lead the way."

Several deputies cracked jokes as the group passed. It did not surprise Brad that there was no one of color. He saw one woman, and she looked like she could take down anything. He also sensed she was Wildborn. Her stare indicated she was startled at seeing him and the others. She was probably not aware she was Wildborn, although her senses would have detected them.

The various technological devices he could connect with highlighted with a blue outline. A quick check on some of the deputies' phones revealed what he considered normal, although one had lewd messages toward the female deputy, who responded in kind. A secret affair.

The computer on one of the deputy's desks served as an entry point, and Brad connected to the network. A poke around revealed various resources, and he linked to his laptop in the SUV. He smiled at Evot's presence. A moment later, he gave her all the credentials and the network topology needed to connect wirelessly and get information.

After they entered the sheriff's office, Paul closed the door and sat behind his desk. He motioned for everyone to sit.

"So Earth Ward," said Paul. "We had one of your special agents stop in a while back. Maria…"

"Guerrara," said Dalton.

"Yeah, that's right. She didn't have your fancy ride or a team, though. Is she involved in why you're here? I haven't seen her around."

"I've taken over the case."

Paul studied Dalton. "And what is that case exactly?"

"I can't say. It's confidential. However, we will be around, and I wanted to inform you as a professional courtesy."

"I appreciate that. I do. What do you plan to do while you're here? That you can speak to?"

Dalton nodded. "We'll most likely visit a few places, talk to a few people, and the like."

Paul rubbed his chin. "Any places I might know?"

"I can't say."

Paul laughed. "I figured. I'm guessing if you're here, there's something bad going on. The feds usually keep me in the loop."

"If I can, I will," said Dalton. "However, for right now, it's best to keep a low profile and information on a need-to-know basis. I just wanted to update you to avoid any surprises."

"I understand," said Paul. "Feds do this all the time, although you have better toys and higher jurisdiction than they do."

"We do, and we have global jurisdiction."

Paul nodded. "And now you're here. All right. Well, if I can help in any way, reach out to me." He motioned at the others. "I'm going to guess you're doing undercover."

"Something like that." Dalton stood and extended his hand. "I'll be in contact if necessary."

Paul returned the handshake. He walked over to the door and opened it. "Don't be a stranger."

Brad followed the others out. While Dalton and Paul talked, Brad had scoured Paul's laptop. It had a wealth of information, and reading through emails had revealed some interesting content but nothing out of the ordinary. He presented as clean.

After a few minutes, they were back in the SUV.

"Paul was all right, but the others didn't like the looks of us," said Todd.

"I didn't notice anything, other than the joking," said Brad. "Oh, and the woman was Wildborn."

"I noticed that too," said Valerie.

"I've been around this type of crowd before," said Todd. "They were being polite and don't trust us. I suspect one or two of them might be Faith Militia."

Dalton nodded. "I suspect that as well. I wanted to meet the sheriff to get an idea of what we might face if things turn ugly. I expect we'll be tracked to some degree, so we'll need to be careful."

Valerie smirked. "Well, I know I attracted their attention. They didn't realize I have better-than-average hearing. Derek wouldn't mind having me in a cell for a night."

"Yeah, I heard that too. Ignore him," said Dalton. He faced Brad. "Were you able to connect?"

Brad interacted with his laptop. "Sure did. I gained entry and gave Evot access. What did you want to know?"

"Were there any unusual murders or anyone missing in the county?"

Brad focused. "Looks like a pastor's son disappeared two months ago. There were also reports of strange cow mutilations."

"Around the Tanner Pack area?"

"Yeah."

Evot perked up. "There was a recent murder in a trailer park as well. The means of death are unknown at this time, and it was also near the Tanner Pack area."

"Interesting," said Dalton. "Let's hope one of their members hasn't gone rogue, although I suspect the Tanner Pack wouldn't allow that."

Todd snorted. "Yeah, definitely not. They would do everything in their power to prevent being exposed."

"What's the plan, then?" asked Valerie.

"We visit the Warehouse first to see what's going on with the Tanner Pack, then we can stop in at these other places."

"Works for me."

Dalton started up the SUV. "All right. We got a game plan."

Dalton studied the Warehouse as they arrived twenty minutes later. The place was nestled off the side of a country road, and the parking lot was nothing more than a dirt area. The building itself appeared to be an actual warehouse, and from what he understood, it had been converted to the unofficial Tanner Pack headquarters.

One thing that caught his eye was the array of motorcycles out front with some tough-looking guys in leather jackets. Their patches indicated they belonged to the Tanner Pack.

"You and Evot need to stay here for this one," said Dalton, glancing at Brad and Evot.

"No issue there," said Brad, shaking a hand out. "Wildborn in an area packed with Outsiders like this? Yeah, no thanks."

"You and Evot can still try to connect and see what you can find."

Brad nodded. "Works for me."

Dalton parked the SUV. He peered back at Todd and Valerie. "I'm not sure what to expect, but be ready in case things go down."

Todd smiled. "Not my first time busting a weregang."

"Or killing some," said Valerie, grinning.

"All right," said Dalton. "Let's go."

They assembled outside as Evot assumed her humanoid form and sat in the driver's seat with Brad on the other side.

The three guys out front stared them down. That was to be expected. Dalton was on their turf, and they had no idea who he was. To head off any potential issues, he approached them with his badge wallet out.

"Inspector Dalton Kingston, Earth Ward. With me is my team."

One of the men with "Dino" patched on his sleeve stood. "So you're him…not quite what I expected after hearing about Hammer."

Dalton nodded. "Hammer fought well; he was just out of his class."

Dino laughed. "Cocky too, damn." He examined Todd and Valerie. "A human and…something else."

"A nice something else," said another man.

"Want to donate blood?" asked Valerie, baring her fangs.

The other men stood.

Dalton extended a hand. "All right. We're here to talk with Jim Duggan."

Dino snorted. "Like that last chick did. Didn't go so well for her."

"I understand someone has to fight Bog in order to talk to Jim."

Dino crossed his arms. "Yeah…I guess that's gonna be you this time. After Hammer, should be easy, right?"

The other men laughed.

"Set it up," said Dalton.

Dino snorted. "Follow me."

Dalton entered the building alongside the others. Half of the interior was essentially a garage, while the other half had eating and pool tables. A bar sat in the far back with a wall of liquor.

The place was packed with various people, and Dalton's Evaran-sense went wild, identifying all the different types of lycanthropes there. Heavy rock blared over the speakers, and the area reeked of body odor and piss. It seemed odd to be this busy in the morning.

Although he recognized a majority of the Outsiders, some were new. He would cross reference it later and see what they were. People cleared a path as Dino moved through the crowd to the back door. Along the way, he shouted that it was breakfast time for Bog. That got everyone excited.

When they exited into the back, Dalton surveyed the environment. A chain-link fence surrounded the massive open area, and various buildings and vehicles lay scattered around.

The bleachers surrounding a rectangular area caught his eye. It reminded him of a fight pit, and he suspected the Tanner Pack used it often. Like inside, music blared over speakers, and the cool wind could not hide the strong fecal smell. The Tanner Pack, with their enhanced senses, apparently did not care. Maybe they liked it.

Dino led them to the open area and pointed out. "Bog will be along shortly."

"What are the rules?" asked Dalton.

Dino laughed. "Don't die." He took off as the bleachers filled up.

Todd exhaled. "They waste no time in getting right to it."

"I know," said Dalton. "I'm guessing they understand that we know what happened to Special Agent Maria, so we're aware of the rules, which we are."

"You sure you can take this Bog guy?"

Valerie grinned. "He took down Hammer. They have no idea what Dalton is capable of."

Dalton nodded at her. "I appreciate the vote of confidence, but I really want to get on with the case. This is a distraction, but it will be a quick one."

Cheers erupted when an older, heavyset man in jeans, a leather jacket, and boots arrived and sat in a fancy chair in a special area on the bleachers.

"I'm guessing that's Jim Duggan," said Todd. "Not sure what he is, though."

"Werewolf," said Dalton.

Todd nodded.

Some of the crowd transformed into werewolves, werejaguars, and other weretypes. Most appeared to be some variant of a dog or cat, although Dalton did see one wereowl.

Some of them growled and glared at Valerie.

She bared her fangs and hissed.

Dalton laid a hand on her shoulder. He sensed her uneasiness, and he was sure the crowd did too. "Easy now. We're guests."

"Right," she said, looking away. After ten minutes, she pointed at a seven-foot mountain of a man approaching the fighting area. "That must be Bog."

Dalton studied him. He was a werecroc, and since there were no rules, he suspected Bog would go into his werecroc form. He wore a gray formfitting suit underneath his jeans, shirt, and boots. That was common among shifters, and it stretched to conform to their bodies. Not all wore them, but some of the larger ones did.

Bog was fair-skinned and had tattoo sleeves on both arms. His long hair, beard, and mustache made it hard to get a look at his face, but he was in good shape. He looked like he had just woken up. It was no surprise he was popular, as he probably won most of his fights. Dalton suspected the fights themselves were rare. Maria going to critical care made more sense now. Per her background, she may have had a superior combat rating, but against someone like Bog, that might not matter much.

Bog entered the open area and raised his hands. The crowd cheered, clanked beer bottles, and slapped hands. An outdoor speaker made a screeching noise.

"We have a fight!" said Jim. "The Earth Ward has sent us another person to beat down." He coughed. "I mean, fight. Welcome Inspector Dalton Kingston."

The audience booed.

Dalton motioned for Todd and Valerie to stand by, then he walked into the open area opposite Bog.

"It's said Dalton took down Hammer. Well…Hammer ain't Bog!" said Jim.

The crowd laughed.

Bog removed his shirt, pants, and boots, leaving just his gray undersuit on.

"And now for the rules," said Jim. He flashed his hands off to the side. "There are none!"

Dalton understood Jim hyping up the fight, and the crowd expected a quick beatdown.

"Without further ado, let the ass-kicking begin!"

Bog pointed at Dalton. "I'm going to do to you what Hammer couldn't." He shifted into his werecroc form.

Dalton's eyes narrowed. Bog now stood nine feet tall and had gained more mass. His green scaled skin sparkled under the sun, and his legs became digitigrade. His fingers formed into massive claws, and his head morphed into a long snout with sharp teeth.

Bog moved his hands to the side and roared.

Dalton went into Scoutspectre mode and adopted a defensive stance.

The crowd murmured.

Bog charged and swiped with his left hand.

Dalton leaned to the side.

Bog tried with his right.

Dalton punched Bog's wrist, then spun into him, hitting him in the face with an elbow. Then he backhanded him.

Bog stumbled back and growled. He ran at Dalton.

Dalton rushed forward and shoulder-slammed Bog back.

Someone tossed a metal bar to Bog. "Get him, Bog! Mess him up!"

Dalton sighed. No rules apparently meant weapons were allowed. He suspected that like Hammer, Bog was probably immune to a heavy stun. If Bog wanted to use weapons, then Dalton would too. He spawned his nanoshield, then grabbed his MH and formed a stun baton.

The crowd gasped.

Bog stepped forward and swung.

Dalton blocked, then shoved the baton under Bog's chin. As expected, the stun only angered Bog.

He kicked Dalton, sending him sprawling back.

Dalton grimaced. Bog had raw power, and it showed. However, he was slow. Dalton focused his Evaran-sense, causing everything to slow around him. When Bog rushed over to stomp, Dalton rolled out of the way while retracting his shield. He jumped up and slipped behind Bog, then applied a choke hold.

They fell to the ground.

Bog thrashed around as Dalton tightened his grip. A few moments later, Bog passed out and morphed back into his human form.

The crowd went silent.

Dalton stood and pointed at Jim. "Can we talk now, or do I need to humiliate someone else?"

The audience laughed.

"I like you," said Jim. "You're every bit what I've heard. Let's talk."

Dalton nodded and walked over to Todd and Valerie.

"Wow, you took him down with ease," said Todd.

"He was predictable. I guess he was used to winning in a few moves."

Valerie grinned. "I liked the way you talked to Jim. You knew your audience."

"Yeah, but I wish we could have talked instead of this ridiculous ritual," said Dalton. "Nonetheless, we can at least discuss the case with him now."

Valerie followed Dalton and Jim back inside. The fight impressed her. If she had to fight Bog, it would have been at range since he would have mauled her up close. Dalton's armored suit proved effective. Most of his weapons were nonlethal, but she knew he could have gone lethal.

She recalled their initial encounter. When she had reached for a gun, he told her to only use it as a last resort. She thought he was being naive but instead learned he had over three hundred kills and simply did not want to add any more. That probably took a lot of restraint on his part, and she understood he could have easily ended Bog.

The crowd had intrigued her. They were gung ho for Bog until he went down. She suspected they thought this would be another lesson taught to the Earth Ward.

Jim had been swilling from his whiskey bottle and had a smug look for most of the fight. His shocked face at the end would be something she always remembered. She figured he had some idea about Dalton, or he would not have asked for him specifically.

They entered a back room and closed the door.

Jim slipped behind a messy desk, with Styrofoam containers lying around on the floor. A window with dusty blinds sat across the room, allowing in some light, but the lighted ceiling fan provided most of the illumination. A slight haze filled the air, and the office smelled like dirty socks and wet fur. He motioned for them to sit on a couch opposite him.

They complied.

Jim eased into his chair on wheels and lit up a cigar. "Damn…that was some fight."

"I'm just glad we can focus on why I was requested," said Dalton.

Jim laughed. "Well, you took down Hammer, who also took down Bog a few years ago. In addition to that, we've had an odd series of deaths and…"

"Kill two birds with one stone. Give Bog a chance to redeem himself since Hammer is put away, and also have someone investigate the deaths," said Dalton.

"You're sharp," said Jim. He cocked his head. "I'll be honest. Not a fan of the Earth Ward. They can eat my ass for all I care, but…I'll admit they're doing better than the Helians. I wasn't impressed they sent that little woman down here, though."

Dalton nodded. "That was an oversight and has been corrected, as evidenced by my being here."

Jim sucked on his teeth. "Well, there you go. I can't sense what you are." He laughed. "Are you a wererobot?"

"Not quite," said Dalton, smiling. "Evolved human."

"Huh, dunno what that is, but it's tough apparently. You got all that fancy stuff like the Helians," said Jim. He eyed Valerie. "And who's this hot piece?"

She grinned. "This *smoking* piece is Valerie Simmons. I'm a part of Dalton's team."

"Oh, well, excuse me," said Jim, chuckling. "Hmm. I can't sense what you are either. Outsider for sure, but I saw fangs earlier like you're a damn vamp."

"I'm Zikarian."

He shook his head. "Zero for two so far."

Name-calling was not unusual to Valerie. *Vamp* was a slur used by Outsiders since it was a waste to say vampire because they were not worth the effort. She did not mind it, but she knew some who did. Jim also made a reference to her attractiveness, something she was intimately familiar with. While it did give her some advantages that she took pleasure in, it sometimes brought out the worst in people who were assholes in general.

Jim studied Todd and shook a finger at him. "He's easy, though. Human. What's your name, boy?"

"Todd Armani."

Jim leaned forward. "Your face is familiar, but your scent isn't."

Todd cleared his throat. "I just have one of those faces."

"I guess so," said Jim. He focused on Dalton. "Saw your ride out front. Armored SUV. No surprise there. You also left some of your team in there. Wildborn and another hot chick. Probably smart to do that."

Valerie grinned, thinking of Evot learning she had been referred to as a hot chick.

"They weren't needed for this part," said Dalton. "Now that I'm here, I'm all ears. What's going on?"

"Right to business. All right," said Jim. He took a puff of his cigar, then pulled out a map with several X markers on it. "The X marks represent the two deaths we've had in the last two months." He reached into a drawer and tossed some images on the desk.

Valerie stood along with the others. The images were horrific. One showed the bottom half of a werebeaver. Another displayed a werewolf that had been twisted like a pretzel.

"As you can see, these deaths were messy. Something with immense strength did this," said Jim. He rubbed his chin. "Not only that, but several members have gone missing. Everyone usually comes back, and I have no way of knowing if it's related to this. We're on high alert here, and our neighboring packs said they ain't seen shit."

Dalton eyed him. "You got some idea, though, of what might be doing this."

"Wildborn, probably," said Jim, grimacing. "That or something new we ain't ever seen before. You took down Hammer, and that shows you're tough. Your dismantling of Bog just confirms that for me. I'm hoping you can take down whatever killed my boys and find any missing pack members you might come across."

Jim's eyes softened a bit. Valerie sensed his pain, and she understood that to a weregang, the pack was everything.

"We tried to hunt in the area, but we found nothing."

"Have you talked to the sheriff?" asked Dalton.

Todd and Jim laughed, then stared at each other.

"The pack won't reveal itself, and the sheriff might be a Faith Militia informant," said Todd.

"That's right..." said Jim, scrutinizing Todd. "We got some wisened in the Waverly police department, and they handled this. Kept it away from prying eyes. But whatever is doing this has eluded everyone, and that's hard to do on our turf. We would have sensed whatever it was, but there was no scent to track. Well, barely any of consequence."

"I understand," said Dalton. "I'd assumed you had some infiltration in the area's law enforcement, and it looks like the sheriff isn't one of them."

Jim laughed. "Did you just use some fancy psychic shit on me?"

Dalton smiled. "I don't know what you're talking about."

"I see," said Jim. "Well, you have the locations. If you want to see the bodies, or what's left of them, I can show you that too."

"I'd like to see them, but do you know what they were doing when they were killed?"

"Hunting like we all do. There's a shit ton of forest around here packed with free food if you can catch it."

"Honing your hunting skills," said Valerie.

"Damn straight."

Dalton stood. "All right, let's check out the bodies."

In another life, Valerie could see herself hanging out with Jim. Although she was an Outsider like him, she would probably never be accepted due to being a vampire. The pack would probably kill her. She followed Jim to a shack out back.

Jim opened the door and stood back. He pointed at some coolers. "They're in bags. I kept that shit ice cold for ya."

Dalton extended his hand and emitted a golden scanning beam.

Jim jumped back. "What the fuck is that?"

"A scanning beam," said Dalton. "I was doing a bio analysis."

"You got Helian tech inside you?"

Dalton shook his head. "No, it came from…far away."

"Yeah, I believe it," said Jim. "So? Did you find anything?"

"Not yet," said Dalton as he continued to scan.

Valerie studied him as he moved his hands around in the air after scanning. It was like he worked with an invisible interface.

"There's something foreign in there," said Dalton.

"DNA?" asked Todd.

Dalton shook his head. "Not so much that but more unusual structures in the blood. It may be the creatures."

"When you say foreign, you don't mean like Japanese or something, right?" asked Jim.

Dalton chuckled. "No, I meant like not of this Earth."

Jim began to grin, then stopped. "You're fucking with me, right?"

"Unfortunately, no. I'm going to need a sample so I can do further analysis. Any concerns?"

"Take what you need."

Dalton glanced at Todd. "Can you get some evidence containers from the SUV?"

"No problem," said Todd. He took off.

Dalton focused on Jim. "Mind having whoever found the bodies meet with us at the sites?"

"Yeah, that'd be Carl. I can arrange that," he said. "I just want this shit wrapped up before the clan goes on the warpath or, worse, another gets killed or ends up missing."

"I'll do my best, and if I succeed, hopefully you'll honor your word to open a dialogue with the Earth Ward."

"My word is my bond."

Dalton's eyes slightly glowed. "As is mine."

"You're one strange bird, but I knew I'd like you, assuming you survived Bog."

Dalton nodded.

Valerie marveled at how Dalton had already formed an unspoken bond with Jim. Dalton was not only a good inspector, but he was a good ambassador. His mere presence made people comfortable.

She wondered if he would investigate Earth Ward personnel if he found evidence of wrongdoing. Her experience told her law enforcement generally stuck together. Perhaps the inspectors being a separate branch was meant to isolate them from that.

She smiled as she caught Jim staring at her ass. He looked away quickly, but she expected that to occur in a place like this. One thing she observed about the pack from her short time with them was that the women were treated as equals. Each pack had its own rules, and the Tanner Pack women appeared tough. A few had even scoped her out. If she had more time, she might have stayed and checked it out more, but the case was heating up.

CHAPTER
SIX

Dalton and the team cruised along a back road as they followed Carl on his motorcycle. He was the werewolf who had found the first body. They were going to a lodge the Tanner Pack used as a base for hunting out in the forest. Dalton was pleased so far with what they had learned on the case, and he was glad the fight with Bog was over. Hopefully, that was not common among other weregangs in the future.

After an hour of driving, they reached a gravel road that led into the forest.

Dalton had enjoyed the ride over with the window down. While Brad and Evot joked around, Todd and Valerie discussed the Tanner Pack. Dalton chimed in every now and then, but he was content to listen. He saw a team forming.

Todd had been cool and calm under pressure even in a building packed with those who would not hesitate to kill him. Brad provided a technological capability that went beyond even Evot. Valerie also had a calm influence, and her knowledge of nonhumans was an important asset.

Dalton suspected her social engineering skills would come into play at some point, and he was thankful to have that option available.

They pulled into a dirt clearing in front of an old wooden house.

"Talk about creepy houses," said Brad.

Dalton nodded. "Evot, leave a servbot here, and use your other one to scout the area. As for the rest of us, it's hiking time."

They assembled outside.

Evot soared into the sky in crow form.

Dalton studied Carl as he got off his bike. He was about six foot or so and had fair skin. A mustache and beard covered his lower face, and a scraggly mess of curly hair flopped out under his helmet. He wore jeans with a sleeveless leather jacket that had the Tanner Pack patch on the back. His arm tattoo sleeves stood out, and his scuffed boots completed the biker-gang look.

Carl took off his helmet, revealing a blue bandanna across his forehead, and joined them. "All right. It's about a two-mile hike through the woods." He gestured at the house. "This is one of our lodges and is usually where we meet up before going hunting. I'm going to change and then wolf out. Any concerns?"

"We're good," said Dalton. "We'll wait for you here."

Carl nodded and headed to the lodge.

Dalton looked around the group. "Okay, we got some supplies in the back, so get whatever you need."

Todd smiled. "I just need my SG-5 and backpack. Maybe some water too."

"SP-8s for me," said Valerie.

"And a Gizmo backpack for me," said Brad. "Oh, and water."

"All right," said Dalton.

Carl returned in his werewolf form five minutes later. "Ready to go?" he said in a grizzled voice.

"Lead on," said Dalton.

"Try to keep up!" said Carl, laughing as he sprinted away.

Dalton grinned. "Don't slow down on our accord."

As they moved through the forest, Evot kept up with Carl and provided an aerial view. Dalton enjoyed being able to have her in the SUV to protect it and to also travel with the group. It crossed his mind that the others did not have the benefit of seeing what she saw except for maybe Brad. Although they could view it on their inner forearm devices, that was a small screen. The goggles could be used as well, but they seemed uncomfortable. Dalton would need to research better options if the group stuck around after this case.

After thirty minutes, they reached a remote spot in the woods.

Evot flew down and landed on Dalton's shoulder.

"Here we are," said Carl. He transformed back into human form and pointed at an area on the ground. "This is where Dean died."

"He's the werebeaver?" asked Valerie.

Carl sighed. "Yeah. I found him out here during my hunt. Although his beaver form is some freaky shit, it's actually pretty damn tough. Those teeth are no joke."

Dalton extended his hand and scanned around.

Carl jumped back. "The fuck is that?"

"A scanning beam."

"What the hell are you, man? Some type of robot or some shit?"

Dalton smiled. "An evolved human with advanced technology, like this beam."

Carl looked at the others, who shrugged.

Dalton studied the readings in his ARI. Although Dean's remains had been carted off, there was still evidence his body had been there. Dalton pulled up the images and saw that Dean had essentially been torn in half. Dalton's scan revealed the presence of an impact on the ground relative to the surrounding area.

"Evot, using the image we saw earlier and our current environment, project Dean's body."

"Of course," she said. She flew up to a branch and emitted a holographic projection from her eyes.

Carl jumped again. "What the hell, man? Your crow can do light shows?"

Dalton grinned. "Yes, Evot is quite versatile."

"That's so cool that you can do that," said Todd, looking up at Evot.

"Thank you," she said.

Dalton walked around the holographic remains. "Nothing obvious about the death other than whatever did this was strong enough to literally slam Dean into the ground, then rip the top half of him off."

"When we found Dean's remains, I got a faint scent, but it didn't lead anywhere. I don't sense anything now," said Carl. "What would be strong enough to do this?"

"I don't think it's strength, although that sure helps," said Todd.

Dalton studied him. "What do you see?"

Todd gestured around. "If something was as strong as we're thinking, it should have left some type of evidence, like footprints, its own blood, or something. However, there is nothing except Dean's bottom half." He pointed up. "Notice the branches around Evot."

Everyone looked up.

Dalton's eyes narrowed. "I see it. Something came down."

"So maybe a wereeagle or something," said Valerie. "It would essentially fly down and hit Dean like a bullet, enough to knock him down. Add in some massive claws, and it could stand on the body, rip it in half, then take off."

Brad shuddered. "That…is a nasty image."

"That might explain this one, but there should be some trace of it, a feather or something, and unless Dalton found that, I don't think that's it. For the other death, that werewolf was tied up like a pretzel," said Todd. "I don't think that was a wereeagle either."

Dalton raised a finger. "Possibly, and it might be a group or completely unrelated. How far away from here is the other location?"

Carl pointed off. "Craig died about three miles that way."

"Lead on."

Carl shifted back into werewolf form and took off. They followed him.

Dalton was sure he would have come to the same conclusion about something airborne having attacked, but having a group to bounce ideas off made that process go quicker. Whatever killed Dean left no trace behind other than the impacts from the fight. Dalton had hoped to find a trace of organic material, but it was like the area had been scrubbed.

After forty-five minutes, they reached the second death site.

Dalton ran a scan of the environment, then had Evot project Craig's twisted body.

Todd pointed up. "Same busted branches. I'm guessing with Craig, he was able to dodge somehow before it got hands or whatever on him." He motioned at Dalton. "You detect anything weird?"

"I don't," said Dalton.

Carl's eyes narrowed. "Yeah, I don't detect shit either."

"Same," said Brad.

"Likewise," said Valerie.

Dalton nodded. "Brad, Evot, when we get back, check to see if there is any satellite imagery of the area during those times."

"Of course," said Evot.

Brad gave a thumbs-up.

"Okay, I think we've done as much as we can here. Let's check out the cow mutilations next," said Dalton. He glanced at Carl. "We appreciate your help."

"I just hope you find and kill the fucker that did this," said Carl.

Dalton grimaced. "I hope we do find whatever is responsible. I suspect whatever did this is most likely just getting started."

Todd felt at ease as the group pulled up to the farm's blacktop driveway. It had been two and a half hours since they visited the second Tanner Pack member death site. The hike back was quicker, as they did not need to stop by the first site, but it was still an hour.

The trip to the farm was relatively short compared to that, and while Todd enjoyed resting during the drive, his curiosity had been piqued about going to the farm. It was 5:00 p.m., and although he could use dinner, he had eaten some snacks on the way out.

Like many other farms he had seen, this one was nestled between fields and forest. A large barn and other support buildings were behind the house, and various shacks dotted the land. The case intrigued him, and up to this point, he had enjoyed working with everyone. He thought there might be some issues with Valerie, but her in-the-present mentality worked well with him.

Brad was an interesting person, and Todd suspected there would be many good discussions to be had if they all stuck around. Evot cracked him up. Her innocence clashed violently with the world he knew at times, but she tried, which was admirable. He had never worked with an AI, so it was a new experience for him. He kinda liked it.

Dalton was mysterious as always, and Todd's initial encounter made more sense to him now. To Dalton, this case was just another in the pile, and the trailer park one was probably viewed the same way. Todd appreciated being on the other side of the case this time, and the farmer they were meeting would be on the side where Todd had been in the trailer park incident.

They parked in front of a garage and exited the SUV.

A young, fair-skinned man with a mop of brown hair came out to meet them. "Hey. Dad's waiting for you over at the spot. He said for me to take you there."

Dalton nodded. "Sounds good. Lead on."

Todd made sure Dalton had called the farm before coming out. While unexpected visits were not unknown, it helped when you were expected. Not only that, but it also gave the farmer time to gather his thoughts and plan what he needed to do. Dalton initially wanted to appear and chat, but having a black armored SUV arrive with this group might be somewhat alarming.

Todd smiled as a cool breeze blew across his face. It was hot out, and the sounds of dogs barking in the distance made the area feel comfortable. He relaxed as he walked down a tractor trail toward a field. Off to the sides, he spotted areas where chopped wood was stored and also a log splitter. The barn they passed had a few tractors in it along with a wagon hitch of some sort.

The young man leading them was chatty and introduced himself as Greg. Brad and Valerie kept him occupied. For

Todd's part, he enjoyed the walk. The trail had trees on the sides to provide shade, and sunlight tried to poke through. He could see himself relaxing here with no problems.

After fifteen minutes, they arrived at a spot near a small lake. A wooden fence extended as far as he could see, and an elderly gentleman with fair skin, green slacks, a blue flannel shirt, and a green ball cap waited for them. If Todd had to guess the man's age, he would say late fifties. The spot he stood over looked like it had been burnt, but leaving a carcass out to rot in this heat made no sense. The man had a manila folder tucked under his right arm.

Dalton walked over and used his badge wallet. "Inspector Dalton Kingston, Earth Ward, and with me is my team: Brad Washington, Valerie Simmons, and Todd Armani."

Goose bumps ran up Todd's arm. He loved hearing how official it sounded to be part of the team.

The old man nodded at them. "Grant Wolf. I'm relieved you came out."

"No problem," said Dalton. "I'm glad you took our call and agreed to meet."

Grant sighed. "The sheriff and local police already been out here. They think I'm nuts."

Todd stepped forward. "Trust me. We've seen the unusual and weird. It's no stranger to us. I'm guessing this is where your cow was killed."

"Yeah," said Grant, adjusting his cap.

Todd glanced at Dalton, who nodded. Talking to farmers was not new to Todd, and he had grown up in a small town, so he understood some things better. The side eye Grant gave Valerie and Brad was not meant as disrespect but more an indication of being uncomfortable with them.

"Why don't you walk us through what happened?" asked Todd.

Grant sighed. "All right, I can do that." He faced Todd. "I was sleeping a few nights ago when I heard something out in the pasture. It was an awful ruckus. I grabbed my shotgun and headed out." He glared at Greg. "I went alone because someone was out partying."

Greg lowered his head.

"As I rushed over to the commotion…that's when I heard it. Wings," said Grant. His lips trembled. "It…wasn't natural. When I got here, I shined my flashlight on Jane, who was on the ground, and…*something*…stood on top of her." He cleared his throat.

"It's all right. We're still with ya," said Todd. He glanced at the others. "Jane was one of his cows."

"Yeah." Grant licked his lips. "I yelled at whatever was on her, and when it turned toward me, its face…" He gazed into the distance.

"Its face wasn't human, was it?" asked Todd.

Grant's eyes misted as he glanced at Todd. In a weak voice, he said, "No. It wasn't. I'm telling ya, I'm not crazy."

"We don't think you are," said Todd, looking over at the others.

They nodded.

Grant handed Todd a manila folder. "All right, well, here are some photos I took. I fired a few times, and that…

thing…flew away. I mean, it jumped up, flapped its wings, and flew away like a bat outta hell."

Dalton and the others walked over and studied the images as Todd went through them.

Jane had been carved up. Whatever the creature was that did this had tipped her over, jumped on top, then tore her to shreds.

Brad rubbed his chin. "I'm thinking out loud. The feet would have to have some massive talons. Check out the pattern."

Grant shook a finger at Brad. "Yeah, it did. They were huge, like chicken feet."

"Look at some of the claw marks," said Dalton. "That gives us an idea of how large this thing was."

"So you believe me?" asked Grant with hopeful eyes.

Dalton smiled. "We do. You're not insane or crazy. You saw what you saw, and we now have an idea of what we're dealing with."

Grant visibly relaxed as he adjusted his ball cap. "Thank the Lord."

"Although I shouldn't mention this, I will to give you some peace of mind. This isn't an isolated incident," said Dalton.

"There's others?"

Valerie smiled. "Several, actually."

"The police didn't mention that," said Grant.

"They wouldn't have known. Earth Ward would, though."

Grant sighed. "Well, whatever I can do to help, let me know. Sometimes the damn cows get out at night, but I'm adding more security and cameras too." He looked over at Greg. "Someone's got a lot of work ahead of him. See, I wasn't crazy."

Greg gave a weak smile and shrugged.

"Do you mind if we stay here a bit and go over this area?" asked Dalton.

"Be my guest," said Grant. He gestured at Todd. "I need to get out of this heat, and Greg needs to get back at it. Iced tea?"

"You know it," said Todd, slapping Grant on the back.

Todd peered at the others and nodded as he walked away. They could scan the area and project holography without having to explain it. Todd felt like he had contributed to the case outside of base knowledge. Grant was easy to talk to, and he relaxed the more they talked. Although Todd was no social engineer, he could lay on the charm as needed.

Dalton presented as an authority figure, and Grant would have been compliant if not uncomfortable. Brad would be considered different, and Grant's son had eyed him a few times, not out of maliciousness but interest. Todd suspected Grant and his son would have a difficult talk at some point if they had not already. Valerie would have been considered wild based on how she dressed. Maybe when they all had uniforms, it would normalize things out.

CHAPTER
SEVEN

B rad surveyed the grungy trailer park Dalton drove into. Trailer parks were a reoccurring theme, one Brad did not care for much. It was where he first sensed Dalton and Valerie six months ago. Now he was in an armored SUV with both of them. Life was full of surprises.

The farm visit yielded a lot of information. Most of it was gathered by Todd. Brad had sensed nothing, but then again, that was not a strong aspect of his ability. While he could sense other nonhumans, it was limited. Brad wished he had done more at the farm, but like Valerie, they were mostly along for the ride on that part.

At least he could watch things from Evot's aerial view. His sunglasses allowed him to use his ability freely, and it was only Dalton, Valerie, and him out at the spot for a while. Brad had relaxed due to the hot sun, a gentle breeze, and, in general, being outside.

They had picked up dinner after leaving the farm, and although there was no Burger House in town, they had a decent alternative. It was now 7:00 p.m., and the sun waned. It would be dark soon, and he wondered where they would hole up for the night. He tensed as he snapped back to reality when Dalton parked the SUV.

Dalton pointed at the yellow police tape. "That's where the scene is." He pointed at Valerie and Brad. "Why don't you two scour around and see what you can find? This is a nonhuman majority trailer park from what I understand."

Brad smiled. "Sounds good to me."

"Todd, you can come with me. Although there's no police on the scene, I suspect they might come, although they should have already been here and left," said Dalton.

Todd nodded. "No problem."

Dalton glanced at Evot. "Keep a servbot in the SUV and one in the air like last time."

"Of course," she said.

"All right, let's find out what we can, then meet back here in an hour."

Brad exited the SUV alongside the others. He joined Todd in the back when he opened the hatch. Although Brad was not planning on any trouble, if there was any, having a SP-8 would be helpful. Once he retrieved his, he holstered it on his belt.

Valerie grabbed two and put one on each thigh. She also took two stun batons and placed them on her back in an X pattern. Apparently, she had no issues with showing off her equipment. Todd had his backpack in case things got crazy, but Brad hoped it would stay calm.

Brad and Valerie took off down the main road, while Dalton and Todd went over to the crime scene.

"So just us this time," said Valerie. "Sort of felt like that at the farm."

"Yeah. I was just thinking about how I couldn't really do much there," said Brad.

Valerie nodded. "What do you think of all this so far?"

"I love it. After spending six months traveling around doing simple things, this feels like a challenge. A mystery to solve."

She laughed. "Yeah, I could sense you were that type." She eyed him. "It's good to be curious."

"What about you?"

"I like it so far," she said. "It hasn't gotten crazy or any-thing…yet, but these contracts pay extremely well, and I'd bet on Dalton every time."

"I'm with you there," said Brad. He surveyed the area. "So this is a nonhuman park mostly. I'm sensing a mix of Daedroulds and Outsiders."

Valerie pointed at a young woman smoking outside her trailer. "She's been eying us since we started walking. Definitely a Raskarian."

Brad studied the woman. "Well, if things get out of hand, I hope you can throw down. Vampires tend to get a little wild around me, present company excluded, of course."

"Who's to say I'm not going crazy inside?" she said, baring her fangs.

Brad's eyes widened.

She laughed and slapped his arm. "C'mon."

They walked over to the young woman.

She wore sneakers, ripped jeans, and a way-too-big T-shirt. Her scraggly, long black hair could use a shower, and her pale skin matched the color of the trailer. If he had to guess her age, he would say early twenties.

Valerie raised her head a bit. "Hey, got a moment to talk?"

The woman eyed her. "Maybe. You're Earth Ward, right?"

"Yeah, and I'm Valerie Simmons. He's Brad Washington."

The woman stood straight. "You can call me Anna." She stared at Brad. "Wildborn. That's new."

Brad cleared his throat. "Yeah, that's me."

Anna showed her fangs. "In the mood for a quick bite job?"

Brad raised his hands. "Uh, no thanks."

"Your loss. What about you?" asked Anna, glancing at Valerie.

"If we weren't here on business, definitely," said Valerie, grinning.

Anna sighed. "Fine. I don't know what you are either. I guess you're here to learn more about what happened to Brady."

"He was the victim at the crime scene?" asked Brad.

"Well, duh. I'm just surprised it took this long for Earth Ward to come out here."

"How'd you know we're Earth Ward?" asked Brad.

Anna pointed at the SUV. "Your blacked-out ride practically screams it. Oh, and the logo on the side." She gestured at Dalton and Todd. "And those two just look like law enforcement."

Brad sensed her defiance. She did not seem to have a lot of love for the Earth Ward, a theme he had seen played out in other areas.

"Were you around when whatever happened to Brady occurred?" asked Valerie.

Anna nodded. "I was blitzed out of my skull, but, yeah, I saw him being a dumbass like he always was. He was high as hell and kept morphing back and forth into his moose form. Some crazy thing swooped down and ripped him to shreds when he was in moose form, then carried him off."

A shiver coursed through Brad. "Something came down and just…took a bite and left?"

"More than a bite," said Anna. "All that remained was the good part."

Brad wrinkled his brow. "Which was…?"

"His big cock."

Valerie and Anna laughed while Brad grimaced.

Anna smiled. "Anyways, the police came out and questioned everyone, and, of course, no one helped them. We know they're tight with the Faith Militia." She motioned at Valerie. "You're not a Daedrould, are you?"

"Nope, Zikarian, but that doesn't mean I don't get hated on by other Outsiders."

Anna sighed. "Damn other Outsiders."

They chuckled.

Valerie and Anna had formed a bond pretty quickly. Anna was rough around the edges, but so was Valerie. Brad was sure if he lived in this park, he probably would not last long.

Valerie gazed off in the distance. "Did you happen to catch which direction whatever it was flew off to?"

Anna pointed southwest. "It went into Ogben witch territory. Crazy bitches down there."

"I've heard of them," said Valerie. "They control a large swath of forested area in the Midwest."

"Yeah, and they're secretive as well, not to mention powerful. As long as they stay out of my shit, I'm good," said Anna. "Oh…you're going to go out there, aren't ya?"

Brad grinned. "Most likely."

Anna eyed him. "You sure you don't want a quick bite job to relax? You're all tensed up."

"I'm good," said Brad, looking down.

"You're cute when you're nervous."

Valerie poked his arm. "Yeah, he is." She focused on Anna. "Before we go, anything else about what you saw that might help us investigate?"

"Yeah," said Anna. "The wings on…whatever it was were a weird mix of, like, a bat's wing and an insect one. Oh, and it wore something. Not a uniform but, like, armor pads and leather straps."

Valerie's eyes narrowed. "Then this might not be a mindless creature."

"Definitely not. It knew how to avoid Brady's antlers."

"And his cock apparently."

They shared a laugh.

Brad was glad to have Valerie along. Although he was a bit nervous around two vampires, he was confident nothing would happen, but his natural instinct was to run. In his two years on Earth, he had become accustomed to that, and now here he was being offered a bite job.

"Anything like that in the Earth Ward knowledge base?" asked Valerie.

"Checking," said Brad.

Anna snatched his sunglasses. "Oh, cool. Your eyes are like little computers."

Brad smiled. "Yeah, sorta."

"So what? You a living computer or something?"

"I talk to technology. In this case, I'm connected wirelessly to our ride and accessing our systems that way."

"That's awesome," said Anna. She licked her fang. "I've had trouble with my router acting up. Maybe you could come inside and check it out?"

Brad focused. He sensed her router and connected to it. There was no doubt what the issue was. A recent firmware update was not playing nice and had scrambled some of her settings. The default update model was automatic, so it most likely happened without her knowing it. He did a quick check of her router type and saw they had rolled back the update. He got the older firmware and downgraded her router to use it.

"Done," he said.

"What? Really?" asked Anna.

"Yeah, you just had bad firmware on it. I've set it so it only updates when you tell it to instead of automatically."

She lunged forward and hugged him a bit longer than he was comfortable with.

His eyes widened.

"This feels nice," she whispered.

He stepped back and smiled. "Glad to be of service." He motioned at Dalton and Todd in the distance. "We should probably check in with them."

Anna studied Dalton. "Something's strange about him. I can sense his raw power even from here. What is he?"

"An evolved human," said Valerie. "And, yeah, he's powerful."

"Sure is," said Brad.

Anna winked at them. "All right. I'll be here if either of you change your mind and want to hang out or play around." She handed Brad back his sunglasses.

"Cool," said Brad.

He and Valerie took off toward Dalton.

"That was interesting," said Brad.

"Yeah, she definitely wanted a bite and then some," said Valerie. "You have a lot of control."

"Well, when you hide from vampires normally, it's not that hard, although I'm good friends with the ancient vampires."

Valerie nodded. "I'm glad they don't have a kill order on me. I still haven't seen or talked to them, but Dalton straightened all that out thankfully."

"They're good people," said Brad. "Definitely not at all what I expected. Might even see them if we stick around on this team."

"Yeah. Now *that* will be…interesting."

Six months ago, Valerie had thought the ancient vampires had a kill order on her. Instead, it was a preservation order since she was the last known Zikarian after her sister died. Brad loved hanging out with Lord Vygon, Lord Noskov, and Mikhail and enjoyed what little time he had spent with them. He also got to meet Evaran, something very few could say. Brad considered it a bonus to being an Earth Ward employee.

For now, he had a better understanding of what they were dealing with. As they approached Dalton, Brad observed a red-faced officer moving his hand around in an animated manner. Brad was not sure what was going on, but he was about to find out.

Dalton sighed as he studied Detective Westin, the hot-headed local law enforcement officer who had come out. He had a bad attitude and questioned what Dalton and the others were doing out there. He had shown his badge wallet and mentioned the rest of the team, but Detective Westin was not having any of it. A quick glance to the side showed that Valerie and Brad had been talking to someone and they were now on their way over.

Dalton focused on Detective Westin. "Look. You can argue all you want, but we have jurisdiction here. I'm not trying to steal your case as you're suggesting."

"Sure you aren't," said Detective Westin. "You might not be Earth Ward for all I know."

"Call the sheriff or your captain if you don't think so, then. I'm curious as to how you knew we were out here in the first place."

"I ask the questions! Let's see what the captain says," said Detective Westin as he huffed off to his car.

Valerie and Brad arrived.

Todd shook his head. "That guy has some issues."

"Yeah, he does," said Dalton. "Nonetheless, I got a good scan of the area." He looked at Brad and Valerie. "You two find anything?"

Brad grinned. "Yep. The victim was Brady, a weremoose who apparently was too high to put up much of a fight. Also, Anna, the Raskarian vampire we talked to, got a look at whatever is causing all this. She said it flew into Ogben witch coven territory southwest of here."

Dalton rubbed his chin. "Interesting. That's a fairly large area."

"If we go in there, they won't take our intrusion as well as the Tanner Pack, I suspect," said Valerie. "I've heard of the Ogben Coven. They're pretty territorial."

"Sounds like it. However, if that's where whatever we're looking for is, then we'll go there," said Dalton. "I'd like to talk with Anna. I need to get rid of Detective Westin first, then we can leave. I suspect Detective Westin's partner is en route, but they'll leave once he is done with his call."

"Works for me," said Valerie.

After a few minutes, Detective Westin had left, and the team met up with Anna.

"Wow, you just radiate power," said Anna, staring at Dalton.

"Thanks, I think," said Dalton. "I'm Inspector Dalton Kingston, Earth Ward, and with me is Todd Armani. You already met Valerie and Brad. They mentioned you got a visual on the attacker?"

"I did, sorta."

"Is there someplace more private we can talk?"

"We could go to the side of the trailer. No one seeing shit there unless they come over."

Dalton nodded. "Lead on."

They assembled between Anna's trailer and her neighbor's.

"Evot, I'll need you for this," said Dalton.

"Of course," she said. A moment later, she landed on Dalton's shoulder in her crow form.

Dalton gestured at Anna. "Okay, start describing it."

She glanced at Valerie, who shrugged. "All right…it stood about nine feet tall."

Evot projected a grayed-out humanoid figure at that height.

"Whoa. What is that?" asked Anna.

"This is holo-sketching. As you describe what you saw, the hologram takes shape," said Dalton.

Brad raised a finger. "It uses natural language processing to convert what you say into something that can be rendered. Typically, that requires a powerful system, but we got Evot."

"A bird is a powerful system. Right," said Anna. "Okay… moving on. It had wings like a bat, sorta."

Wings appeared on the projection.

"Bigger. Also, they had an internal part that sorta looked like an insect's wing," said Anna. She studied the change. "That looks about right. Let's see… It had large claws on its feet, and its legs were bent."

"Digitigrade?" asked Dalton.

"I…I don't know what that is."

"Like a dog's back legs where they walk on their toes. Humans are plantigrades."

"Uh-huh," said Anna. "It was digitigrade, then. Oh, and its skin was smooth for the most part, but I only know that because of how reflective it was. Well, there was some fur too but not much."

The projection updated.

Dalton studied it. "Interesting. Did you glimpse its hands or face?"

Anna shook her head. "Not the hands. The face had a snout or something, but I didn't get much more than that. Oh, and it had pads held together by straps on various parts, like the shoulder and chest."

"It wore light armor?"

Anna shrugged as the hologram updated. "That's what it looked like to me."

"Then this is possibly a sentient creature," said Dalton.

Todd walked around the projection. "This is impressive. Creating a hologram from a verbal description."

"I take it that's standard with the Earth Ward?" asked Anna.

"Not even close. This is specific to Dalton and Evot."

Anna squinted. "Oh. Well, that's about all I saw of it. It was fast, like, in and out in under a minute. I heard Brady scream, then he went quiet, and the only thing after that was bone crunching."

"Were you able to sense if it was an Outsider?" asked Brad. "I shoulda probably asked that the first time we talked."

"You were too nervous that you might enjoy a bite job," said Anna with a sly smile.

Everyone focused on him.

"Uh…yeah, that musta been it," he said.

Anna raised her head a bit. "It wasn't an Outsider, Daedrould, Wildborn, or anything with exotic energy. I did sense it was powerful, though, sorta like Dalton except nowhere near his power level." She studied Dalton. "You're planning on going after it I heard."

"If it went into the Ogben territory, we have no choice," said Dalton. "Do you know how we can contact the Ogben Coven?"

Anna laughed. "Yeah, but you're not gonna like it."

Todd grimaced. "The Ogben Coven is hostile even to nonhumans. They'll most likely attack first before talking."

Dalton sighed. "So we'll probably have to fight them first like Bog."

"Bog?" asked Anna. "You fought that werecroc asshole?"

Brad gestured at Dalton. "He not only whooped Hammer, but he beat Bog down too."

Anna eyed Dalton. "Then you're *way* more powerful than you let on."

"So I hear," he said. "Any place we should start?"

"You got a map?" she asked.

"Evot can display one."

The projection changed to an overhead view of the area.

Anna studied the map, then pointed at a location a few miles off a trailhead entry point. "I've heard that's where you go, but I've never checked it out myself. I thought the Earth Ward would know about that."

"We have no formal relations with them. This could be a chance for that," said Dalton.

Anna shrugged. "Good luck with that."

"All right. I think we have enough for our next move. Did we miss anything?"

Valerie shook her head. "I'm good."

Brad and Todd indicated they had no more questions.

Dalton extended his hand to Anna. "Thank you for your help."

Anna returned the handshake. "I'm not sure pointing to where you'll most likely die is helping, but whatever."

After a few minutes, they were in the SUV. Evot morphed into her cat form and hopped up on the dashboard.

Dalton began to drive. "This'll be interesting."

"Are we all going, or are any of us staying back?" asked Todd.

"We can all go," said Dalton. "Evot will leave a servbot behind in case she needs to drive off. The other servbot will be with us."

"That's so cool she can do that," said Brad.

Valerie nodded. "Yeah, what he said."

"I am cool," said Evot with a toothy grin.

Brad and Valerie laughed.

Dalton went over the case in his head. From what he understood at this point, something had killed the Tanner Pack members, the cow on the farm, and now the weremoose, which should not have been an easy fight. Anna had mentioned Brady was high and in no condition to fight back, though. With her holo-sketch, everything pointed to a strange creature that came from the Ogben-Coven-controlled forest. That was definitely within the Earth Ward's domain.

After a thirty-minute drive, they pulled into the isolated trailhead.

Dalton studied the cracked lot and overgrown vegetation on what he figured was a concrete bathroom. The wooden signs that pointed into the forest were defaced, and even the trail entrance was covered in underbrush. The light posts had busted bulbs.

"Yeah, no one's been here in a while," said Valerie.

"It's as far as we can go with the SUV," said Dalton.

Todd gestured outside. "It's going to get dark in about an hour and a half. Should we wait until tomorrow?"

"I'd prefer to meet them now, but if everyone wants to wait, we can."

"I'm good," said Brad.

"Same," said Valerie. "Plus, I can see in the dark."

Todd nodded. "Works for me. I grabbed goggles that have night vision if anyone needs one."

Brad perked up. "I could use one. This would also be a chance to work with Gizmo."

"All right, then," said Dalton. "Let's get geared up for a fight and head out."

CHAPTER
EIGHT

Todd concentrated on his surroundings as the group trekked down the beaten hiking path. Nature usually comforted him, but he also understood where he was entering. There was a good reason that slayers never entered a forest with a known nonhuman population, especially an hour or so before it got dark. If they were still inside, the chances of surviving became much less. It made sense that nonhumans ran to forests when trying to escape something, although the Ogben Coven was known for killing trespassers regardless of who or what they were.

Dalton walked up front with ease, and Todd appreciated his leadership qualities. He was tough but fair, and Todd sensed Dalton was a good person trying to do right. Valerie was not what Todd expected. She was quick-witted and had an insight that he had not expected. He was glad she put the past aside for this opportunity. Brad struggled a bit to keep up with the group, but his strength was more mental than physical. Evot flew above in her crow form.

Todd slipped on his goggles and smiled. A small window appeared where he could see a map that Evot updated. The Earth Ward possessed advanced gear, and he suspected he only scratched the surface of what was in stock. He made a note that if he was accepted on the team long term, he would spend some time researching what was available.

The hiking trail proved to be a bit tougher than Todd expected. The negligence allowed for it to be somewhat overgrown, although it was still easy to see the general outline. The rays of the setting sun descended through the treetops and created a spectacular display, and the low tree density allowed movement off the trail if necessary. There were some rotted signs along the way, and he was thankful there was a wooden bridge in decent shape over a small creek.

After thirty minutes, Dalton stopped to point out into the forest. His eyes glowed. "I suggest you leave."

Todd did not see what Dalton pointed at, and the hairs on Todd's neck rose.

"I don't sense anything," said Valerie.

"Me either," said Brad.

"It was a Displaced," said Dalton. "She has left, though."

Todd rubbed his arm. Displaced were essentially ghosts, the remains of exotic energy that still had some essence of its former host. Although he had read up on them, he had never seen one. It was apparent Dalton could. Displaced were known to be mischievous, and they could interact with things to some degree. To see or even interact with Displaced required great power, and it was used as a measuring stick among powerful entities. Dalton passed that test with flying colors.

After another thirty minutes, Dalton paused at a clearing. He raised his hand.

Todd went on alert as he surveyed the scene. It was now dark out, and he and Brad had slipped on their goggles. Todd did not have the sensory capabilities of the others, but his heartbeat ramped up. Something was off with the trees, and the silence had become more noticeable. Maybe it was more Displaced.

"Outsiders and Daedroulds," said Valerie.

Brad nodded. "Yep, although I can't sense where."

"There," said Dalton, pointing at a small cluster of trees on the edge of the clearing. "Get your weapons ready."

Todd drew his SG-5. Although he did not sense anything, he would take Dalton's lead if it came down to a fight.

Brad opened his backpack and set Gizmo on the ground. He rose up on four legs and faced where Brad did. He grabbed his SP-8 and joined Dalton. Valerie pulled out her dual SP-8s.

Everyone assembled around Dalton, who popped into his Scoutspectre mode and spawned his nanoshield.

Todd loved that Dalton could do that. He looked like an alien with advanced technology. Although Todd knew Dalton was an evolved human, it was hard not to think of him as somewhat alien. His technology was the stuff of science fiction stories.

Evot flew overhead and scanned the area with yellow beams from her eyes.

After Dalton pulled out his stun baton, he marched into the clearing toward the trees. He also moved his hand about, emitting a golden beam.

Although Todd saw some of the scan results from both of them in his goggles, it did not make sense. He was glad the group could even scan in the first place. Dalton must have been a fearsome inspector to try to hide or run from.

The group reached the trees.

Dalton re-formed his stun baton to his MH and put it back on his thigh. With his now free hand, he raised it toward the trees. "I can sense you. There is no need to hide from me. I'm Inspector Dalton Kingston, Earth Ward, and this is my team. We're investigating an unusual creature in these woods."

An older woman with pale skin, scraggly hair, and a tattered robe made of foliage walked out of the forest. "Earth Ward…begone!" She let out a bloodcurdling scream.

"Wait!" said Dalton.

The area came alive as trees slithered out of the forest. Large roots erupted from the ground and reached toward the group.

Todd's heartbeat shot through the roof as he took aim and fired a stun beam at a root.

It coiled back and shrieked.

Dalton reformed his stun baton and burst into action, knocking a small tree away that had tried to hit him with a massive branch.

Valerie and Brad fell back and unleashed a hailstorm of stun shots at the roots. Gizmo moved around in sync with Brad and shot where he did.

Todd's mouth went dry as the woman walked through all the chaos without so much as a hint of fear. His pulse quickened when he tried to stun her, and his beam hit what appeared to be a bubble shield.

Brad cried out as a tree grabbed him and held him in the air. Gizmo tried to shoot the branch.

Evot flew down and landed on the branch, then did something with her feet that caused the branch to drop him.

Todd was not sure what happened, but her feet had become a blur.

Valerie tried to catch Brad, but they both tumbled to the ground.

Todd rushed over and upped the SP-5's stun setting. He let loose beams everywhere in an arc to keep the front clear.

Dalton danced and whirled while fighting four trees and two large roots at once.

Todd thought Dalton might get pushed back by the bubble shield as he approached the woman, but his eyes glowed, and he marched through the shield right up to her.

Dalton tapped her with his stun baton.

She collapsed.

Todd and the others provided focused stun beams on the trees that rushed to aid her.

"Stop!" bellowed a voice from the forest.

The trees paused.

Todd took a moment to catch his breath. This would have been a fatal encounter if it had been a slayer group. Evot hovered over Dalton and shone a light on a young woman who walked toward the older one on the ground. The approaching woman wore a black tunic with an open robe that had white-and-green embroidery. It looked like a battle outfit. She wielded a staff with an odd crystal at the end, and a bow and quiver resided on her back. Her black hair snuck out of her hood.

"Inspector Dalton Kingston, I'd like to talk," she said.

Dalton checked around. "I would too, but you preferred to fight instead."

"That wasn't me. It was Sima, my aunt, and she's... different. Part of what happens when you're over nine hundred years old. I sense she is merely unconscious, and I appreciate you not killing her. I'm Ranasa, a witch initiate of the Ogben Coven."

Dalton approached her and extended a hand. "Then let's start this off the right way. Inspector Dalton Kingston, Earth Ward, and with me is my team: Brad Washington, Todd Armani, and Valerie Simmons."

Ranasa studied his hand, then shook it. "I've heard rumors of you. I never expected you to show up here, though."

"Sima knew we were Earth Ward."

Ranasa smiled. "You're more known than you might think. You make an impression. Why are you here?"

"It's a long story, but in summary, we're investigating a strange creature that has been roaming around and killing cows and nonhumans and I'm sure some humans who haven't been reported yet. The last attack was on a nearby trailer park, and a witness had the monster flying here."

Ranasa sighed. "I know of the creature you speak of. However...perhaps you should talk with High Priestess Kreelah. She'll know how to help you. I can take you to her and the coven if you're interested."

Dalton nodded. "We definitely are." He faced the group. "Is everyone okay?"

Brad rubbed his chest. "Hurt a little here, but other than that, I can walk."

"Same," said Valerie, holding her side. "I'll heal."

"I'm good," said Todd.

"All right, then. I think we're good to go," said Dalton.

Ranasa studied Brad. "You're a Wildborn!"

Brad smiled. "So I've heard."

She walked over and touched his face.

Brad grimaced. "Uh…hello to you too?"

She smiled. "You're the first one I've ever seen. I'm sorry if I got excited."

"It's cool."

Ranasa faced Valerie. "You're an Outsider, but I don't know—"

"Zikarian and last of my kind. Oh, and vampire."

Ranasa grinned. "Interesting mix." She scrutinized Todd. "Human. *That*, I am familiar with."

Todd shrugged. "I'm the only pure one in this crowd."

"I see," said Ranasa. She scrutinized Dalton. "You're something else. Not an Outsider, Daedrould, or Wildborn."

"I'm an evolved human."

Ranasa nodded. "Right. Kreelah will be interested in talking to you. C'mon." She took off into the forest.

Todd followed the others as they moved off. The various tree shifters in the fight shuffled away, and one carried Sima. He had never met an Ogben witch, but their introduction had been like a handshake and a punch to the face. Hopefully, the rest of the coven was not as crazy as Sima.

This was a unique opportunity to get an inside look at a coven. In the past, it was done with a shotgun. He had no doubt that even a well-equipped slayer unit would die in these woods. Learning about all the cultures he had only heard of was one aspect he looked forward to, assuming Dalton kept the team intact. Todd hoped so, as he liked everything so far.

Sima had surprised Valerie. Although she was aware of shapers—those who controlled a bubble-shaped area around them—that was a power usually granted to warlocks and other specialized strains. To see a witch with it was rare. From Valerie's experience, most witches were able to focus their control on an object near them.

Ranasa was a good example, as she effortlessly moved branches and the like out of the way with but a wave of her hand. Sima was powerful, and Valerie did not think she would have survived an encounter like that alone. That spoke to Dalton's power. He had waded into the fight without a hint of fear, and he seemed to know exactly how to deal with shapers. Most did not.

Valerie had tried to catch Brad when he fell, but as fast and strong as she was, she could not get there in time. Instead, she became a cushion, but at least Brad was not seriously hurt. Both of them took a hit, though, and her bruised shoulder ached.

Gizmo had moved easily along with Brad's movement. She saw how powerful that could be if there were heavier versions or a swarm.

Valerie was not sure where they were geographically headed, but Evot tracked everything, which would be relayed to Dalton. Various Outsiders and Daedroulds had appeared during the trip, but they kept their distance. Valerie bet most sensed Dalton and were wary. That was to be expected. He had some type of energy that was not just different but powerful.

It intrigued her that the coven had tree shifters that were Outsiders, yet Ranasa was a Daedrould. The only other major group she knew of with mixed types like that was the Ollikrin nation. There were other shifters, and unlike the Tanner Pack, most appeared to be weremoose, wereboar, or forest related. However, she mostly sensed Daedrould, which indicated witches and warlocks for this area. Most covens were small, but the Ogben Coven was anything but.

Valerie enjoyed the investigation up to this point. Todd was definitely used to fighting, whereas Brad was not. However, she saw how powerful Brad's ability was. There was no animosity on the team, although everyone could be trying to put their best foot forward. The fight with Sima showed what working together was like, and so far it was somewhat clumsy. Still, she got to travel somewhere she would never visit alone.

After a thirty-minute hike, they reached a clearing surrounded by large trees. Stone benches resided on the edge.

It was some type of speaking area. Valerie had seen something similar when she had spent time with the Ollikrin nation. Posts with torches ringed and lit the area, but she could see well in the dark. Todd and Brad had taken off their goggles, and she made a note to see if they provided any value to her.

Ranasa ushered them to the center. "Wait here. High Priestess Kreelah will be out shortly with the others."

They moved to the center.

Valerie noted that Evot chose her crow form instead of her human one. Maybe it was so she could perch on Dalton's shoulder. Valerie's senses flared as witches and Outsiders appeared at the fringe of the clearing. They probably wanted to know what was going on. If it got messy, it would be a tough fight. Although Todd was normally cool and calm, he held his SG-5 close.

An elder woman flanked by several others approached.

Valerie suspected she was High Priestess Kreelah. She wore a black tunic with a robe and a hood that covered most of her pale face. Her silver hair peeked out, and a staff adorned with an unusual crystal at the end complemented the outfit.

The other women wore similar outfits, although most of their embroidery was silver and blue, whereas Kreelah's was gold and green. The colors probably indicated some sort of hierarchy.

Kreelah raised her staff, and everything went silent. "The Earth Ward has sent Inspector Dalton Kingston to us."

The coven murmured.

"And he has brought his team. A human, a Wildborn, and a Zikarian, who is the last of her kind," said Kreelah. She gazed at Dalton. "I heard some of why you're here, but I'd like to hear it from you."

Dalton cleared his throat and stepped forward. "A creature has been attacking nonhumans. I'm sure it has also been doing the same to humans. The Tanner Pack requested Earth Ward assistance, so I came with my team. We've tracked the creature to this area."

"We know of this foul demon you speak of," said Kreelah. She glanced at her sisters, then back at Dalton. "It is tough and has evaded us. It's also intelligent and appears to have some knowledge of armor."

"Do you know where it came from?" asked Dalton.

Kreelah shook her head. "It appears for an hour or so, then disappears. It can fly, and recently, it took Skylka from us."

Dalton looked at Evot.

"Skylka is registered as the granddaughter of Circe, an Outsider with the Greek Pantheon," she said.

"Your crow talks," said Kreelah.

Evot flew off to the side and morphed into her human form. "I do."

Kreelah and the others stepped back. "You're a werecrow, but I don't sense you."

Dalton raised a hand. "Evot is my artificial intelligence. She controls a swarm that allows her to create different forms."

"You possess Helian technology, then," said Kreelah.

"I'm more advanced than that," said Dalton. "Back to this creature. Did it look like this?"

Evot projected Anna's holo-sketch.

Kreelah stepped forward and waved her staff through it. "You control light. Impressive."

Evot started to say something, but Dalton motioned at her with his hand down. He faced Kreelah. "It's a tool to help me perform investigations. If you have any additional details, it will help shape the hologram."

"I see," said Kreelah. She studied the display. "Yes, it did look like that. However, the arms were bulkier, and the face was a cross of a dog's and a bat's. It had fur on some parts of its body outside the pads." She scrutinized the changes. "Yes, that's it."

Valerie shuddered at the final hologram. The creature looked like it flew out of some darkened hell. Its massive claws on its feet and hands were very noticeable. The face resembled a jackal's.

Dalton nodded. "If you can point me to where you last saw this creature or where it last attacked, I'd like to go there and camp out until midnight."

"You want to use yourself as bait," said Kreelah. "Skylka is a demigod, but she is our demigod, and she is powerful. Do you believe yourself stronger than her?"

"I don't know. The most powerful nonhumans I've fought to date are Hammer and Bog."

Kreelah studied him. "And how'd that go?"

"Hammer is in a dimensional prison and is maimed, and Bog was defeated yesterday," said Dalton.

"You may be powerful enough, then, but they didn't fly."

Valerie had not expected that Kreelah would know who Hammer and Bog were. She probably had a good information network, although maybe not a current one.

"I have to try," said Dalton, his eyes glowing.

Kreelah and the others stepped back. Some gasped.

"What are you exactly?" asked Kreelah.

"An evolved human."

Kreelah shook her head. "I've sensed your energy type before, but it was from Evaran, the god of time."

Dalton smiled. "I traveled with him recently. He actually brought me here to this Earth."

"Then you're his high priest, similar to my role."

"Not quite. He's more like a brother to me and a close friend."

Kreelah fidgeted with her staff. "Then it is no coincidence you arrived in our time of need. We need Skylka back, and I think your destiny is to return her."

"We'll try," said Dalton. "We're ready to go."

"Before you do…" said Kreelah. She examined Valerie. "I'm sorry to hear you're the last of your kind. I'm guessing your kind fell prey to both humans and nonhumans."

"They did," said Valerie, sighing.

Kreelah examined Brad. "And a Wildborn. How rare and, more importantly, older than eighteen."

Brad smiled. "I like to think I am."

"You, too, are a survivor," she said, eying Todd. "And a human but not a normal one. You're wisened and at ease with nonhumans, which suggests a history with them. Most humans with that level of confidence are usually ex-slayers."

Todd looked down. "That was the past." He raised his head. "I'm here to help Dalton with this case."

"How noble. You wish to atone for your past actions."

Todd glanced away.

Valerie was not sure how Kreelah picked all that out, but apparently, she had a good ability to read people.

"One other thing. The Kaz Lodat has been seen in the area," said Kreelah.

Dalton's eyes narrowed. "I'm not familiar with them."

Valerie grimaced. "The Helians, who took on the appearance of angels to humans, branded the Kaz Lodat as demons. Since then, their black eyes, above-human strength and speed, and other gifts have been…demonized."

"A branding effort by the Helians," said Todd. "I'm not sure what they're doing here, but there aren't a lot of them globally. However, they are a tight unit. I've read the slayer reports on a few encounters."

Dalton interacted with his forearm interface. "Interesting. There aren't many registered with the Earth ward."

"By design," said Valerie. "They operate in the shadows."

"If they interfere, then we will deal with them," said Dalton.

Kreelah nodded. "If they come any farther into our territory, they will be dealt with." She reached into a hip bag and pulled out a round stone. "This is a binding stone and

is bound to Skylka. It glows in whatever direction she's in."
She grimaced. "As you can see, it's not glowing now, but I
refuse to believe she's gone yet." She offered him the stone.

He grabbed it and fidgeted with it. "Thank you."

She snapped her fingers. "Ranasa! Take them to where
they need to be." She tilted her head at Dalton. "I hope
you find Skylka and deal with this monster. I think your
appearance here has always been fated."

"More than you might know," said Dalton with a grin.
He motioned at Ranasa, who stood at the edge. "All right,
everybody, let's go."

Valerie enjoyed the interaction, and she understood how
rare it was. The other witches had already cleared a path for
Ranasa and Dalton. Valerie followed them and listened to
the varied conversations as she passed the coven members.
Some called Dalton the god of time's brother, while others
said he was a demigod. She suspected he might enter the
coven's mythos if he rescued Skylka.

Dalton could see in the dark, and the half-hour trek to the
last sighting of the creature was a lot easier due to a cleared
path. It was 10:40 p.m., and the moon provided decent
illumination. The clearing they reached revealed a grassy
field. He tried to sense if there were other Ogben Coven
members around, but only Ranasa registered. The creature
must be tough to not only fight the coven but also take
Skylka.

Ranasa pointed to the middle of the clearing. "If you want to get this creature's attention, just wait there. Although its appearance is random, we think it comes nightly."

"We could do a campfire, then," said Todd. "That'd definitely get its attention."

Dalton nodded. "Possibly, but I can shoot a light up from my MH which is more powerful and can be seen easily. It will use about five charges an hour, but I have about eighty charges left. Plus we won't have to build a fire."

"This will leave you without your stun baton," said Evot.

Dalton shrugged. "I can grab it if needed. As long as I have my nanoshield, I can deflect any potential air attack. That would give me enough time to grab my MH and form my stun baton. Besides, I still have my RSG." He surveyed the area. "All right, let's go set this up. Ranasa, thank you for guiding us here."

She nodded and took off.

The rest of the group walked out to the middle of the clearing. Gizmo scuttled about.

Dalton saw potential in Brad's ability to control drones like that. In the earlier fight, it had performed well, and the thought crossed Dalton's mind to look into better applications of that in future fights. Maybe a swarm of microbots could be designed.

He pulled out his MH to adjust it so the top part formed a wide spotlight, with a small blade for the bottom. Once configured, he plunged it into the ground, then activated the light.

A bright beam reached into the sky.

"That's seriously impressive," said Todd.

Dalton nodded. "Well, now we can wait and admire it."

They sat around it in a circle.

Todd grinned. "Nothing unusual about sitting around a light at night in order to attract a demonic creature in witch-filled woods."

Everyone laughed.

"I suppose it does sound odd when you take a step back," said Dalton.

"Are you sure you'll be able to fight this creature if it comes?" asked Todd.

"We'll see when it arrives. Based on what we know of it, I believe I've fought stronger."

Todd eyed him. "I know you haven't talked much about your past…but what would compare?"

"I don't mind telling you all," said Dalton. He pointed up. "Before I came here, I fought against a space empire known as the Tenagrin Hegemony in the Horologium-Reticulum super cluster, which is very far away from here. I was traveling with Evaran and the gang at the time, and we assaulted an entrenched Tenagrin fortress. The Tenagrins were snakelike, and one unit in particular, a juggernaut, stood about twelve feet tall or so and weighed over fifteen hundred pounds. Juggernauts wore heavy armor and wielded massive two-handed weapons. They would have easily crushed Hammer or Bog. Nonetheless, I took on two juggernauts at the same time."

"No shit?" asked Brad.

Dalton smiled. "I prefer not to fight if I can. However, some situations require it. This is one of those times unless the creature wants to talk."

Brad laughed. "Yeah, I don't think that's likely."

"Well, if it comes, we got your back," said Todd.

Dalton liked having Todd on the team. Although he may have been nervous during the fight, it did not show or affect his fighting ability. The SG-5 had proved its value, and Todd operated it with ease. It also assuaged some of Dalton's concern with Brad and Valerie. Although they had performed well, it might have been worse without Todd there. His cool manner helped keep things calm.

"I appreciate that. We know this thing likes to fly in," said Dalton.

"Wish we had brought a net," said Todd.

"That would help, but we can try stunning it first," said Valerie. "Why do you think it only comes out at night? Maybe it lives in a cave and hates light."

Dalton rubbed his chin. "That's a good point." He showed his palm. "I can emit bright pulses from my scanner to disorient it."

"Really?" she asked.

"Observe," said Dalton. He aimed at the ground and emitted several pulses of blinding light.

"Whoa," said Todd, squinting. "Yeah, that's pretty handy."

"And bright," said Valerie, grimacing.

Dalton smiled. It felt good to have a team. The last six months had been rougher than he had expected. Although he could handle the cases tossed at him, there was little room for error. He thought about if he had to face this creature by himself. If something went wrong, that would be it. A team opened up other options.

After several hours, Dalton sensed a presence. It was now 1:00 a.m., and Valerie and Brad had snoozed off. Todd remained on high alert as expected. Whatever approached was on the edge of his senses, so that was about fifty feet. The fact it was in the air and not something he recognized most likely meant it was the creature.

"Evot! It's coming! Try to highlight it!" he said.

"Of course," she said as she flew up.

Todd stood and pulled out his SG-5. "Not seeing anything."

Brad and Valerie woke up.

"What's going on?" asked Brad.

"It's here," said Dalton.

Valerie jumped up and pulled out her SP-8s. Brad joined her.

As they looked up, Evot bathed the creature in her lights. It chased her, but she was more nimble and able to evade.

"Evot, bring it here," said Dalton.

"On my way," she said.

Dalton's heart raced as it approached. Based on the holo-sketch, it was a little different but not by much. The wide wings, clawed feet and hands, and jackal-like face were true, but the body was covered in a mix of armor and fur, an unusual combination. He suspected the shine Anna mentioned was from the armor pads. Two massive fangs also jutted out from its snout.

"Oh shit!" said Todd, firing away.

Dalton went into Scoutspectre mode and spawned his nanoshield. After forming his RSG, he shot at the creature.

It shrugged off both stuns and barreled down at him.

He raised his shield. The creature landed on him, slamming him into the ground.

Brad and Gizmo unloaded stun beams at it.

It roared as it raised its clawed hands toward them.

Valerie switched to her stun batons and rushed in. She dodged the beast's strikes and slipped behind it, then kicked it off Dalton.

He jumped up and charged the creature. His shield-bash knocked it to the ground.

Everyone fired a stun beam at the beast.

It growled and faced them.

Dalton flashed it with a series of blinding light pulses.

It shielded its eyes, then turned and leapt into the air.

"Evot, track it!"

"Of course," she said as she took off.

Dalton grimaced, realizing he had some bruising. The creature was heavier than he thought, and one of its foot claws had cut his arm.

"Well, we know bright light works," said Brad.

Dalton placed a hand over his wound. "And it has sharp claws and is heavy." He morphed back to his official mode. "There's also some type of paralyzing poison on its claws, but my super cells are fighting it. No wonder this thing is so effective."

"Poisoned claws. Awesome," said Todd, shaking his head.

"It's chasing me again," said Evot over comms.

Dalton sighed. "Come back."

"Okay," she said.

After a few minutes, she appeared in the air with the creature on her tail. Once it saw where Evot headed, it turned around and flew away.

Evot rejoined the group and assumed humanoid form. "I think it's intelligent."

Todd wrinkled his brow. "How so?"

"It knew it was being followed, so it dove into the forest and tried to ensnare me. Although I was faster, it chased me to a specific clearing where I detected another creature."

"So there's more than one, and it tried to corral you with its bud," he said.

Evot nodded. "I believe so."

Dalton looked around. "All right. We can check it out tomorrow...in the daylight. For now, let's get a motel room for the night. This poison is ravaging me. I was poisoned on the case before this one, and it was much stronger, so I should be okay. I just need to rest for a bit."

"Motel sounds good to me," said Brad.

Dalton pointed at Valerie. "Nice kick you did back there."

She smirked and moved her hands off to the side. "It couldn't handle all this."

They laughed.

"No, it couldn't," said Dalton. He glanced at Brad and Todd. "You two held under pressure. That's a good sign."

"I just wish we coulda stunned it," said Todd. "We'll need nets or something next round or at least a different plan."

"Yeah," said Brad. "The fact it just shrugged off our stuns is crazy. It must have stun-resistant skin."

Dalton held up some of the beast's hairs. "Maybe, but it did cause some damage. Evot will be able to analyze this and the data on the poison in me when we get back. Everyone ready to go?"

"I am," said Brad. "These mosquitoes are playing games out here."

Valerie nodded. "I'm good to go."

"Same," said Todd.

"All right, let's move," said Dalton.

He pulled out some small bags from his belt and collected evidence. Although it would be contaminated, Evot should be able to filter it out. The fight did not go as planned, but that was somewhat expected because the creature was unknown. Its stun immunity most likely meant it was much more powerful than initially known. Chasing after it in the dark woods was not ideal, especially now that there was more than one.

Although he did not want to say anything in front of the group about the pain the poison caused, it hurt more than Azua's, but he could already feel it beginning to wear down. If any of the others had been hit, they would be down. It was time to regroup, lick their wounds, and plan their next step.

CHAPTER
NINE

Brad understood Dalton's choice to stay on the outskirts of town, but that also meant staying in a cheap motel. Its low-tech nature meant less opportunities for surveillance, although the rooms could be bugged. Brad surveyed the motel room and did not detect any hidden cameras or surveillance equipment. The room had two beds and a connecting door to Dalton and Todd's room. Valerie was his roommate for the night.

Their unit looked like it had seen better days. The green carpet was not an aesthetically pleasing choice. The beds had brown covers, and a rotary phone sat on a dresser between them. Opposite the dresser was an old television. He was not sure he wanted to check out the bathroom unless absolutely necessary.

Adrenaline still surged through him from the fight. If Dalton had not been there, that creature would have made quick work of the group. Brad suspected the monster calculated Dalton as a risk, but Brad did not think that extended to the others. Gizmo had turned out to be easy to control, and Brad had some ideas to enhance him. Brad's hands had shaken on the way back to the SUV. He had been less than ten feet away from potential death.

Valerie plopped down on her bed. "This ain't too bad."

Brad sat on the edge of his bed. "It'll work."

She eyed him. "You okay?"

He sighed. "Yeah, I am. I just didn't expect the creature to fire up some old feelings."

"Like…?"

"Like when I'm around an executioner android. Both represented death if within ten feet."

"Ah."

He raised his head. "And you must be fearless. You walked up to it and literally kicked its ass. I liked that."

Valerie shrugged. "This is a good gig, and I don't want to lose it because of some overgrown bat thing."

Brad studied her, then they laughed.

Dalton and Todd entered through the connecting door.

"I heard laughter in here," said Todd.

Brad smiled. "Yeah. We were just talking about Valerie kicking the monster in the ass."

"It was well played," said Todd. "I'm gonna get some bourbon. We have about forty minutes before we can't buy any."

"I'll go with you," said Valerie, hopping up.

Dalton nodded. "I'll be here. I want to have Evot analyze the samples I took."

"I can help her," said Brad.

Dalton tilted his head. "You don't want to sleep?"

"I do, but a few hours analyzing won't hurt. Besides, we have all day tomorrow to check out where that thing went, right?"

"We do," said Dalton. He grabbed his wallet and pulled out several hundred-dollar bills. He faced Todd and Valerie. "Consider this an advance."

"Works for me," said Todd as he took the money. He bowed toward Valerie and did a flourish toward the door. "After you."

Valerie opened it and grinned. "As expected."

They exited.

"They seem to be getting along well," said Brad.

Dalton sat opposite him. "They do. When I first met them, they got into a shouting match in that trailer park where I first sensed you."

"That's crazy to believe that the trailer park incident would lead to this."

"Hopefully, a good type of crazy."

Brad nodded. "Definitely."

Evot sat next to him. "I have scanned the samples and recreated them digitally. Do you want to view them on your laptop?"

He rubbed his chin for a moment, then faced Dalton. "Are you able to connect to her unsecured space?"

"I would hope so, considering she's anchored in me."

"All right. I'm thinking it might be faster if we meet in there." Brad glanced at Evot. "If that's okay, that is. If not, we can use my laptop."

Evot smiled. "My unsecured space is optimal for analysis."

"Sounds good," said Brad. He lay on the bed.

Dalton stretched out on the other one.

Evot morphed into her cat form and settled on Brad's chest.

"Comfy, are we?" asked Brad.

Her ears twitched. "I am. My space is ready."

Brad closed his eyes. The last time he had done this with Evot, they had gone through some stolen data. When he opened his eyes, he stood on a platform with a tiled floor. There were no walls, and the platform hung in space. He understood why they were there when Dalton, who appeared as a glowing energy figure, waved his hands around.

Holograms of the various pieces of evidence were displayed outside the platform.

Brad studied the data labels, graphs, and charts that flew off to the side of each piece.

He pointed at the fur sample. "So it shows that this thing is not from this Earth, at least based on its...what I think is DNA, but what are those weird things on it?"

Dalton nodded. "They're referred to as i-motifs and G-quadruplexes. Humans have them, but I've never seen them in this density before. It's the other strange formations that tell me this creature is not from this Earth. I did not sense any exotic energy either, so I'm thinking this creature is an alien."

Brad cocked his head. "So if it's an alien...*how* did it get here?"

Evot pointed in another direction, and a hologram of her pursuit of the creature displayed. "I chased it into the forest but detected another creature there. Perhaps they have a ship nearby."

Brad examined the other highlighted monster. It hid behind a tree and was in position to nab Evot as she flew by. It was obvious these creatures were intelligent.

"It's a good thing you didn't go down there, then," said Dalton.

"Yes, and when I didn't fall for their trap, the one we fought pursued me back to the group."

"We'll check out that area during the day. My bright-light pulses drove it off, although if it was an alien with a ship, I would have expected more advanced gear. This is not adding up."

Brad browsed the database of results and picked one. He pointed to the side, and a visualization of the data appeared. How it was able to convert raw data into what he saw without any sort of visible transformation impressed him, but then again, Evot was an AI.

"Check this out," he said. "Evot's scan shows that their skin can handle light, but your pulses would hurt it."

Dalton examined the data. "We can use that to our advantage. It also means that wherever they come from must be dark or twilight. The poisoned claws are probably an offensive adaptation."

Brad shuddered. "Yeah, sounds great."

Dalton laughed. "We need more information. This encounter gave us a lot of insights, and we now know what we're up against. I'm not surprised it took down two Tanner Pack members and a cow, and I suspect the kill list is actually longer. The goal is to find out where it's coming from, and I'm beginning to think it came through a localized space rift."

"You mean like a portal or something?"

"Yep," said Dalton. "From what I learned on the *Torvatta*, portals can either go through space or time or both. I don't know which one these creatures are using, but if I can find the portal they are coming from, I can seal it permanently."

"You mean these things could not only be from another place but another time?" asked Brad.

"Potentially, yes."

"That's nuts." Brad glanced at Evot, then back at Dalton. "How would you seal the portal?"

Dalton raised his hand, which erupted into a blue glow. "I have what is called a Torvatta-touch. It allows me to open, close, and seal any portal or rift I can sense. Also, if I'm in another timeline, I can open a portal back to this timeline at any time. Oh, and I can open a portal to another nearby one, assuming I can sense it."

Brad took a moment to digest what he had just heard. Dalton was already powerful, but this Torvatta-touch ability was unusual compared to his other abilities. Brad understood the *Torvatta*, Evaran's ship, had given Dalton the ability, which in itself was hard to believe. He was uniquely qualified to deal with cases of this nature. Maybe Kreelah suggesting it was Dalton's destiny to save Skylka was not far off.

"You with us?" asked Dalton.

Brad cleared his throat. "Oh, yeah. Sorry. I got caught up in my thoughts." He gestured at Dalton. "Yeah, that Torvatta-touch sounds like it would do the job, but…"

"But what?"

Brad licked his lips. "What if Skylka is alive and on the other side? Jim also mentioned there were others missing. Maybe they're over there too. Are you going to go after them?"

Dalton smiled. "Of course, assuming they weren't torn up like the others. For Skylka, the stone Kreelah gave me should help. For the others, I'm not sure how to find them."

"And the only way to find out is to explore, so we can't just shut down the portal if we find it."

"Unfortunately, no. However, I can extend the binding stone through to see if it glows. Maybe they were all taken to the same place."

Brad nodded. "That might work, but how do we prepare for some place we've never seen?"

"Very carefully," said Dalton, grinning.

They laughed.

"We do know something of the creature, so it's not completely unknown," said Dalton.

"You would think the Ogben Coven would have more information," said Brad.

Evot tilted her head. "They do not possess the necessary technology to evaluate what they faced."

"Yeah, but I'm sure they sensed it, and they should be plenty strong enough to handle it."

Evot nodded. "This assumes they know when it attacks and where. Their demigod being captured most likely has shaken their confidence."

Brad sighed. "Yeah, I guess so. It'd be like if Dalton were taken out. I don't know what we'd do."

"Hopefully, get me back," said Dalton.

"Yeah, but, I mean, how? I guess we have our communication interface on our undersuits, but how would that work through a portal?"

Dalton eyed him. "Let's hope we don't get separated."

He laughed. "Yeah."

Dalton peered out into the dark. "All right, let's work on seeing if we can construct this creature's environment."

Brad loved being able to have these types of conversations in Evot's unsecured space. He understood how rare someone like Evot was, and Dalton was even rarer. They were by far the two most unique people Brad had ever met. Maybe this was a reward for all the hell he had been through. He much preferred this to being chased by exterminator androids or doing menial work for the Earth Ward.

Todd focused on the fight as he drove with Valerie to a nearby liquor store. The creature was right out of a horror movie, and he could not shake the image of it when it had looked at him and roared, as if saying to come and get some. The fact that one cut from its claws would incapacitate him scared him. Although he always felt like he had nerves of steel, that moment made his knees weak. He recognized the creature for what it was: a predator.

The SG-5 had performed admirably against the Ogben Coven but did not fare well when fighting the creature. His tendency was to use lethal weapons, but he would try to abide by Dalton's wish to use nonlethal ones. Still, a shotgun would have turned that monster into mincemeat, or so he thought.

Brad fought admirably, and Valerie fascinated Todd. She was fearless and had no hesitation in kicking the creature in the ass. Dalton was one tough cookie. He not only took a full hit from a dive-bomb, but he got back up and shield-bashed the winged attacker. Todd was curious what Dalton, Evot, and Brad would find from their samples. Hopefully, something that could be used against it the second time around.

He grinned at Valerie in the passenger seat. She had one of her feet up on the dash, and she had relaxed in her chair. He was glad there was no animosity between them and wished he had come to the realization earlier that nonhumans were people too. It still troubled him that he was a factor in so many nonhuman deaths. Half of them were not deserved.

"So what do you think so far?" asked Valerie.

Todd glanced at her. "I'll be honest. I'm kinda liking this, although I could do without the flying poisonous monsters."

"Yeah, me too. I mean, the money's good, and there's definitely no shortage of action, but I like working with Dalton."

"Same," said Todd. He cast a sidelong glance at her. "I never looked into it, but…what happened when Dalton rescued you from the Faith Militia?"

Valerie sighed. "I killed Zeke, as you already know. Then I got surrounded by a group of around ten slayers. I'm tough but not that tough."

"I heard it was a fight and a half, the type that makes hair grow on your chest. Well, not yours obviously."

Valerie smirked. "I'd hope not. Anyways, they put me in that damn building, then Craig tortured me for hours."

"That sucks."

"Yeah, but when Dalton came, he did his robot armor thing, took a direct shot, then stunned Craig. After that, Dalton let me feed on Craig to get my strength back."

Todd shook his head. "That's some crazy shit right there. I remember running up and seeing Dalton in his Scoutspectre mode, as he calls it, pointing some advanced gun at me. I was like, yeah, not messing with that."

They laughed.

He cleared his throat. "I'm angry that Zeke killed your sister and niece and made you the last Zikarian on the planet."

Valerie gazed out the window. "It's life. I told my sister she needed to hide, to blend in, but she was always an optimist and tried to see the good in people. I told her humans were an apex predator species and if given a chance, they would prey on her. She didn't listen. Her husband was tough, a werebadger, but not much you can do when eight slayers open fire with assault weapons."

"Damn," said Todd. "I heard when they found Zeke in his trailer, you cut off his balls and stuffed them in his mouth?"

Valerie smiled. "Sure did. I also stuffed his heart up his ass since that's where it always was."

Todd chortled. "I remember hearing about it, but I didn't go see the body. I just heard it was some nasty shit."

"He deserved it."

"Yeah, I know that now. I still can't believe I bought into all that bullshit. The Faith Militia preys on those who are angry and looking to lash out. Mix in religion, and you got an explosive cocktail."

Valerie nodded. "I tried to stick to assassinating people and killing slayers between contracts for sport."

"I'm glad I didn't cross paths with you until now, then."

They pulled into the liquor store's parking lot.

Todd enjoyed talking with Valerie. She turned out to be the most laid-back, fiercest person he had ever met outside of Dalton. Confidence oozed off her, and although he thought he could never be with a nonhuman, he found her attractive. He would not pursue that, as you never got involved with your teammates if you could help it.

They exited the SUV and approached the liquor store's entrance.

"Damn!" said a drunk guy with his arm hanging out of a truck. "You got some fries with that shake?"

Another man in the truck laughed.

"Sure do," said Valerie. "You got a napkin for that drool?"

The man drew his head back.

"C'mon, they're just drunk assholes," said Todd.

"Maybe I'll be one soon too," said Valerie as they entered the store.

Todd made a beeline to the whiskey section, while Valerie went to check out the wine area. He quickly found some bourbon. She joined him a minute later with what looked like an expensive wine bottle. Dalton giving them an advance was unexpected. Todd had figured he would get a six-pack but not when he had cash to spend.

As they were paying, the drunk man from outside staggered in.

Todd gave him a quick look. He was overweight, and his belly peeked out under his shirt. One of his hiking boots was unlaced, and his pants were stained. His ball cap did not hide his greasy hair, and his pale skin had a sheen on it, as if he exhausted himself by entering the store.

"Hey!" said the man. "I...I think you were..." He struggled to keep something down. "Making fun of me."

Valerie eyed him. "We never talked. Who are you?"

"We...we did! I think..." he said.

Valerie shook her head. "No, I'm sure I'd remember talking to someone of your caliber."

"That's right! You would!"

Todd shook his head as he paid the cashier.

The drunk guy stared at Valerie. "Damn! You got some fries with that shake?"

"You got a napkin for that drool?" she replied.

"Oh, no, I don't," he said. He wiped his mouth.

They moved past the man and got back into the SUV.

As they backed out, the drunk stumbled out and pointed at them. "Hey! You...you already said that!"

Valerie rolled down her window and winked at him. "Who are you again?"

The guy stared at the ground in confusion.

Valerie laughed as they drove out of the parking lot.

"Glad that didn't escalate," said Todd.

"Nah, he was in no condition to fight. I'd easily snap his neck if he tried," said Valerie.

Todd's eyes widened.

"Well…maybe I'd just break a bone or two. This is the new Valerie."

"Right."

She pulled out her wine bottle and opened it, then chugged it.

Todd was not sure if she was kidding, as he did not know her that well. She could have easily caused a scene and destroyed the drunk and probably the guy in the truck too. He was glad she restrained herself, or maybe she really was taking a new approach to life. From what he had heard after looking her up from the trailer incident, she had been a highly effective assassin and had taken down some tough marks.

"You're gonna be wasted before we get back," he said.

"Unfortunately, I'll just get a buzz. Zikarian and all that. Besides, if I did get drunk, you might try to take advantage of me."

"What?"

She scrunched her face as she laughed. "Your face!"

Todd puffed his cheeks as they continued on. Valerie liked to tease, and he suspected she enjoyed stirring the pot to get a reaction from others. He was used to being around people like that, so it did not bother him. She must have felt comfortable enough in his presence to let her guard down some, although it could also be that she did not care. Non-humans were hard to read, and Zikarians were completely unknown to him. He liked what he saw so far and looked forward to seeing how she, and the team, evolved over time.

CHAPTER
TEN

Valerie sat on the roof's edge over the room the others were in. It was 2:45 a.m., and she should probably sleep, but she had wine. Dalton, Brad, and Evot were in some trance state, although Evot had her cat form out and mentioned they were researching and discussing things. Todd had gone to his room and planned to have a nightcap before sleeping. Valerie decided she would enjoy her wine outside in the fresh air. Climbing up to the roof was not hard, as there were plenty of handholds.

She swung her legs as she took a swig. The wine was good, and she enjoyed the light breeze and the moon illuminating everything. Although she could have joined Dalton, Brad, and Evot, she was not in the mood for anything technical. Some alcohol and relaxation were on her mind, and after the fight, she needed something to cool down with.

When she was an active assassin, she always made time to drink something of the victim's at their place of residence. Her fellow assassins said it was sloppy, but she viewed the drinking as its own reward. Most of the contracts she took were real pieces of work. She had no qualms about killing them. Although the pay was good, the contracts were dangerous, and the more famous you became, the more enemies you made.

She wondered how her reputation would change by joining Dalton's team. Perhaps if she helped resolve the toughest cases, others might reconsider bothering her for revenge or having a contract placed on her. Her assassin acquaintances from the past would still see her as one of them, and they would probably think she had an angle to get to a hard-to-reach target. She did not care what they thought, though.

Teaming up was easier and paid well, or so she hoped, and she surprisingly liked the members of the team. From where she came from, sleeping with them would speed up getting to know them better. Unfortunately, humans had a strange take on morality, and the chemical reactions in their brains, compared to hers, made that type of bonding out of the question. It usually destabilized them, the opposite of what happened in her home dimension.

Companionship was one thing she did not have much of as an assassin. It was get in, kill, drink something, then hop out. Hiding in the shadows was essential, as was moving around a lot. Her friends were few, and those she had were fellow assassins who knew how to survive. Her throat constricted as she thought of her sister. If she had only prepared better, she might still be alive.

She sensed something on the edge of her senses and perked up. It was human, which was not unusual, but whoever it was, they were across the parking lot and behind some trees. The spot would provide a decent view of where the group stayed. She continued to act like she did not sense the human as she figured out what to do.

In the past, she would have slunk away, only to reappear and either gut the person or torture them for information. As part of Dalton's team, she had some options. He should be made aware and then decide what the next step would be. She grinned as she hopped down and entered the room. Once she closed the door, she tapped Dalton on the shoulder.

He snapped out of his trance and faced her. "You all right?"

Valerie crooked a thumb at the door. "I think we're being spied on. There's a human across the lot, hiding in the bushes behind some trees. I figured I'd tell you instead of torturing them."

"Yeah, let's not do that," said Dalton. He stood and activated his camouflage shielding. "Okay. I'll check it out."

"Wait!" she said. "You need to make it look normal. Let me go out first and then climb back on the roof. Whoever it is will think I went to use the bathroom."

Dalton nodded. "Good call. After you, then."

Valerie exited the room and climbed up to the roof's edge. She sensed Dalton even though he was invisible. That was a great skill to have to fool humans, but for nonhumans like her, she had a general idea of where he was and also his relative power. The human would have no such luck unless they had advanced gear.

After five minutes, a zapping sound filled the air. She hopped down and tapped on the door.

Brad, Todd, and Evot rushed out.

"What's going on?" asked Brad.

"Oh, you know, Dalton just zapping a spy, I think. Let's go!"

They assembled around Dalton, who stood over a stunned man.

"Brad, can you check to see what tech he has on him?" asked Dalton.

Brad nodded.

Todd shook a finger at the man. "Hey, this guy was at the sheriff's station."

"Derek," said Valerie, grimacing. "How could I forget that face?"

"Looks like he's a slayer too," said Brad. "His phone shows several numbers that match up with the Earth Ward slayer database."

"And he was out here tracking us. Hopefully not for a fight," said Todd.

Dalton rubbed his chin. "Here's what we'll do. Brad, use Derek's phone to text the sheriff. I assume that number is in the contacts."

"It is," said Brad. "What should I make it say?"

"That he's out of his mind and needs help."

Brad laughed. "Done."

"As for the rest of us, we should be wary if the Faith Militia knows our location," said Dalton.

"I'll sleep in the SUV," said Todd. "It has a place for that, and it's bulletproof. If we need a quick getaway, I'll be in position."

"Won't you get cold?" asked Brad.

Todd shook his head. "There's blankets in there. I made sure of that before we left."

Dalton nodded. "I'll join you. Brad and Valerie can use the room, and Evot can patrol the area in crow form. She can use her cat form in the room in case we need visuals, although I could send it to your suit interfaces as well. Evot, you good?"

"Of course," said Evot. She swapped to her crow form and took off while another servbot jumped out and formed a cat. She sauntered away with her tail swishing.

"Damn, now I'm feeling all paranoid," said Brad.

"I understand," said Dalton. "It may be nothing, but it's better to be prepared than not to be."

"What are we going to do with Derek?" asked Valerie. "Just leave him here?"

Dalton studied him. "Let's lean him against a tree but take his binoculars. Evot, when the sheriff arrives, try to get nearby so we can listen in."

"Of course," she said over comms.

"All right, everyone. Let's get moving," said Dalton.

Valerie grinned as she thought about the sheriff coming out to find his deputy unconscious outside a motel. She did not think the sheriff was compromised, so Derek most likely would not spill what he was doing out there, assuming he woke up. She looked forward to listening to what Evot picked up.

Dalton relaxed in the rear right seat of the SUV. Todd had the left chair, and he had lowered the back so it formed an almost horizontal surface. He lay down and sighed. Dalton had no doubt the chairs were comfortable, and he could see himself nodding off with ease if need be. The important thing was that if required, he could move to the driver's seat and drive.

Derek spying on them was not completely unexpected. Dalton operated under the assumption that the Faith Militia would track them somehow; he just did not know who would be doing it or where and when. Now he had all that information. Although the Faith Militia was entrenched in the area, there was also a sizable amount of powerful nonhumans.

"I can't wait to hear what the sheriff has to say to Derek," said Todd, placing his hands behind his head.

"Me too," said Dalton. He glanced over at Todd. "I wanted to say thank you for taking my offer to try out for the team."

"It's cool," said Todd. "I'll be honest—the offer came at the right time."

"I'm aware of your financial issues."

Todd laughed. "Yeah, no surprise there. With Evot, you've got access to a ton of information."

"She selected you, actually."

Todd perked up. "She did?"

Dalton nodded. "It was you and several others. That trailer park was more important than I realized."

"Yeah, I guess so. I remember seeing you in your Scout-spectre mode and thinking, 'Holy shit.'"

"I bet," said Dalton. He stared out the window. "There was another purpose for my wanting you on the team."

Todd propped himself up on his elbow. "Yeah?"

Dalton faced him. "You were a leader in the military, then in the Faith Militia. Should I go down for whatever reason or if I'm not available, I need you to step up."

"I take it, then, my membership is going to last past this trial?"

"Unless you do something crazy or die."

Todd's eyes widened. "Yeah…let's hope that doesn't happen."

"Evot has protocols to defer to you should I be down."

Todd gestured toward the front. "What about Valerie? She's older than I am by far and probably has more experience in general."

"She does her own thing, and I don't know enough about her to say what she would do. As for Brad, he's never commanded before," said Dalton.

"I get it," said Todd. "I just hope we never run into that situation."

"I hope we don't either, but it's important that there is a chain of command in place."

Todd smiled. "Tactical. I can relate."

Dalton expected Todd would have no issue with being a second-in-command. His easygoing but serious-when-needed nature would serve the team well. Dalton figured Brad would defer without issue, and Valerie would too after possibly a few snarky comments. Nothing would be official until after this case, but Dalton was confident in his team.

Brad provided technical support along with Evot. Todd came with leadership and experience in combat. Valerie's fearlessness had already shown itself, and he counted on her to defend the team. It was a far cry from the Scoutspectre teams he led in the past, but he suspected this team would evolve into a tight-knit one.

"Sheriff Paul Jackson has arrived," said Evot over comms.

Dalton grinned and extended his right hand. A projection shot up with a view from Evot, who sat on a branch over Derek.

"That's so cool," said Todd, sitting up.

Dalton focused on the display.

"Derek! What the *fuck* are you doing out here? Derek?" asked Paul. He shook him.

Derek groaned as he moved around.

"Are you drinking again?"

Derek's face scrunched. "Paul?"

"Yeah…Paul. Who else did you expect after you texted me?"

Derek shook his head. "I…I never texted you."

Paul sighed. "The hell you didn't. You said you were going crazy and needed help. I come out here, and you're sleeping in a motel lot."

Derek used the nearby tree to stand. "I…what? How…? I don't understand what happened."

"What do you mean? Why are you out here?"

"I don't know," said Derek. He checked his pants and pulled out his cell phone. A moment later, his eyes narrowed. "I never sent that text, but it's there."

"Uh-huh," said Paul. He grimaced. "I've known you for a long time. I'm gonna let this slide…but don't test me. I was about to bang the shit out of my goddamn wife before you texted me with this bullshit." He pointed at Derek. "Go home and get your shit straight!"

Derek looked down. "I will. I'm sorry. I…I don't know what came over me."

Paul jumped back in his police car and peeked out his window. "I mean it. Get going!" He drove off.

Derek stared at the SUV before going to his car and leaving.

The projection ended.

Todd held his side as he laughed. "That's hilarious. I guess the Faith Militia will need to get its updates another way."

"Apparently so," said Dalton. "Still, they know where we are. I'm not sure, though, if they view us as a threat or are just checking us out."

"Well, I can tell you with some certainty that they view the Earth Ward as a nonhuman-infested organization, so our presence here has probably put them on edge."

Dalton sighed. "Then we will need to be careful. Why don't you get some rest? Evot will alert us if anything pops up, and if it does, we can handle it."

"All right," said Todd.

Dalton got comfortable and closed his eyes. The day had been busy, and his mind raced with thoughts about the creature.

CHAPTER
ELEVEN

B rad yawned as he woke up. A quick check showed it was 10:30 a.m., which usually meant he had overslept, but the night had been long. After all the action earlier that morning, he figured they would have a later start to the day.

He grinned at the presence by his hips. Evot had curled up against him. He was not sure why she did that. But he was careful not to assign normal human emotions to AIs. On his world, that was how they lured you in before trying to kill you. He tried to think of Evot in terms of what subroutine and variables she ran, but it was hard to do since she was unique and, more importantly, his friend.

Valerie chowed down on what appeared to be an egg and bacon biscuit. The smell of fast food permeated the air, and his stomach growled. He slid off the bed and nodded at her, then went to the bathroom. After getting cleaned up, he investigated the paper bag on the table near the TV.

"These yours?" he asked.

Valerie grinned, her mouth full. "For the group. Drinks in the mini fridge."

Brad wasted no time in selecting a hash brown and a biscuit sandwich. He was hungrier than he thought. It was also not lost on him how much had been bought. A quick check on the nearby receipt showed fifteen biscuit sandwiches and hash browns. In the refrigerator, he found some orange juice in a cup with his name written on it. He was not going to complain about a free breakfast.

After thirty minutes, Dalton and Todd joined them.

"Good to see everyone is up," said Dalton.

Valerie smirked. "I'm ready for another day of monster ass-kicking."

Brad loved her attitude.

Dalton nodded. "We're going to go out to where Evot flew yesterday. I doubt those creatures are there during the day, and if there's a portal there, we can check it out."

"Maybe the portal only opens at night," said Brad.

"I considered that. It could be natural. I'm not sure. We'll find out," said Dalton. "Let's pack everything up and get moving."

After twenty minutes, they were on their way.

Brad enjoyed sitting in the passenger seat. The place they visited was about five miles from the nearest parking lot, so he figured it would be a good hour-and-a-half hike. He was sure it would be hot and humid, and he was thankful he was fit.

"Does the area we're going to belong to the Ogben Coven?" he asked.

"They claim the forest," said Dalton. "However, I suspect they have a few places where they congregate and live. I'm not aware of any near that area, though."

Valerie's eyes narrowed. "They probably know of our presence and are watching us. This is a test."

Brad sighed. "Great. How are we going to fight two creatures if they're there?"

"I'm bringing my pistol," said Todd. "Don't worry. I won't shoot to kill, but it should be a good deterrent if we need it. They require wings to fly, so putting a few holes in them should work."

"I got my knives," said Valerie.

"Slicing their wings might work. I hope we don't need to go lethal, but if we do, my MH can form that type of weapon," said Dalton. "If it comes to that, let me strike the first blow, then everyone else can follow."

Todd nodded. "Works for me."

Brad eased back into his chair. He hoped it did not become a lethal fight, but the group might not have a choice. The creatures wore armor, so they were probably used to fighting and killing. The wing-slicing sounded good, and they also had the bright light from Dalton, although that might not be as effective in daylight.

Gizmo was great, but if stun failed, Brad would not have much to work with. Maybe some type of enhancement could be worn, like a clawed gauntlet that could not only pierce tough material but also deliver a stun. Brad smiled as various ideas floated through his mind.

After an hour, they arrived at the deserted trailhead.

From what Brad understood, trailheads were scattered throughout the area as a starting point for hiking trails. He figured the lot builders would have shit their pants if they knew the trailheads were being used as a staging point to hunt winged nightmares from someplace else.

They parked and exited. After grabbing their gear, they entered the forest. Evot assumed her humanoid form to walk with them and used her crow form to scout ahead. After an hour-and-a-half, they reached the spot she had last encountered the creatures.

Brad surveyed the environment. Although there was a small clearing, the trees were somewhat dense, a far cry from the sparse layout he had seen earlier. The underbrush was also thicker, but that proved no obstacle to Dalton scanning around. Brad was glad they were there in the daylight.

Todd motioned at some broken branches. "They were here." He gestured at the ground. "And they walked away."

The claw marks on the ground were hard to miss. How strange it must be to be light enough to fly yet powerful enough to leave marks and also flatten Dalton.

Dalton nodded. "Let's check it out. Evot hasn't picked up any sign of the creatures, so we're in the clear for now." He motioned at Todd. "Lead on."

Brad admired Todd's tracking skills. He seemed to be in his environment.

After twenty minutes, they came upon an overgrown trail.

"Tracks appear to lead here," said Todd.

"Yes, and that's because there's a portal here," said Dalton.

Valerie studied the trail. "Where?"

Dalton walked to the middle of the trail and extended a hand. "Where my hand is. It's closed at the moment."

Brad did not sense anything either, but he trusted Dalton.

"Okay, everyone move about fifteen feet away and prepare for a fight. I'm going to open the portal, and I'm not sure what we'll see or what might try to pop through. If it's something dangerous, I'll close it."

They complied.

Brad's heartbeat raced. There could potentially be another fight, or maybe some Cthulhu-like tentacle would slip through the portal. He had never seen a portal before, not even the one he came through from his Earth.

Dalton raised his arm at a ninety-degree angle and clenched his fist. Blue flames erupted around Dalton's hand.

Brad gulped.

Dalton's eyes glowed, and a small, bright point of light ahead of him shimmered. A moment later, the point had expanded to a large, oval-shaped portal that showed another place on the other side.

The other world had reddish-gray skies, and the hellish ground looked like it was made of black basalt columns. Lava pools appeared in the distance. Although Brad did not believe in hell, if he had to picture it, this is what it would look like.

"What is this place?" asked Todd, licking his lips.

Valerie stepped back. "I don't know, but it doesn't appear friendly."

Dalton grabbed the binding stone given to him by Kreelah, then extended his arm through the portal. "I'm getting a reading of the environment."

Evot landed on Brad's shoulder.

He was glad she did not fly through. It made sense if she was to explore, but the thought of an army of the flying creatures played in the back of his mind.

Dalton withdrew his fist and faced the group. "Some good news and bad news. The good news is that Skylka is alive and she is definitely over there. The bad news is the environment is hostile to human life. Skylka, being what she is, has some protection, but I'm afraid I will need to go alone for this part."

"What?" asked Todd.

"My super cells and suit will protect me from the environment. I'll take one servbot and leave the other here. Evot can merge back when I return."

"Okay," said Evot.

"No way you're going in alone. I'm coming with you," said Valerie.

Dalton projected a hologram of the air composition on the other side. "This is what's over there."

She shrugged. "So there's less oxygen. From where I came from, there's even less." She walked over to the portal and stuck her head through, then pulled it back out. "Yeah, I can handle that." She gestured at Todd and Brad. "They most likely couldn't, not without a suit."

"Fine," said Dalton. He focused on Todd. "I'll need you to coordinate things out here. I'm not sure how long we'll be gone, but Evot should be able to relay any messages once the portal opens naturally. Make sure to time it."

Todd nodded. "You got it, chief."

Brad wrinkled his brow. "What do we do until then? Wait here or at the motel?"

"We'll figure it out," said Todd. "Evot will be here in some form, I'm guessing, so we can camp out in the SUV until needed."

"Works for me," said Brad. He swept his gaze across Dalton, Valerie, and Evot in crow form, who had landed on Dalton's shoulder. "Good luck in there."

Dalton grinned. "I got Valerie and Evot. What else do I need?"

Valerie eyed him while Evot cawed.

Dalton entered Scoutspectre mode. "All right, let's go."

Brad swallowed hard as they entered the portal, which closed once they were through. The fact Dalton could even do that impressed Brad. Valerie's fearlessness was once again on display. Going through a portal to an unknown place that looked like hell was no problem for her. It also did not surprise him that Todd was the point person when Dalton was gone. Evot stood next to Brad, acting like this was all routine to her.

Brad had no desire to be a leader, and Todd had years of experience under his belt. It was probably why Dalton chose him to unofficially be a second-in-command. There would most likely be an official designation if the team stuck around after this case.

"So what now?" asked Brad.

Todd nodded. "Let's scout the area, see if there are any places we can hole up in or extract to if this place becomes hot."

"You think we might be attacked out here?"

Todd smiled. "I always think we'll be attacked. This is out in the open, so I just want a lay of the land and to identify points we can move to if needed."

"Got it," said Brad. "For the record, I'm glad he chose you to coordinate. That's not my thing."

Todd slapped him on the back. "C'mon. We got this."

Brad appreciated Todd's easygoing nature and confidence. Hopefully, they found a few places before going back to the SUV, where they would probably spend the night. Evot morphed into a crow and flew around. Thanks to his connection with his interface, he could see the data she streamed from her view. He followed Todd as he took off. It was time to assess their position.

Dalton surveyed the environment. The reddish-gray sky cast gloom everywhere, and his senses told him this was not a dimension but a planet. Usually there was a dimensional energy he could detect but not here. This was definitely a planet or possibly a moon. Something must be in the atmosphere to cause the twilight appearance, but some light did break through.

The glistening black basalt-like rock columns he and Valerie stood on surprised him. They were on an arc-shaped platform that jutted out of a mountain. Looking over the edge, he made out lava flows, parched ground, and sand in the distance.

The hot temperature was noticeable, and he suspected that must be normal to the denizens here. As he turned, his gaze was drawn to the worn-down temple carved into the side of the mountain. Unusual symbols appeared to have been half removed, and a broken-down stairwell led up to a doorway that had massive ruined pillars on each side.

Valerie pointed at the temple. "Okay, I wasn't expecting that."

"Me either." Dalton pulled out the binding stone. "Looks like Skylka is not here since it's pointing off the edge of this area." He handed it to Evot. "Scout out where the stone leads to."

She gripped the stone in her claws and flew off.

"As for us, let's see what this temple is. I don't think the portal's location is coincidence."

Valerie's eyes narrowed. "You think whoever built this temple did so because the portal was here?"

Dalton moved his hand out in an arc. "Look around. The portal is in the center of a large outcropping, and if you look at the ground, there were some structures in place around it. Maybe they worshiped it."

"Could be."

"Let's check this temple out while Evot finds where Skylka is," he said.

They walked up the stairs to the doorway.

Dalton scanned the pillars. Data labels popped up on various parts, but what caught his eye was the pillars' age. The pillars had been around for thousands of years and did not match the composition of the surrounding rock. They had been hauled up somehow. He peeked off to the side of the outcropping, then at the doorway. How that was done was not immediately obvious.

"Well, one thing's for sure, this place is ancient," he said.

"How long we talking?" asked Valerie.

"Thousands of years old."

Valerie ran a hand over her mouth as she studied a symbol. "I guess that makes sense. Although most of it is worn away, this symbol has a unique part to it. It's Kaz Lodat."

"Really?" asked Dalton. He scanned the symbol. "I can see that."

"That means the Kaz Lodat were here at some point," said Valerie. She examined the area. "Maybe this is their world. It certainly fits their demonic branding."

Dalton shook a finger. "Perhaps they crossed over thousands of years ago, got stranded, and made the best of what they had."

Valerie shrugged. "Which isn't much. The Helians hunted them nonstop. If you do hear about the Kaz Lodat, it's usually some isolated incident."

"They must think the recent killings are a sign of some type and are investigating it," he said. "Another possibility is they have some connection to this place and were drawn to the portal when it opened."

"They'd shit their pants if they discovered a way back here, or maybe there is something here they want to bring over…"

Dalton nodded. "With that in mind, let's inspect what's inside."

They entered through the massive stone doorway.

Dalton's helmet automatically adjusted to the darkness. He was not worried about Valerie, as she could already see in the dark. The long hallway they stood in was huge, and every fifteen feet or so on each side were other doorways.

He was starting to get used to visiting places inside mountains. One aspect that immediately stood out was the cooler temperature. It was times like this that he wished he had Evot's other servbot. It would make exploring much quicker.

"Hey, check this out," said Valerie, standing near one of the doorways.

Dalton joined her and peered inside. The room was octagonal, but each side contained vertical strips of symbols of some type. It appeared to be a crude form of a library.

"Let's investigate," he said.

They entered and walked around. Dalton used his MH to create a standalone light, then placed it upright on the ground so it shot an illumination beam to the ceiling. Shadows danced around the wall, making it appear like the symbols moved.

"No idea what these are," said Valerie.

Dalton scanned the symbols and studied them in his ARI. Although he did not have the on-demand universal translator from the *Torvatta*, he did have a translation program and part of the *Torvatta*'s knowledge base. All it took was a query to find matching symbols, then the translation program did the rest.

"This wall segment describes the temple, who they worship, and some protocols to observe," he said.

Valerie drew her head back. "You…you can read that?"

"Not quite, but I do have a good knowledge base to work with along with some advanced programs. It doesn't know everything, but when it comes to anything Earth related, there is a ridiculous amount of information available. Usually Evot handles this."

"Must be nice."

"It can be, although if I want to converse in a different language, I still have to speak it."

Valerie smirked. "I'll take your word for that." She pointed at a segment on the back wall. "These are remarkably preserved, but I know that symbol."

Dalton studied it. The symbol was a circle that had another segmented circle around it. Each section had a spike extending out. A pair of horns resided in the middle, and the overall feel of the symbol was odd.

"That's the emblem of one of the Kaz Lodat factions. This is definitely one of their temples," said Valerie. "Let's hope, then, that Skylka is not only alive but has all her body parts."

Dalton raised a finger.

"I'm being chased," said Evot over comms.

"Okay, come back to the portal," said Dalton. He glanced at Valerie. "Let's go!"

They hustled back to the stone platform.

Three winged creatures chased Evot. Based on her scans, they were similar to the ones they had fought earlier. He knew stun did not work on them, so he formed a vibrating blade with his MH and spawned his nanoshield.

"That's what I'm talking about," said Valerie, pulling out two daggers.

"I don't want to kill them. They could be controlled by something. Let's try the wing-slicing thing and bright light first to drive them away."

Valerie adopted a defensive stance. "Rather just kill them, but your way is more challenging, so why not. Be nice if I had an armored suit too."

Dalton nodded and stood next to her, his shield raised.

After a few minutes, Evot flew down, gave Dalton the binding stone, and merged back into his upper arm.

The first monster landed while the other two circled above.

Dalton pointed his blade forward. "Don't make us do this."

The creature moved its clawed hands off to the side and roared, then it charged.

Dalton pulsed blinding light at it. When it raised its arms to cover its eyes, he dashed ahead and cut several slits in its wing.

It shrieked and tried to fly away but fell to the ground off the side of the platform.

The second creature slammed into Dalton, but he whirled around and blocked with his shield against its poisonous claws.

Valerie used the distraction to repeat Dalton's wing-slicing, and the second beast suffered the same fate when it tried to escape.

The third one grabbed Dalton from behind and attempted to fly over the side to drop him. He clutched its leg.

As it dangled him over the edge, it sank.

Dalton's eyes widened as Valerie jumped off the side and perfected a landing on the back of the creature. She cut a slit in one wing as the creature tried to shake her off.

When they hit another platform farther down, the attacker flew away. Its wing was not as badly damaged as the others'. The unconscious bodies of the other two monsters lay nearby.

Dalton took a moment to catch his breath. The fall hurt since he had landed on his back with the creature and Valerie on top of him. Getting smashed into the ground was beginning to be a reoccurring theme. The poison made its way through his system, but his super cells went to work. He tasted blood as he shifted back into his official mode.

Valerie knelt beside him. "You're hurt, and you got scratched."

"I'll be fine. I just need a moment," said Dalton. He eyed her. "You jumped off that platform and rode the creature down. Your fearlessness is admirable."

She smiled. "I was an assassin, remember?"

"Yeah," he said, grimacing.

"You sure you're going to be okay?"

He nodded. "My super cells will tend to the poison and bruising." He looked up. "The wing-slitting works. However, now we're fifty feet or so lower than where we started, and we need to vacate this area before those two on the ground wake up."

Evot jumped out and formed her humanoid form. "I discovered Skylka's location, and we're now closer."

Dalton nodded. "I guess that's a positive. Show us."

She extended her hand and projected a holographic map.

Dalton studied the overhead view. She had marked where they were and where Skylka was. It was about an eight-mile hike across a sea of sand, and Skylka resided in a large stone fortress. They would need to go down the mountain slope for half a mile. Getting back up would be interesting.

"Wow, talk about ancient. A fortress!" said Valerie.

"I was able to scan it in detail," said Evot.

"And we'll check that out. But first, let's find a cave or someplace we can rest that's not out in the open," said Dalton.

Todd had never seen a portal before, and after witnessing his first one, he was still not sure what to make of it. He suspected few ever saw Dalton's eyes glowing and his hand erupting in blue flame. The hairs on Todd's neck had risen when he looked through the portal. Another world sat on the other side, one that was not friendly to humans. It amazed him how much more he had learned as an ex-slayer compared to an active one.

Valerie jumped right in about going over with Dalton. She continued to impress Todd. A part of him wondered if she had a death wish in doing some of the things she did, but it could just be that she was that tough. For his part, he was content to handle the situation Earth side, and with Brad and Evot, he was not alone. Being a part of a team was something Todd had missed.

His left inner forearm device beeped. He tapped at it. "Go ahead, Evot."

"I have surveyed the surrounding area, and it appears to be clear. I have marked several areas we can move to if needed."

"Great," said Todd.

"I know we've only scouted two areas, but there's quite a few more. We going to check out the rest?" asked Brad.

Todd rubbed his chin. "I think we're good with knowing they're there. Most are probably like the ones we scouted already. We can head to the motel. Dalton paid for a week, so we have a place to rest and wait. However…I'd like to hang out at one of the spots during the day and spend nights in the SUV so we're close by if needed. We can use the motel room to shower and eat and whatnot."

"Works for me," said Brad. He looked around. "I'd say if we're going to wait out here, we pick up some chairs or something on the way to the motel."

Todd grinned. "Yeah, my thoughts exactly." He tapped at his forearm device. "Evot, what about you?"

"I plan to periodically survey the area," she said over comms. "I can alert you both when you're not around if the portal opens and Dalton contacts me."

"Okay. I think since he won't be contacting us right away, we have time to pick up some chairs and maybe some other things at the local retail store along with a motel visit."

Brad motioned off in the distance. "Lead on."

They took off through the forest back to the SUV.

Todd appreciated that Brad did not get upset over not being in command. He seemed to prefer Todd take the lead, so that worked out. Although slayers operated as units, they usually had quarrels over who was the leader since the structure was so informal. He still could not believe he had wasted a chunk of his life on that madness.

He wondered how much the Ogben Coven knew of his slayer past. In one incident, he and three others had gunned down a teenage witch in Michigan. Although she dressed in all black and subscribed to a goth lifestyle, she was not a threat. It angered him that he was so brainwashed that he saw her as the harbinger of end-times. That was one of many cases he hoped he could put behind him, but they haunted him now.

After an hour-and-a-half, they reached the parking lot where the SUV was.

Todd's eyes narrowed at the pickup next to the SUV. The three men outside in camouflage outfits with guns on their backs indicated they might be a threat.

"Brad, drop Gizmo and have him stay out of sight. Try to get him to the back side of these guys. Evot, we may need you as a distraction," said Todd. "Activation word is *doughnuts*."

"Of course," said Evot.

Brad laughed. "Doughnuts?"

"It's out of place in the conversation we're about to have with these guys," said Todd. He pulled out his SG-5. "Hopefully, I won't need this."

Brad let Gizmo out, then grabbed his SP-8. "I'm with you there."

They walked up to the men.

A heavyset man with a red beard stepped forward. "This yer truck?"

"Sure is," said Todd.

The man sucked on his teeth as he eyed Todd's SG-5. "Whatcha got there?"

"Prototype gun I was testing."

"Mm-hmm," he said. "You seen anything odd out here?"

Todd wrinkled his brow. "Not that I'm aware of. What do you mean by odd?"

The man glanced back at the other two, then faced Todd. "They say these woods have some crazy bitches in them. Some call 'em witches even…"

"You're hunting witches?" asked Todd.

"Maybe…and if we find any, we'll kill 'em," said the man.

"Well, good luck with that," said Todd as he moved toward the SUV.

The man stepped in front of him. "I think you're a little different too."

"How so?"

"Armored SUV…fancy weapons…that ain't normal out here."

Todd sighed. "We're Earth Ward and working a case."

"Earth Ward?"

The other men laughed.

"What is that? Some club for hikers? You protecting the environment or some stupid shit like that?"

Todd wished he had a badge wallet. "No, it's a UN-approved law enforcement agency with global jurisdiction."

"Uh-huh. Got a badge?"

"No, we're new, so we haven't gotten them yet."

"I see," said the man. He studied Brad, then faced Todd. "I think yer full of shit, and I think you know what's out there. Maybe that's why you're here."

Todd saw Gizmo under the SUV by the right rear tire. "Well, we need to get going, and you're in our way, so…"

"Go around me."

"What if I told you…that there's a dozen doughnuts in it for you if you move?"

"What?" asked the man, laughing.

Evot generated a ferocious growling noise. Eyes wide, the men looked around.

Todd took aim and stunned the first man.

Gizmo popped out and stunned another, while Brad got the third.

Todd shook his head. "These assholes just couldn't leave it alone." He glanced at Brad. "You get anything from their phones?"

"Oh, they're slayers," said Brad. "And now they know we're here. They had to have known what the Earth Ward was and were probably messing around with us. Plus we got a big ole logo on the SUV."

"Yeah," said Todd, sighing. "We'll need to cover our tracks when we come back out here." He heard another vehicle coming their way. "Let's go!"

They jumped into the SUV and took off.

Todd checked the rearview mirror. A sporty black sedan pulled up next to the men. That was definitely not slayer style. Men in business suits hopped out, shot two of the men, then loaded the one Todd had talked to into their sedan. From everything he had read about the Kaz Lodat, this fit their profile. What they wanted from the slayer was unknown, but the slayers may have been hunting the Kaz Lodat as well.

Todd grimaced. The slayers did not have a fighting chance. A part of him wished he had put them in their truck, but he did not want to stick around if more were coming. Now two were dead, and he was directly responsible for that. Then again, if they had not pressed their luck, all this could have been avoided.

Brad shook his head. "I'm going to say those were not more slayers."

"They're Kaz Lodat. On a positive note, I don't think we were tracked, but I hate that stunning the slayers made it like shooting fish in a barrel for the Kaz Lodat."

Brad shrugged. "That's on the slayers. They decided to be assholes, and, well, actions have consequences."

Todd cast a sidelong glance at him. "That's a hardened view."

"I'm no stranger to death. Where I came from, if I talked to anyone, they usually ended up dead within a week. Yeah, I felt bad about it and went out of my way to avoid people, but that wasn't my fault. It was those asshole executioner androids. Those slayer deaths aren't on us; they're on the Kaz Lodat."

Todd noted Brad's mental toughness. He must have seen things that forced him to keep it together in such a harsh environment.

"All right. Let's regroup at the motel," he said. He tapped at his inner forearm device. "Evot, you seeing any more traffic in the area?"

"There is another black sedan nearby," said Evot.

"Sounds like the Kaz Lodat are swinging their weight around. We can figure out our next move over some grub."

Brad nodded. "Works for me."

"I'll stay out here by the portal and alert you if anything changes," said Evot.

"Excellent," said Todd. "Okay, talk to you in a bit. Out."

"Out where?" asked Evot.

Todd and Brad chuckled.

"I mean, the communication is over," said Todd. "We usually say 'over' after every communication, then 'over and out' at the end. But this communication is just us, secure, and stable, so I omitted the 'over' part."

"Oh. I see. Okay, then. Out."

Todd grinned. He liked interacting with Evot. She had a childlike innocence, but he figured she had probably seen horrors while traveling with Dalton. He attracted tough cases. Todd focused on the road as they continued on. He wondered what the Ogben Coven's and the Tanner Pack's takes were on the Kaz Lodat in the area.

CHAPTER
TWELVE

Valerie surveyed the cave she and Dalton had found. It was large and opened up some farther in. Perhaps it was an entrance to something that went much deeper. The important thing was it was high enough that they could stand but creatures would not be able to fly in and around.

Dalton had taken a beating, and she understood that if the monster had landed on or scratched her instead of him, it would have been lights out. He was tough, and it amazed her that he could still move.

The fight ran through her mind. When she had seen Dalton sinking, she went with her urge to jump down on the creature. Looking back, she realized how crazy that must have seemed to him. At the moment, everything told her that she needed to get it off him. It was only when the creature flew away that she had noticed her adrenaline was through the roof. There was no shortage of action being around him.

She gestured at him as he sat against the rocky wall. "So is every case with you like this?"

He chuckled. "No, but this case is definitely different. I'm glad I have a team with me on this one."

"I can see why you wanted to put one together. I have no doubt you could probably do the case solo, but…yeah, some crazy shit for sure."

Dalton nodded. "I didn't expect there to be three creatures this time."

Evot popped out and formed her human shell. "Your injuries are healing, but the poison will take some time."

"Yeah, and thanks to Valerie's quick thinking, it's not as bad as it looked."

Evot faced her. "You jumped off a cliff without knowing if you would land on the creature."

Valerie smirked. "I couldn't let Dalton have all the fun."

Evot smiled. "He does like to have fun."

Valerie laughed.

Dalton shook his head. "Evot, let's take a closer look at what you found."

"Of course," she said. She extended her hand and showed an aerial view of a massive stone fortress.

Valerie's skin crawled the first time she had seen it, but now she realized how sinister it appeared. The place was ancient. It stood tall among a forest of twisted trees with gray leaves. Red vines snaked around the outer walls.

Strange lights flickered in the towers, and a mist rolled through the grounds. Each corner of the structure had a skeletal face carved in it with lights where the eyes would be. Sand dunes loomed outside the forest. The whole area reminded her of a graveyard in the middle of a desert.

Several of the beings walked around. They had digitigrade legs, red skin, and a goatlike head with horns. Others looked like humanoid skeletons who wore a bare minimum of armor. They had some type of glistening rubber-band-like strip that ran over all their bones and connected them.

"That place doesn't look inviting at all," she said.

"Sure doesn't," said Dalton. "Evot, when you were being chased, you were in crow form, I assume."

"That is correct," she said.

Dalton rubbed his chin. "Maybe you can go in as a swarm of insects. You'd be able to scout inside with the binding stone."

Evot transformed into a swirling mass of flies.

"Also, if you stretch it out and make it sparse, it would be hard to detect."

She did so.

Evot's shape-shifting ability fascinated Valerie. She understood it was a swarm of nanobots that could form anything, and this was yet another example of its utility.

Valerie cocked her head at Evot. "You could actually find Skylka, then we could talk with her."

"That's the goal," said Dalton. He eyed Evot's swarm. "But the moment you're in danger, you get out. Are we clear?"

"Of course," she said. "Also of note—I detected a subterranean network that connects this area to the fortress."

Dalton offered the binding stone to Evot. "Interesting. Traversing that would be preferable to trekking over sand for eight miles. While you're out there, try to get more information on that underground system."

"Understood." She consolidated around the stone and then flew off with her swarm following her.

Dalton stood and watched her fly away. "If we can establish communication, the next step will be to retrieve Skylka."

"So we're going to infiltrate that dark fortress," said Valerie.

Dalton nodded. He pulled off a small cube and set it on the ground. "This can relay what Evot sees. I'd use my hand to project, but this will free it up."

Valerie sat opposite him. "Sounds good. Did you see those others walking around outside there? They resembled guards, although those skeleton ones creep even me out."

"I did. They don't look anything like the Kaz Lodat."

Valerie smiled. "It's said that when they first came over, they looked very different. It was the hybrids that survived the Helian purge, mainly because they appeared human, and the only way to know otherwise was a DNA scan. I'm guessing this is where the pure Kaz Lodat live, and they might be some type of parasite. I guess if they created a hybrid, only the DNA would tell you if they descended from a pure Kaz Lodat being."

Dalton nodded. "Maybe that's how their mind control works. They infect you somehow."

"Could be," she said.

After thirty minutes and some light chatting, the projection showed Evot approaching the fortress.

"Looks like she's almost there," said Dalton. He studied the projection. "She hasn't been noticed yet."

Evot flew into the eye of one of the large skeletal faces carved at the base of a tower.

Valerie's eyes widened at the diamond-shaped red crystal. It gave off the unusual light. It hung in the air, which confused her. Unfortunately, the door to the room was sealed, so Evot had to leave. She flew around outside until she found an open area to fly in. The room she entered was long and had a black stone dining table that spanned the area. Valerie frowned at the fancy plates and silverware.

"Okay, I was not expecting that," she said.

"Nor was I," said Dalton. "More importantly, there's an open doorway that will allow Evot entry into the interior."

Valerie watched the projection. She loved that she could do this, and one of the things she did as an assassin was observe people and their patterns. Usually, she did the reconnaissance, but having Evot do it worked well.

Evot passed some guards who were oblivious to her. It also helped that she flew close to the ceiling. Some of the guards peered around, but they did not appear motivated to do much of anything. Their dead eyes made it seem like they were not all there.

The variety of guards intrigued Valerie. While most resembled the goat-humanoid or skeletons from earlier, some were large humanoids that resembled wereboars with big tusks and a nose horn. She was not sure if the parasite controlled how the body appeared or if it only took over a body and used it.

"Those are some crazy-looking guards," she said.

Dalton nodded. "Per Evot's scan, the only thing connecting them is some type of worm thing inside them. At this point, I think it's fair to say the Kaz Lodat are a parasite species. They must propagate by taking over a host, then reproducing via the host's system."

Valerie shuddered. Her heart accelerated as Evot flew into a massive throne room. A large being sat on a huge chair at the end. The horns on its head were sharp, and its clawed hands suggested they could do some damage. It sat almost stonelike on its throne, which appeared to be made of bones. Its black eyes, red skin, and black battle armor made it look menacing. If she had to guess, it probably stood over twenty feet tall when standing.

"What is that?" she asked.

Dalton shrugged. "No idea, but let's hope we don't encounter it."

Evot exited and continued down several stone hallways until she found a set of stairs. She flew down them to another level.

According to a data label, Evot went down at least four hundred feet. It was almost like entering another facility, and the stairway was the connection.

The new area ended in a massive tunnel. Hallways led off to destinations unknown, and the only light was red crystals hanging from the ceiling. A few guards and other beings moved around. Moans and groans floated through the dusty air.

"I'm going to guess this is a dungeon or something," she said.

"Looks that way," said Dalton.

After fifteen minutes, Evot paused before a steel door. It had a small window filled with a mesh at eye level. "The binding stone indicates this is her cell."

Valerie found it interesting that the doors were steel when everything else was stone. Even more puzzling was the fine-mesh window, indicating a somewhat elegant design.

"Can you slip in through the mesh?" asked Dalton.

"Yes," said Evot. "However, I don't think the binding stone will fit."

"I understand," said Dalton. "You can hide it somewhere nearby and then go in. Once inside, you can use your human form and project us so we can talk with her."

"Okay," said Evot.

She flew around until she found a place to tuck the stone away. The glow needed to be accounted for, so she left it near a red crystal in another hallway. Since they now knew where Skylka was, the binding stone would not be needed, but it was still good to have in case she got separated during a rescue attempt. Evot flew back to the door and approached the mesh.

Valerie was not sure how they would rescue Skylka, but being able to communicate was a big first step. It showed Valerie how unique it was to be on Dalton's team, and up to this point, she was even more impressed than she thought she would be.

Dalton studied the cell as Evot filtered through the mesh. Her control unit was too big to fit through, so it rested on the outside of the mesh, while the rest of the nanoswarm formed a tendril to her humanoid form.

He got a good view of the dismal inside. A red crystal in the ceiling provided a dim glow to the room. A stone slab jutted out from the back wall, and a hole in the ground on the side most likely was the bathroom. There was a faucet of some type near the hole but no cloth or towel in sight.

Skylka resided on the slab. She was naked and curled into a fetal position, facing away from the door. Evot's scan indicated she was awake, but her life signs were weak. As if on cue, she rolled onto her back and peered at Evot's human form. Skylka sighed and looked away, then back at Evot.

"Are you…real?" asked Skylka.

Evot nodded. "I am, and I have someone who wishes to speak with you."

Dalton adjusted the projector box to include him and Valerie. "Go ahead, Evot."

She projected a hologram of them from her hand.

Dalton flashed his badge. "I'm Inspector Dalton Kingston, Earth Ward, and with me is my teammate, Valerie Simmons. The woman projecting this is Evot, an artificial intelligence, and she controls a nanoswarm that can morph."

Skylka sat on the edge of her slab. "Earth Ward? I…I haven't heard that name in a long time." She scrunched her face. "How do I know this isn't a trick?"

Dalton wondered what torture she had undergone to come to that conclusion. "This is no illusion or trick. We are outside the fortress where you're being held, but I wanted to verify where you were first. High Priestess Kreelah gave me a binding stone, which Evot used to track you."

"You are real!" said Skylka. She immediately ducked her head, as if expecting to get hit, then looked back up. "Are you here to rescue me?"

"We are," said Dalton. "How did you get captured?"

Skylka leaned back against the wall and crossed her legs. "It was one of the Dagothian scouts. It scratched me, and I must have passed out because when I awoke, I was here in Barguul's castle."

"Dagothian. I'm guessing that's what species the Kaz Lodat are."

She nodded. "On Earth, they're known as demons, and their alliance there is known as Kaz Lodat. Also, they're not pure like here. The Dagothians are parasites that can control a body. The Kaz Lodat are humans where a Dagothian controlled a body, then used it for reproduction while sneaking in their own DNA. They're not fully Dagothian and not fully human. The Dagothians here call themselves pure and can body hop, and the ones on Earth are known as lessers and are bound to their bodies. The lessers are supposed to serve the pure ones, not be on their own with their own lives and thoughts."

"Interesting but twisted," said Dalton. "I'm not familiar with Barguul. Is he some type of commander?"

"He's a pure Dagothian, one of the powerful old ones. He captured his current body from some large creature that used to roam these lands. He recognized me for what I was and kept me alive for his amusement. Apparently, wherever here is, the place is divided into old ones and their clans. Barguul is particularly ancient and claims he is over ten thousand years old," said Skylka.

"You know quite a bit about this place."

Skylka scowled. "I do, actually. Barguul liked to talk to me while he ate something alive. Naturally, I probed to see if there was anything that might help me escape, but once I learned I was no longer on Earth, I knew it was a lost cause." She surveyed her cell. "I don't know how long I've been here, but I can't sense anything like I could on Earth. It's like the planet is corrupted. I do understand, though, that I came through a portal, one of many on this planet."

"You did," said Dalton. He motioned at Valerie. "We both came through it."

"This place is a hellscape," said Valerie.

"Yes, yes, it is," said Skylka. "If you rescue me, will you be able to open the portal and get us back?"

Dalton smiled. "I can. It's one of my abilities. The hard part will be reaching you, then escaping. What do you know of the guards?"

She shrugged. "Most are not that smart. They're lessers, and they obey Barguul and carry out his wishes. It's not like they have an education system here. The pure ones occasionally take on a body to reproduce lessers as slaves and servants, like the guards, then the pure ones return to their main body."

"Sounds great," said Valerie.

Dalton rubbed his chin. "What about the guards' senses? Are they enhanced?"

"I...I don't know. Why are you asking?"

Dalton activated his camouflage shielding. "Because I can do this, but if they have enhanced senses, they'll still be able to track me."

Skylka sat up. "That's a powerful ability."

"Yeah, it is," said Valerie.

Dalton became visible again. "Maybe with a combination of Evot as a scout and camouflage shielding, we can reach you undetected. Leaving will be another issue. Once outside, we'll need to go eight miles back to where we are now and then up a mountain to reach the portal. There's an underground network we might be able to use, but it still needs scouted. The goal is to get at least within fifty feet of the portal so I can sense it."

"An ambitious plan," said Skylka. She grimaced. "I'm sorry. I'm not used to being in such a weak state." She took a moment to catch her breath.

"It's all right," he said. "You've already been a big help, and we now know where you are. Evot is going to scout around so we have a better idea of what we're dealing with."

Skylka frowned. "I think Barguul will be able to sense you. I didn't detect any exotic energy on him, but his senses are different from the others. Maybe because he's an old one. He poked me with his finger, and there's something fighting inside me, but I've been able to keep control."

Her fear of Barguul was evident. Dalton wondered what abilities she had. One thing he had learned from traveling with Evaran was that powerful planar beings with no exotic energy could have abilities. Dalton remembered Bob and Sam, powerful beings who could mimic anything they touched. Getting Skylka out without attracting Barguul's attention was ideal, as Dalton did not want to fight an unknown like that.

"Have you sensed any others here? Outsiders or otherwise?" he asked.

She nodded. "I sensed three Outsiders a while back, but since then, only one, although I can't detect them from here. Only when I was taken to the throne room."

"Okay. Conserve your strength until we come. We'll figure something out," he said.

She smiled weakly. "I appreciate your effort even if you fail."

Dalton nodded. "Evot, get the layout for the rest of the facility, then check out that subterranean network."

"Of course," she said. The hologram ended.

Valerie shook her head. "The Kaz Lodat are known to have minor mental abilities. I can only imagine what a pure old one must have. I bet they use some type of injection that messes with the mind. That's probably what's affecting Skylka. Then again, her resistance to it might be why she's still alive."

"I think so too," said Dalton. "She seemed like she's already convinced herself that the rescue will fail. Maybe that's a side effect."

"Speaking of which…what's the plan? We going to look for that other Outsider while we're in there?"

Dalton gestured toward the fortress. "Evot will continue to gather reconnaissance data. Once we know the layout and what we're dealing with security-wise, we'll go from there. She can also try to locate the Outsider. However, I suspect it will be me sneaking in and getting Skylka, and potentially the Outsider, out."

"If we can use those tunnels, it would be a huge advantage. Otherwise, we're going across sand, where we'll stick out."

"Overland might be preferable, depending on what's underground, but I prefer the subterranean network at this point. Once we get to the fortress, we can try something." Dalton eyed her. "How much do you weigh?"

CHAPTER
THIRTEEN

Todd glanced in the SUV's rearview mirror to admire the new folding chairs he and Brad had purchased. While at the store, Todd also got some minor things to help make their stay out in the woods more comfortable. Bug repellent was high on the list, as was a shield lantern that could keep mosquitoes at bay. Although the product said fifteen feet, his experience was it was hit or miss outside ten.

Brad had gone wild on the snacks, and he had secured a small box of beef jerky. Todd had thought Brad would grab one stick, but apparently he thought about the long haul. He also picked up a small bag to carry some items. The idea was that Gizmo would become a workhorse. Todd was not fully sure how that would work, but Brad insisted it would.

As they approached the motel, Todd's thoughts changed to Dalton and Valerie. How they had no fear about entering a hellish-looking place still amazed Todd. It made him and Brad buying beef sticks and supplies appear comical.

Evot being able to be in two places at once was powerful. Todd saw a real-world application on this case, and it impressed him. She had not heard anything, but Todd planned on staying the night near the portal. He suspected it opened naturally on a periodic schedule. Perhaps then she could get an update.

"Whoa, check it out," said Brad, pointing at the motel parking lot.

Todd had not pulled in yet, but he slowed down and looked over. A black sedan sat next to where they would normally park. He sighed. Maybe the Kaz Lodat had somehow discovered where they stayed.

"All right…let's not jump to conclusions," said Todd. "They may actually just be renting a room. It might not even be them."

Brad nodded. "Maybe, but I'd feel a lot better if we asked the motel owner about it."

"We can do that," said Todd as he parked next to the main office. "You coming?"

"Yep," said Brad. He grabbed his SP-8 and holstered it on his side.

Todd eyed him. "You all right?"

Brad licked his lips. "I know what it's like to be hunted, to be prey." He glanced at Todd. "I'm just bringing backup in case things get wild."

"Okay. Let's go."

Todd made sure his concealed carry was on him as he got out. Brad continued to amaze him. His initial assessment of Brad was that he would try to avoid conflict, but that melted away when he had a team. It could be that he was more comfortable with a group, but Todd saw how having killer androids stalking around might change someone's perception.

They entered the motel office.

Todd tapped the bell on the desk. His eyes narrowed at the thin, pasty man who came out of an office. His appearance suggested he was confused or maybe had started drinking early.

"Hey, have a question if you got a moment," said Todd.

The man glanced at Brad, then Todd. "Sure. How can I help?"

Todd pointed at the black sedan outside. "Did whoever drives that get a room next to ours?"

The man peered through the window. "Drives what?"

Todd drew his head back. For a moment, he thought maybe he was confused or hallucinating, but then he remembered Brad had seen it too.

"The car right there," said Todd, gesturing emphatically.

The man eyed them. "You two been drinking?"

"I was going to ask you that," said Brad. "You really don't see a black sedan outside?"

"No…should I?"

Todd adjusted his hat. "Yeah, you should. Have there been any recent check-ins?"

"Nope. Y'all were the last ones in."

"All right. Well, thanks for the information. Have a good day," said Todd.

They left and got back into the SUV.

"Yeah, that guy's not quite all there," said Brad.

"I suspect it's the Kaz Lodat messing with his mind. That's their thing."

Brad wrinkled his brow. "I didn't know they could do that."

"Yeah, they're sick bastards about it too. From what I understand, the more powerful a demon is, the easier it is to mess with minds. Humans are easy prey to them, but I'd suspect nonhumans, not so much. That would be a helpful skill if you want to remain undetected," said Todd. He motioned at the office. "We just saw a live example. Let's just be glad the guy's alive. Kaz Lodat incidents tend to be violent and oftentimes sexual in nature."

Brad shuddered. "Then I'm glad that guy's pants were still on."

Todd laughed. "Well, I didn't look over the counter." He glanced at the black sedan. "All right. I don't think it's safe to hang out in the room."

"What's the plan?"

Todd tapped his thumb on the steering wheel. "We can camp out in the SUV anywhere, which is awesome, but I think we'll be hunted. The Kaz Lodat probably got some intelligence on us from this guy and maybe even law enforcement. Maybe even that slayer who was nabbed back at the forest. I think it's time to call a friend if we're going to rough it somewhere."

"Who you got in mind?"

Todd smiled. "Rick, a good bud of mine. He's normally two hours away from where I live but only an hour from here. He'll be all we need for an extended stay in the woods."

"Works for me," said Brad.

Todd nodded and pulled out his cell. After dialing Rick, he sat back.

Rick picked up. "Todd. How's it going?"

"Bit of a bind, actually," said Todd. "Thinking we may need to lie low in the woods for a bit. You available?"

"For you, of course. Is Dalton in trouble?"

"Not quite. He's…on another world at the moment."

"Come again?" asked Rick.

Todd sighed. "It's complicated, man. It's just me and Brad out here, and there's Kaz Lodat lurking around. Black sedan outside our motel, actually."

"Kaz Lodat…" said Rick. "All right. Tell me where you need me, and I'll be there in a few hours with supplies. If we're dealing with demons, then I'm bringing something to even the odds."

Todd grinned. That was Rick's way of saying he was bringing his custom suit and weapons. Todd looked forward to not only seeing his old friend but also getting some support. Although Brad could help in a fight, Todd suspected if things got hot, they would be outnumbered. Rick would even things and then some.

"All right. Let me pick a spot, and then I'll text you the location," said Todd.

"Sounds good," said Rick. "See you then."

Todd ended the call and faced Brad. "We're about to get some much-needed help out here."

Brad nodded.

"I wish we didn't need to call him, but I had no idea what to expect with this case. Now that I do, I'll make sure we're equipped to handle situations like this better, assuming we're around for another case."

"I hear ya," said Brad. "Where are we going to camp out at?"

"I'm not sure yet," said Todd. He gestured at Brad's laptop. "You and Evot would probably find a secure and defensible spot faster than I could by a wide margin."

Brad smiled and opened his laptop. "I got this."

"Until then, I'll move us out of here, and once you've selected a spot, we can head there. I'll shoot Rick the location, and then we can set up camp."

Brad went to work.

As Todd drove out, he went over the situation. The Kaz Lodat were an immediate threat, but so was the Faith Militia. He had considered asking the Ogben Coven to keep those factions at bay, but he suspected they were already trying. There was no love lost between those two groups. The Tanner Pack could help too, but he doubted they would. It would be a sign of weakness. For the moment, they had a game plan.

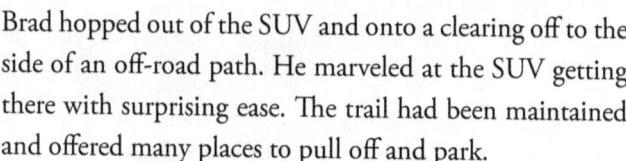

Brad hopped out of the SUV and onto a clearing off to the side of an off-road path. He marveled at the SUV getting there with surprising ease. The trail had been maintained and offered many places to pull off and park.

Rick had been given the location, and Todd was on the phone, guiding him to their spot. Brad was not sure what to expect when Rick arrived, but the area was remote enough that it should prevent any sedans from cruising by.

Brad stretched and took in the forest air. It felt good to be outside. It bothered him that the Kaz Lodat were involved. Everything he had read about them indicated they were bad news. Todd apparently knew more about them than Brad did. He would make an effort to study them more in detail after this case, assuming he was still on the team.

After an hour, Rick arrived.

Brad scrutinized the worn-down pickup truck. It wheezed like it was out of breath. After the truck parked, Brad studied Rick. He wore camouflage pants with black boots and a tight black T-shirt. His red beard and shaved head stood out. Brad suspected he was ex-military of some type, as he had that look.

Todd and Rick walked over to Brad.

"Brad, this is Rick, and, Rick, this is Brad."

They shook hands.

"I hear you two have some demon problems out here," said Rick, looking around.

Brad grinned. "Yeah, some. We're also in Ogben Coven woods, with slayers out and about and a monster from a hell world."

Rick arched an eyebrow at Todd.

Todd grinned. "He's not lying."

"All right, then," said Rick. "It's going to be dark soon. I brought some supplies, but if your SUV is bulletproof, we should sleep there."

"Yeah, makes sense," said Todd. "I'm guessing a campfire might attract too much attention."

"Definitely, but that doesn't mean we can't sit outside. I brought a small grill," said Rick. He walked over to the truck bed and pulled back a metallic cover.

Brad noted the variety of supplies. A large black container caught his eye, but Rick avoided that and grabbed the grill.

"You can get the lantern repellents," said Rick, glancing at Todd. "I brought four, so we should be covered."

"I got it," said Todd. He gestured at Brad. "I could use some help with that."

"No problem," said Brad.

He grabbed two while Todd got the others. It made sense that a campfire might be too bright, but some lanterns with a grill was perfect.

After thirty minutes, the grill had been set up with foldable chairs around it. The lanterns were placed in a square formation encapsulating the area. Everyone sat and had grilled hot dogs.

Brad liked that, if needed, they could hop into the SUV at a moment's notice. Any type of sneak attack could be deadly. The night had begun to settle in, and a quick check on his watch showed it to be 8:20 p.m. The lanterns did their job and kept bugs at bay. He bit into a juicy hot dog and eased back into his chair. The light chat did him good, and it was obvious Todd had a lot of respect for Rick.

"Well, I better get suited up," said Rick, standing.

Brad wrinkled his brow. "Suited up?"

"Just wait," said Todd.

"All right…"

Rick headed for his truck and returned ten minutes later.

Brad's eyes widened. Rick had on a custom black-and-dark-gray suit with dual blades on the back in an X pattern. His first layer was black cargo pants and a loose black shirt. The second layer was armored pads of various types scattered around. Some were on his shoulders and upper arms, while others were on his quads.

Each upper thigh had a pistol holster, and he wore a utility belt packed with gadgets and pouches. His bandolier crossed his chest and also had pouches and what looked like large rounds for something. But it was the helmet that stood out. It had a fiberglass-like appearance, similar to some of the pads. Two eyeholes were cut out as well as openings on the side, but the helmet appeared sturdy. Brad also sensed technology in it.

Brad stood. "Uh…what's all this?"

"I'm Executioner," said Rick in a deep, digitized robotic voice. "You have nothing to fear."

"Right," said Brad.

Todd laughed. "Executioner was one of the most feared slayers out there until he reformed."

"Less reformed and more freed," said Rick. He took off his helmet and sat, then motioned for Brad to sit. "I didn't want to alarm you, but in this environment, it doesn't hurt to be prepared."

Brad sat back down. "I guess not. I'm surprised I never saw your name pop up in the Earth Ward knowledge base."

"That's because I stopped executing nonhumans," said Rick. "I'm sure I'm there, but maybe it's not current."

Brad nodded. "I have experience with being hunted by executioners. The cyberpunk Earth I came from had the android version. They didn't like that I could talk to technology."

Rick smiled. "So you're nonhuman…and from another Earth."

"Yeah," said Brad, eying him. "That's not a problem, is it?"

"Maybe long ago but not now," said Rick. "I'm going to guess you're Wildborn."

Todd pointed at Brad. "He can do some amazing shit. It's really helped us out."

Rick studied Brad. "I bet. And this other Earth…I guess, then, that the multiverse *is* real."

"Oh yeah," said Brad. "Dalton came through, like, ten before coming to this one."

Rick glanced at Todd. "You have an interesting team."

Todd shrugged. "Yeah, but I like 'em."

Brad gestured at Rick. "Why did you stop slaying, if it's not too personal?"

"He doesn't really talk about that," said Todd.

"Oh."

"It's fine," said Rick. He smiled. "Brad shared his background openly, so I'll do the same."

Brad perked up.

Rick gazed off into the distance. "It all started when I left Special Forces and went into mercenary work. I got into some shit and almost died. I was sent to a facility, where a group known as Kargus Tech experimented on me. They enhanced me…superior strength, speed, and regeneration, in addition to better cognitive skills. I became an elite mercenary after that."

Rick did not have any exotic energy, but he had some of their benefits, although the cost seemed to be almost dying and being experimented on. Brad shuddered.

"I did that for a few years, then Kargus Tech was taken down by the ancient vampires. One of the side effects of my experiment was they conditioned me to hate nonhumans. I naturally fell in with the Faith Militia and then faithfully executed anyone they needed me to. Hence, my name."

"How many executions did you do?"

Rick grimaced. "One hundred and sixteen."

Brad's skin crawled. Clearly, Rick was no stranger to death.

"I regret them."

"And you just stopped slaying after doing that?"

Rick sighed. "It wasn't by choice. I ran into an ancient vampire enforcer named Blake Brown. He was by far the toughest fight I'd ever had, and I lost. He should have killed me, but instead, he bit me." He circled a finger in the air. "Hypnotic bite or something. Whatever it was, it broke the Kargus Tech conditioning. He said it was a gift, but I think he probably found it tactical and hilarious to turn me against the Faith Militia. I was free, and, of course, I left the hate-filled Faith Militia."

"Blake Brown…" said Brad. "I've read about him. He's a badass. Lord Noskov's right-hand man. Unfortunately, Blake was exiled from Earth a while back."

"That would explain why I haven't seen him around," said Rick. "I talked to him once after the bite wore off, and I told him what happened. He said I could atone for my actions by helping others who left the Faith Militia and protecting nonhumans from other slayers. Obviously, nonhumans wanted nothing to do with me, but I did help ex-slayers, like Todd."

"And I'm glad you did," said Todd, slapping hands with him. "His reputation was so fierce that when the slayers tried to kill him, half just ran away."

"And I killed the other half," said Rick, grinning. "Then I cleared out a ten-mile radius of any slayers and began recruiting a network of those who had left."

Brad ran a hand over his mouth. "Damn, that's crazy. And now you're here, right in the thick of all this."

"To be honest, I miss the action, not the slaying part, though. This hell monster sounds like a challenge, and the Kaz Lodat are no friends of mine. Their mind tricks don't work on me, as a few I killed found out."

Brad felt safer with Rick around. It was obvious now why Todd called him. With that type of skill and experience, they stood a much better chance of not only coming out of this alive but being there for Dalton as needed.

"Well, we'll need to visit the portal site tonight to see when it opens, if it does," said Brad.

Rick put on his helmet and stood. "I'm ready to go when you guys are."

Brad noted the assault weapon on Rick's back as he cleaned up. He must be strong to not only carry an armored suit but also various weapons. Rick was an unknown variable to probably many others' plans. Todd mentioned evening the odds, and Rick definitely tilted things in their favor.

CHAPTER
FOURTEEN

The half-hour trip back to the portal went without any issues, and Todd felt better about the situation. He expected the Kaz Lodat to leap out of the shadows. The moon provided decent illumination, but he relied on his goggles. Brad wore his, and Todd knew Rick's helmet had night vision. Todd wanted to look into getting a suit similar to Rick's, although it might stick out. Maybe there was a compromise.

"We're here, Evot," said Todd. "I take it that we've had no visitors."

Evot landed and assumed human form. "We haven't." She studied Rick. "Hello, I'm Evot." She extended her hand.

He shook it. "Rick Westmoreland."

"You're Executioner."

He nodded.

"I like your suit," she said, smiling.

"Thanks, but, uh…what are you?"

"I'm an artificial intelligence that is shackled to Dalton. However, I can control two servbots, each being a nanoswarm with morphing ability."

Rick drew his head back. "That's seriously impressive."

"She definitely is," said Brad.

Todd looked around. "All right. Now that we all know each other, here's the plan. The suspicion is that this portal opens on a periodic basis, so it could be any moment. We're exposed out here in the open, and Evot can hide in crow form in a nearby tree to communicate. For the rest of us, let's pick a spot that's not so vulnerable."

Rick pointed at a dense cluster of trees. "I'll wait over there."

"I'll hold the tree's base down," said Brad.

Todd grinned. "All right, I'll join you. Let's go."

They moved into position.

Todd was glad he sprayed on repellent, but the mosquitoes did not care. They were thick, and June bugs were also out. He hated that they were clumsy, and they appeared to like the dim glow of his goggles. Brad hunkered down next to him, not appearing to like the bugs either. Todd could barely make Rick out in a tree. He must have been fearsome on a hunt.

An hour later, a light shimmered where the portal would be.

"Heads up," said Todd.

"I've never seen a portal before," said Rick.

"Just don't hop through, and you'll be fine," said Todd.

After a moment, the portal formed.

"You're up, Evot."

"Of course," she said over comms. "I have made contact with myself on the other side. Dalton is requesting a visual. The area is still clear."

"Okay. We'll meet in front of the portal, then," said Todd.

Everyone assembled.

Evot changed to human form and projected a hologram of Dalton and Valerie.

"It's good to see you're all in one piece," said Dalton. He scrutinized Rick. "I see you brought some backup."

"Rick Westmoreland," he said, nodding.

"You're Executioner. I'm familiar with you, although your involvement is strange."

"It's a long story," said Rick. "Besides, Todd's my bud."

"I understand," said Dalton. He surveyed the group. "We found Skylka and talked with her via Evot. Skylka's being held in a fortress owned by Barguul, an ancient Dagothian, which is the Kaz Lodat's species. As expected, there's no sign of exotic energy; they're just alien. We're about eight miles out, so Valerie and I are going to infiltrate the fortress and get Skylka out."

"So the Kaz Lodat are aliens, then," said Rick. "That's interesting."

Dalton nodded.

"Where are you now?" asked Brad. "Looks like a cave."

"Because it is," said Valerie. "We got jumped by three of those scouts."

"Scouts?" asked Todd.

"The winged creatures."

"Oh."

Dalton made a cutting motion. "We cut a rip in their wings, which made them try to flee."

Todd gestured at Rick. "Well, we may not have the luxury of getting close enough to do that, but he might be able to."

"Right, and you need to do whatever is needed to defend yourselves should they attack," said Dalton. "I'm thinking this portal is only open for an hour, maybe two, tops. Have you had any issues on your side?"

Todd sighed. "Brad and I ran into some slayers, and we had to take them out. Then the Kaz Lodat picked them up, and they also had a car at the motel. That's when I called Rick."

Rick glanced around. "I don't think we were followed, but if the Kaz Lodat have some connection to where you're at, do you think they can sense the portal's location? I know some nonhumans have a bond with one another, and although these Dagothians are alien, they still might have one too."

"That's an excellent question and something I pondered too," said Dalton. "Maybe no one will come, but I wouldn't plan on that. They're drawn to this area, and the only thing of note is the portal. Just be alert."

Todd nodded. "Will do. If I had a suit to go where you are, you know I would be there right beside you."

"It's all right," said Dalton. "I think this rescue will go well. We'll be back on your side in no time."

Todd wanted to share Dalton's confidence, but infiltrating a heavily defended fortress on a demon world with just him and Valerie sounded nuts.

"Okay. We'll be around out here if you need us," said Todd.

Valerie saluted, then smiled.

"Out," said Evot.

The projection ended.

Todd pointed at Evot. "There you go." He focused on Brad and Rick. "I guess we wait until the portal closes, then come back tomorrow night."

Rick gestured at the tree. "Sounds good. I've got my spot all set up."

Brad sighed. "I'm glad our undersuits stop bites, but we don't have coverings on our hands and face." He raised a finger. "After this case is over, I think we need to assess some new gear."

"I want something that's a mix of our undersuit and what Rick has," said Todd. "I'm sure the boys in the Earth Ward R&D can come up with something."

"My suit is an original," said Rick, raising his head.

Todd nodded. "I know, but the Earth Ward has some fascinating tech." He motioned at Brad. "Show him Gizmo."

Brad opened his backpack, and Gizmo jumped out.

Rick took a step back. "A drone."

"Yeah, and I can control it as if it's an extension of myself, although it does have its own rudimentary programming," said Brad.

Gizmo beeped at Rick.

He laughed. "This is probably the most unique group I've ever encountered. Hot damn." He glanced at Todd. "This is a good gig. Crazy but good."

"Yeah," said Todd. "We're not out of the woods yet. Figuratively and literally."

"No, we're not," said Rick. "All right, back to my spot, then."

As they went back, Todd reflected on the situation. He thought they had enough to hold the spot if attacked, but he did not know how long they would need to be out there. Things could get hairy if a Dagothian scout came through. Rick's observation about the Kaz Lodat sensing the portal had been unexpected, but Todd saw that as a possibility.

Hopefully, Dalton would rescue Skylka and reach the portal without issue. He and Valerie seemed to be in good spirits, although Dalton had been seated against a cave wall. Maybe he conserved his strength, but Todd suspected the fight may have been rougher than explained. If something did attack the portal area, they now had the means to defend it.

Hanging out in the woods on a summer night was not Brad's idea of fun. Nonetheless, he enjoyed the banter between Rick and Todd. They were clearly old friends, and Rick reaching out to help Todd after he left the Faith Militia probably strengthened that bond.

Brad had talked with Evot some. She had been interested in Gizmo. He had basic programming, and Brad had updated some aspects of it. In some respects, Gizmo was like a highly trained dog that could be controlled as needed.

Evot had been curious if Gizmo would be upgraded to a full AI or stay as is. Brad was not sure, as he had never created an AI before. Although he could talk to technology and even affect a codebase, designing an AI was another world.

Evot had been in curiosity mode, as she also had questions about Rick. Brad suggested she ask him directly, but she said he did not have a comms system to link to. He grinned when he told her she would have to do it the old-fashioned way and talk to him face-to-face. She made a note to do so. Brad enjoyed discussing topics with her. She was open and honest, and she was a departure from the AIs he knew.

After an hour, Evot contacted the group. "There are six people moving toward the portal."

Rick jumped down from the tree.

"Kaz Lodat?" asked Todd.

"I'm not sure," she said. "They have business suits and sunglasses and are carrying assault weapons."

"Sunglasses at night?" asked Rick. "What? They trying to do their best rendition of an '80s song?"

Todd laughed. "Probably not." He swiped his inner forearm. "Check out the map."

Brad and Rick studied the red dots moving their way on the tiny screen.

"Damn, I need a way to hook into your system," said Rick.

"It'd be nice to have this information available in a headset," said Todd.

Brad studied Rick's helmet. It had a rudimentary system, but it could be integrated. That would have been helpful earlier when Evot wanted to chat with him. "Headsets would be nice, although Rick has an existing system I can update to work with ours."

"Really? If you can, go for it," said Rick.

Brad focused on Rick's system and updated it. As it was already constrained on resources, Brad made sure to leave a small footprint.

Rick drew his head back. "How…? That's incredible!"

Brad smiled. "Now we just need to get something for the rest of us."

"Definitely," said Todd.

Something flew out of the portal and into the sky.

"Um…I think a scout just came out," said Brad.

"I'm tracking it now," said Evot.

Brad's heartbeat ramped up. First the Kaz Lodat and now the creature, and they were headed toward each other. He wondered if they would fight.

After ten minutes, the scout landed near the Kaz Lodat men.

Evot had perched on a branch a bit away, but she zoomed in on the meeting.

The Kaz Lodat were not frightened by the creature. The strange language the Kaz Lodat used was not recognizable by Evot, but the scout understood it. Brad was bewildered that the scout talked, although it was a deep, growling voice, and its words sounded similar to the Kaz Lodat's.

"What the hell are those things talking about?" asked Rick. "Sounds like a growling match."

"No idea," said Todd, chuckling. "As long as they talk and aren't causing trouble, I'm okay with that."

As if on cue, the scout flew in the group's direction.

"Um…it's coming our way," said Brad.

"So are the Kaz Lodat," said Todd. "Let's move back some."

They moved half a mile off.

"They're still coming, and the scout is almost on us," said Brad.

His mouth went dry. It appeared the scout and Kaz Lodat were working together, and they were now actively seeking them. That could only end in disaster.

"Maybe they want to talk," said Todd.

Rick laughed. "Yeah, I don't think so."

"We have to try. That's what Dalton would do, I bet," said Todd.

Todd was right. Dalton would try to talk things through first, but Brad was not sure the Kaz Lodat were in the mood to chat.

"Why not have Evot as a go-between? She can hide in the trees but still relay communication," said Brad.

"Worth a shot," said Todd. "Evot, that work for you?"

"Of course," she said. "I am going to them now."

Rick shook his head. "All right, we can try that, but if we discover they're here to push our shit in, we'll need to fight. If that happens, let me take the scout. You two and Gizmo can use your stun magic on the Kaz Lodat."

"You want to fight the scout by yourself?" asked Brad.

"I can handle it," said Rick.

Brad appreciated his bravado, and given his history, he may be one of the few qualified humans on the planet who could handle the scout.

After a few minutes, Evot landed on a tree out of the Kaz Lodat's line of sight. He loved that he could see through her eyes via the link she had with his forearm interface.

"I am ready to relay you," she said.

Todd straightened and took a deep breath. Brad gulped. It was not every day you talked with a monstrous creature and demons. Brad hoped there would not be any fighting, but everything told him that was what would happen. The fate of the slayers roamed around in Brad's thoughts for a moment. He did not want to end up like that.

Todd normally had nerves of steel, but the situation could get ugly. He liked being able to talk to the Kaz Lodat without them seeing him, but he also understood that the creature probably already knew where he and the others were, as it flew directly toward them. Looking at his forearm interface, he saw what Evot did. Although it was dark out, it appeared like daylight, and he had a zoomed-in view of the men's faces. He gripped his SG-5.

"All right. Evot, I'm ready."

"You are live…now," she said.

Todd nodded. "Kaz Lodat. What is your purpose here?"

They stopped and looked around. One stepped forward while continuing to search for the source of the audio. "You speak for the group that attacked one of our scouts?"

"I do, but we didn't know it was one of yours. All we knew was it was killing things it shouldn't have."

The man scoffed. "Whatever it killed had the *privilege* of dying to a pure Dagothian."

"Yeah…I don't think so. I ask again…what's your intent here?"

The man smiled. "To welcome an old one to this world. We know your group is trying to interfere with that; therefore, you *will* be eliminated. Surrender now, and your death will be quick."

"Not happening," said Todd. "Besides, I don't think the Ogben Coven is going to allow an old whatever to walk around their woods."

"One of their most powerful has already been captured," said the man. "If they had the strength, they would be here now instead of cowering in the safety of their grove."

"I think this conversation is over," said Todd.

"It will be once we find you."

Evot ended the communication. "I have detected another group going to the portal. The ones we talked with are approaching us."

"Damn demons coming out of the woodwork," said Rick.

Todd raised a finger. "I have an idea…"

After ten minutes, everyone was in their positions and the scout had arrived.

Todd surveyed the situation. The clearing was large enough that the scout would be able to come from above. Thanks to Evot, a hologram of Rick stood in front of a tree in the southwestern part of the clearing. He was behind the tree, so the scout would still detect him. Todd and Brad hid in the southeastern part, with Gizmo in the northwestern area. The Kaz Lodat approached from the northeast.

The scout dove feetfirst at Rick and flew through the hologram and into the tree. The creature lay dazed on the ground.

Rick popped out from behind the tree with his dual blades. "Not so smart, are ya?" He sliced its wings off.

The scout shrieked and clawed the ground as it tried to get away.

Rick faded back into the forest.

Todd grinned. The ruse had worked. Now there was the approaching Kaz Lodat to deal with.

"Okay, first part done! Get ready for the second!" said Todd.

The six-man group of Kaz Lodat arrived. Three of them checked on the scout, while the other three spread out, facing west, north, and east.

Gizmo crawled out onto a branch and shot a stun beam at the one facing north. Todd stunned the one facing east, while Rick grabbed the one facing west, then tossed him at the three by the scout. The Kaz Lodat members sprawled to the ground.

Todd, Brad, and Gizmo emerged and bathed the fallen in stun beams. The scout crawled out from under the bodies and ran off.

Rick laughed. "Well, that was easier than expected. The only thing still conscious is the creature."

"And we wanted it that way," said Todd. He tapped some of the Kaz Lodat with his boot.

"We gonna let that monster thing run away?" asked Rick, gripping his blades.

"It may not have had a choice in this. I prefer to show mercy. If it comes back, all bets are off. Besides, Evot is tracking it from the sky. As for the rest of these Kaz Lodat, let's put them together. They'll wake up after a while, but we'll be gone by then."

Rick waved a blade around. "Or you could not worry about all that and deal with it now."

Todd shook his head. "Let's not make it worse than it already is."

"I'm with him," said Brad, crooking a thumb at Todd.

Rick shrugged. "Your call."

Todd suspected that if Rick was left to his own devices, there would be a dead scout and six decapitated Kaz Lodat. However, the fight had gone smoother than Todd expected. The scout would cause a disruption when it reached the other Kaz Lodat at the portal, but he and the others would be back at the SUV. Evot would update Dalton on the other side about the scout talking with the Kaz Lodat. He would also know the area was a hot spot.

For now, hunkering down near the SUV was the goal. It was obvious that the Ogben Coven's help would be needed to secure the area for when Dalton and the others returned. That would be a challenge in itself, but Todd suspected the Ogben Coven did not want Kaz Lodat walking around.

After thirty minutes, they reached the SUV. The darkness provided some cover, and Todd looked forward to resting. Evot had responded that Dalton and Valerie were on their way to the Dagothian fortress. Todd was still amazed they planned to go there.

Thankfully, the portal had closed, and the scout had gone through before it did. The other Kaz Lodat at the portal went to the ones who were downed. Apparently, they had some method of tracking them. Todd now knew there were at least twelve Kaz Lodat in the area and, at most, two sedans, maybe three.

After a good night's rest, they would head for the Ogben Coven to convince them to help. It would be much easier with Dalton around, but maybe this was why he chose Todd. For his part, he would try his best to do whatever was needed to ensure that when Dalton, Valerie, Evot, and potentially Skylka came back through the portal, they were not walking into a Kaz Lodat trap.

CHAPTER
FIFTEEN

Dalton was confident that he and Valerie could rescue Skylka. The only concern was crossing the sand dunes. Evot had detected multiple types of creatures that Dalton did not want to mess with. It also did not help that Dagothian scouts patrolled the area.

It had been six hours since Evot left Skylka, and Dalton had wrapped up a quick discussion with Todd and Brad on the other side. It was 10:30 p.m. Earth time, and he had rested enough that he was ready to go.

He had studied the subterranean network Evot had flown through. It would allow them to get close to the fortress. A nagging thought in the back of his mind asked why the tunnel system appeared abandoned. The temple they had seen upon arriving also had been in disrepair. Perhaps the Dagothians had lost interest.

It was an odd choice for Barguul to not fortify the portal. If he knew Skylka and others came through there, and the scouts were bringing back specimens, the portal would be of great value. However, Skylka mentioned there were other portals, so maybe Barguul was stretched thin or his resources were being used to fight other old ones.

Dalton focused back on the underground network. Part of it led up to the temple via a long, angled stone tunnel. The cave they were in went up to the tunnel, but the connection was sealed. If opened, it would provide an entry point.

It worried him somewhat that the other end of the network near the fortress ended in a deserted underground city. There was an entry point into the fortress from there, but he suspected the city held some secrets.

He morphed into his Scoutspectre mode. "All right, let's get to that tunnel."

Evot jumped off and formed into a cat. She scouted ahead.

He glanced at Valerie. "This is going to be rough. We can go back to the portal once we're in the tunnel. It leads to the underground network to the fortress, but if we walk up, it goes to the temple. I can get you to Earth, then."

She eyed him. "Really? After I jumped on a Dagothian scout for you?"

He chuckled. "All right. I appreciate the support."

"It'll take more than that to get rid of me. Besides, we got Evot."

Evot peered back and gave a toothy grin.

Dalton enjoyed having Valerie along. Most would have been scared and for good reason, but she had been around for so long and had seen so much that this did not faze her.

They walked deeper into the cave until they reached a dead end.

"Okay, stand back," said Dalton.

Valerie complied.

Dalton extended his hands, then vibrated his hand armor. As he touched the wall, it began to crumble. It took some effort, and he had to clear some areas out before others, but after thirty minutes, he had cut out a hole to the long, downward-sloping tunnel.

"That's new," said Valerie. "I didn't know your hands could vibrate like that."

He nodded. "They always could, but it wasn't until I traveled with Evaran that I discovered a different use for that ability, like this."

She laughed. "I'm sure there's another use that's friendlier."

He eyed her.

Evot tilted her head. "Which way are you suggesting?"

Valerie laughed. "Oh, Evot. So much to learn."

"I do."

"I'll fill you in later."

"Thank you."

Valerie winked at Dalton as she stepped through the opening.

Although she flirted with him and the others at times, Dalton could never be in that type of relationship with her. His super cells would try to heal her, effectively killing her. Plus, he did not like to mix romance and work. He had seen that be the cause of multiple problems in the past. Maybe one day he would enter a relationship, but he was content now with where he was in life.

He stepped through and analyzed the environment. Evot took off down the tunnel and scanned. The stone appeared worn down, and the ground was solid rock that was most likely smooth at one point but was now broken up. There was no light anywhere, and he was thankful he could see in the dark like Valerie. The temperature was also much warmer than expected.

"Wow, this place stinks," said Valerie.

Dalton nodded. "I'm sure it does. My scans indicated a hint of sulfur in the air."

"I really wish I had a helmet like yours," said Valerie. She ran a hand up and down in front of him. "Actually, I'd love a suit like yours, although maybe a little less robotic looking."

"When we get back, we can look into it," said Dalton. "Assuming you want to stick around, we have the entirety of the Earth Ward Research and Development team at our disposal."

Valerie smiled. "I'd love that. As much as I like what I have on, it's not really cutting it out here."

"I hear you," said Dalton.

"Should I be in crow form to provide illumination?" asked Evot.

"I think we're okay since we can see in the dark, and light might attract unwelcome visitors." He waved forward. "Let's move."

They reached the bottom of the sloping tunnel, which led into a larger leveled one. As they ventured into the dusty passageway, he checked for life signs. There were some small ones—most likely insects. Although debris littered the main path, it was clear for the most part.

Valerie pointed at the ceiling. "Notice those smaller holes?"

Dalton studied them. "They look too precise to be natural but not precise enough for a machine."

"Yeah, now watch it be some nasty boring creature."

"So far we haven't encountered anything."

She nodded. "I bet there's a good reason these tunnels were abandoned, and we haven't run across it yet."

"Let's hope we don't."

They continued on without incident for the next hour.

Dalton had received a final communication from Evot's servbot on the other side. Todd and the others had fought a scout and some Kaz Lodat, and the group had retired to the SUV. He was glad they could handle themselves, and the increased Kaz Lodat presence indicated a threat. According to Todd, they wanted an old one back, but Dalton had no intention of letting that happen.

They came across an open hole in the floor that had something lighting it up from within.

Dalton paused and peered over the side. Lava flowed freely far below. That explained the unusual temperature rise he had sensed. A narrow ledge along the wall allowed for passage, but it would be a tight walk.

Evot morphed into her crow form and flew across, then changed back to her cat form.

"Of course there's an open hole with lava in it. Wish I could fly like Evot," said Valerie. She hopped onto the ledge and inched her way across while facing the wall.

Dalton admired her courage. Most would balk at trying to cross but not her. He joined her, and after ten excruciating minutes, they reached the other side.

Valerie peeked back at where they had come from. "If we do bring Skylka here, I hope she can make it across. If not, one of us will have to hold her against the wall while we cross."

"We'll deal with that when we get there," he said. "Makes me wish I had a grappling hook. When I traveled with Evaran and the gang, they had some type of energy one that could be shot anywhere."

"Must be nice," said Valerie.

"It was," said Dalton, sighing. "Let's add that to the list of things to obtain for next time. A normal grappling hook, not an energy one."

"I got ya."

They continued on, and after another thirty minutes, they paused.

Dalton raised his hand. The chittering noises made his skin crawl, and whatever created them sounded large enough to potentially be a threat. He spawned his nanoshield and pulled out his stun baton.

Valerie grabbed her dual ones.

"I have detected multiple life-forms approaching us through the holes in the ceiling and sides," said Evot.

Dalton looked around and narrowed his eyes. "I sense them too. We might be able to avoid them."

They ran.

Valerie peeked back. "Oh, that's awesome. Spiders with a wasp's face. Oh, and they're the size of Evot's cat form."

"Focus!" said Dalton.

He had a visual from Evot. The large white insects poured out of every hole. No wonder the Dagothians gave up the tunnel. There were too many creatures to use his stun on, and he might need it later. The one advantage he and Valerie had was they were faster than the insects. If it came down to a fight, he would most likely go lethal.

They came upon an open area with red crystals jutting out of the sides.

Dalton was impressed at how luminous they were. A quick scan of the environment showed another opening not too far away. The floor was a mix of dirt and blue-green ceramic tiles.

They rushed to the center of the room. The insects froze at the entrance.

"They're scared of the light," said Valerie. "To be fair, those crystals do have a sinister vibe to them."

Dalton nodded. "Whatever works. I should have tried my light pulse earlier." He sighed. "It's times like this I wish I had an illumination orb that could follow me. I saw one in action, and they're quite useful."

"Yeah, that would've been helpful. Let me guess, another thing you saw when traveling with Evaran."

"Yep."

"I have the schematics for one," said Evot. "I can also perform similar functionality."

"Right, but then that takes you out of a scouting role. We'll assess this case later and determine what we'll need going forward. As a good friend once told me, learn, adapt, and evolve."

Valerie smiled. "I like that."

"Me too," said Dalton. He motioned forward. "All right, according to Evot, we're close to the city under the fortress."

"Great."

Dalton grinned as they took off.

Valerie did not think the case would have them running in the dark while being chased by big bugs. However, she still felt confident about where they were and their goal. She suspected most would have already run screaming back to the portal, but this was the most exciting event she had experienced in a long time. She was rarely surprised by something, but it happened nonstop on Dalton's team.

It only took thirty minutes to reach the edge of the tunnel before it exited into a massive cavern. A city carved out of stone covered the landscape. The decayed gargantuan statues in the distance resembled the goatlike humanoids she had seen earlier. Maybe they were consumed by the Dagothians. It would be cruel to not only take over the race but also build over their city as if it never existed.

Light emanated from a massive hole in the center of the city. The way the light reflected off the ceiling gave the area a strange glow. Although everything appeared calm from where they stood, she knew from the bugs that may not be the case.

Evot formed into a crow and took off.

"Wow, this place is huge, and it smells rotten," said Valerie.

Dalton studied the area. "I bet it does. Evot says the hole in the city has a lava flow deep inside it. Based on the cart tracks leading from the hole to the fortress's entrance, I'm guessing this is their waste-disposal system."

"That's one way to do it," she said. "Now all we have to do is cross a dead city."

"We got this," he said. "Evot, keep scanning."

"Of course," she said.

They exited the tunnel onto an uneven stone-tiled street. Red crystals jutted out at various heights from the rock walls, and some were embedded in crumbled buildings. It gave the cavern a dim glow, and she was thankful it would not be filled with bugs, assuming they avoided red crystals because of the light. It could be the crystals attracted something the insects feared. She pushed those thoughts out of her head.

The stone structures looked primitive, although she saw signs of elegant pillars in the distance. Whoever lived in the city was apparently well versed in working with stone. The streets were wide, but they all angled down slightly toward the hole, as if it had opened and pulled the whole city toward it. The tilt of various buildings attested to that.

The fortress entrance was easy to see. Evot had already morphed into an insect swarm and entered the large tunnel. The uneasy silence disturbed Valerie, and the foul stench that assaulted her nose made her nauseous.

After thirty minutes and more than halfway to the fortress entrance, Dalton paused. A rattling noise echoed.

"What's that?" she asked.

"I don't know," said Dalton. He adopted a defensive stance.

Valerie followed suit.

"I sense movement all around us," said Dalton. He pointed in various directions. "There, there, and there."

Although she sensed something, she did not see anything moving. Dalton's senses must be on another level.

Strange creatures resembling a black, gooey snake with bones for legs emerged from behind buildings and under debris. It was like the main body found whatever bones it could use and integrated them into its snakelike body. They resembled larger versions of the parasitic Dagothians she had seen earlier.

One rushed forward and snapped at Dalton with its sharpened bone mandibles.

He blocked, then kicked it back.

Some of its bones fell off, and it slithered away.

"What is that?" asked Valerie, dodging a charge from another creature. She spun in a circle and came down hard with her dual batons, breaking a few of the attacker's bones off.

The creature shrieked and fled.

"I'm not sure, but there's a lot more coming. I think there's a reason this city is abandoned. Let's move!" said Dalton. He surged forward with his shield out.

Valerie stayed close to him as he bulldozed through a mob of the monsters. Although there were many, they were physically weak. However, they were persistent. She had to watch all angles as the creatures tried to jump off buildings and onto her. Thankfully, she was much faster than they were, and with her dual batons, they were not going to get her unless she got swarmed.

Dalton made a good tank and cleared the path ahead. After ten minutes, they reached the fortress's entrance. Some of the creatures had peeled off and scampered away. A few determined ones tried to attack, but Dalton and Valerie held strong.

As she and Dalton walked backward, the creatures hesitated to approach them. She was not sure if it was due to them being afraid of the fortress or of her and Dalton's fighting skills.

They entered the tunnel leading to the fortress. The creatures stopped their attack and returned to the city.

"I wasn't expecting that," said Valerie.

"Same," said Dalton. He shook his head. "I don't think they were afraid of us. Probably the fortress."

Valerie sighed. "Makes you wonder why."

"Let's catch our breath, then we'll continue on."

Valerie took the moment to reflect on the situation. If they were going to go back through all this with Skylka, at least they had an idea of what to expect. It would be more difficult with having to protect Skylka, who was greatly weakened.

After a few minutes, Dalton motioned at Valerie. "You ready for a piggyback ride?"

She laughed. "I was wondering why you wanted to know how much I weighed."

"I can extend my nanobots to you, but I will have less defense. That's okay, as camouflage mode is not meant to be defensive in that regard."

She smiled as Dalton faced away from her and knelt. Once she climbed on his back, he stood. The sensation of his nanobots covering her was one of the strangest things she had ever felt. It helped that a small platform jutted out from his lower back to provide support. After she was covered except for her eyes, he took a few steps.

"Not bad at all," said Dalton.

"This would be so much more fun in another situation," said Valerie.

He laughed. "Let's not get crazy now." He went into camouflage mode.

Her eyes widened as she moved her arm. Although she could see the slight blur of her arm, it was invisible for the most part. His camouflage mode was as advertised. When they reached Skylka, they would not be able to do this, but it was preferable to be detected while escaping rather than breaking in. If someone had told her she would ride Dalton, this was not the image she had. Nonetheless, she relaxed as he took off.

CHAPTER
SIXTEEN

Dalton did his best to move quietly, and although Valerie was on his back, he had no issues in that regard. It did slow him down considerably, but he would rather fight on the way out as opposed to in. Hopefully, it would not come to that.

Evot had helped guide him through the dungeon-like maze. The grimy stone tiles had a green shine to them, which was illuminated by red crystals. He would have thought there would be red illumination, but whatever was on the walls appeared green.

The initial tunnel they had entered led to an area with crude carts. Massive side-by-side holes that sat a few feet off the ground covered the right wall. Based on the refuse on the ground, he suspected the holes were some type of sewer pipe ending. A few Dagothians shoveled the mess into the carts.

Past the room were smaller tunnels that sloped upward. At some parts, it leveled out into an area with some stone tables and chairs. Maybe they were rest stops or even rudimentary guard posts. Thankfully, they were empty.

After an hour, they reached a large tunnel that had doors similar to the ones he had seen Skylka behind. Along the way, they had discovered a storage room of some sort, and they paused to grab some sheets with a hole in the middle. Dalton suspected they were the bare minimum used to cover prisoners.

Sounds of despair haunted him. His gut instinct was to free them all, but that would be suicide. In addition to the strange creatures in the cells, there was an Outsider nearby.

"I'm sensing an Outsider," said Valerie.

Dalton nodded. "Let's check it out since it's on the way."

"Okay," she said.

They reached a door similar to Skylka's.

"Evot, take a peek at what's inside."

"Of course," she said.

Dalton studied the cell in his ARI. It was dismal, and a naked man cowered in the corner.

Evot projected Dalton's head toward the man.

"I'm Inspector Dalton Kingston, Earth Ward. I sense you're an Outsider. You're not related to the Tanner Pack by chance, are you?"

The man stood. "What the?" He studied Dalton, then cleared his throat. "I am, actually. I'm Gary Turner. What the hell's going on?"

Dalton nodded. "Good. Then we'll be rescuing you. Jim Duggan is anxious to get you back."

Gary perked up. "Jim…yeah, I'd like to get the hell out of here."

"And we plan to. There is another person we need to retrieve first, and then we'll stop by here and unlock this door. Be ready to go."

"Why not open it now?"

"Because I'm in stealth mode. Evot, an artificial intelligence with a nanoswarm that can morph, is projecting my head to you. We'll become visible once we get the other one we came for. At that point, we may need to fight our way out."

Gary morphed into a humanoid bull. In a deep voice, he said, "Good. I'm ready for another round. These assholes poisoned me last time or something."

"They used paralyzing poison. Hopefully, we won't have to deal with that. Sit tight, but be ready to go."

Gary snorted as he nodded.

Evot pulled back out of the cell.

"Well, we found a missing member of the Tanner Pack," said Valerie as they continued on.

Dalton frowned. "Yeah, but Jim mentioned several missing. I suspect Gary is the only one who survived and has a story to tell."

He focused on Evot's scans as he crept through the tunnels. The guards did not patrol and instead occupied various checkpoints. Even then, there were not many of them. The dungeon's design was such that if someone escaped, they would run into the monsters below or deal with those above. It was easy for Dalton to see why many would lose hope.

They reached Skylka's cell after fifteen minutes.

Dalton leaned against the door and tapped it. "Skylka?"

A rustling sound came from the other side.

"I'm here," she said. "Is it time?"

"Yeah. Stand back. I'm going to open this door. Once out, we need to make one more stop, and then we're out of here. Are you standing back?"

"I am."

"Okay," said Dalton. He knelt and turned his head toward Valerie. "Time to hop off once my nanosuit has pulled back in."

"I enjoyed the ride," she said.

He chuckled. "I'm sure you did. Evot, watch the nearest checkpoint."

"Of course," she said and flew off.

After he pulled his nanosuit off Valerie, he went into Scoutspectre mode. He vibrated his hand near the lock mechanism, which chewed through the thick metal. It was louder than he expected, and although he tried to use his body to muffle the sound, the view from Evot showed the guards had been alerted.

"Shit!" he said as he opened the door.

Skylka rushed out and hugged him, then Valerie.

"I hate to cut this short, but we need to move," said Dalton, handing her a sheet.

Skylka stepped back and studied the sheet before transforming into a wooden humanoid. Small branches poked out at various points. Her green eyes slightly glowed.

"Whatever you are, thank you. I won't need a covering, though. Let's go!" she said.

Dalton nodded. "We have one more stop. Evot, stay on the guards. We're on our way to Gary's cell."

They hustled to Gary's cell.

Dalton tapped the door. "You ready?"

"Hell yeah, I am!" said Gary.

Dalton opened the door and handed Gary a sheet.

He wrapped it around his hips, then stared at Dalton. "You're a robot?"

"No, armored suit," said Dalton. He gestured at the others. "With me is my teammate Valerie Simmons and Skylka of the Ogben Coven. Skylka, this is Gary Turner of the Tanner Pack."

Skylka and Gary nodded at each other.

A loud, guttural roar echoed through the hallways.

"I think that's their alert system. We need to move! Now!" said Dalton. He tossed the spare sheet on the ground.

They hustled to the entrance, arriving in forty minutes. Two guards waited for them. Valerie stunned one while Gary gored the other.

Dalton appreciated that Skylka, even in her weakened state, had kept up. Her tree form was powerful, but she was probably tired due to being imprisoned and tortured and her sleep cycle being disrupted. It did not help that it was 3:50 a.m. Earth time. She ran like her life depended on it, which in this case, it actually did.

Gary was eager to fight, and the guard he ran over stood no chance. Valerie performed as expected and took down the other sentry with ease. The dead look in the guards' eyes made Dalton uncomfortable. Even while being defeated, they did not appear to care, as if the body was merely a shell.

Gary drew his head back as he gazed over the stone city. "What is all this?"

"Waste disposal, we believe," said Dalton.

"It's a prison for lessers," said Skylka.

Everyone stared at her.

"Barguul liked to brag about what he did to them before leaving them here to feed on waste. Sometimes he'd come down and hunt them, then eat them while they were still alive."

"That guy's an asshole!" said Gary.

Dalton pointed at the exit. "That's where we need to go. The only thing you need to worry about is the centipede-like Dagothians here, which I guess are the prisoners. They're not strong and don't have poison, but they are numerous. I'll charge forward, and you all follow."

Gary picked up a club from one of the downed guards. He snorted through his big bull nose. "Ready when you are."

"I wish I could help," said Skylka, grabbing the sword from the other sentinel. "Not really skilled with this, but I can try. My form should help protect from some blows, I hope."

"Just stay behind me," said Dalton. "Valerie, you got the rear."

She nodded.

Dalton pointed up. "Evot, aerial view."

She took off toward the ceiling.

Dalton held his nanoshield out front and gripped his stun baton. Maybe the creatures that attacked them before would remember the last time. He doubted it and planned on having to fight. There were also most likely more guards on their way down. It was now or never. He burst forward toward the city exit.

Several creatures initially tested them, but Dalton busted through one, and Gary knocked another far away. Valerie dismantled two of them, and Skylka knocked the bone legs off another.

A swarm had formed by the time they reached the exit. The fortress entrance was now packed with sentries of various types who had rushed out and now fought the creatures. The lessers condemned to this forgotten city had no qualms about attacking the guards.

Part of the swarm surged toward them. Dalton and the others would be pushed into the dark tunnels with rabid insects, which was where they were headed. Dalton was not sure about Gary's or Skylka's ability to see in the dark, but it would be known shortly.

Dalton wished he had some type of explosive to seal the tunnel or anything that would impede the oncoming horde. The group would essentially be trading swarms the farther they got into the tunnel and the closer to the temple.

Dalton motioned for everyone to follow him. As they rushed on, he contemplated various strategies. A bright light from his stun baton and a light pulse from his hand might be all that was required. Maybe the red crystals in the room before the dark tunnels could be used somehow.

Valerie gripped her dual stun batons as she followed Dalton and the others. Skylka had been able to keep up, and Gary looked like he was ready to murder something. Valerie could not fathom what must be going through their minds. They were held in cages like animals, with no end in sight, and now they had a chance at freedom. Without

Dalton and the team, Skylka and Gary would have been written off as dead or missing, and life would have gone on.

They continued toward the red crystal room Valerie and Dalton had encountered. Valerie wondered if they could somehow bring the red crystals into the tunnel, although she was uncertain how much would be needed to keep the insects at bay.

While Dalton could use his MH and hand for light, there were not a lot of other options. When the case was over, and if Dalton allowed her to stay on, having some form of light generation was on her list of things to get.

The swarm from the dead city had thinned, as fewer bugs chased the group. She paused every now and then to knock a few back, and it seemed the lessers knew enough to avoid where the group was going.

After thirty minutes, they reached the large open area with red crystals jutting out along the walls. The swarm had stopped its pursuit, leaving the group with a moment of peace.

"Whoa. What is this place?" asked Gary.

Dalton scanned around the room. "It's a place that divides this tunnel system. It's dark beyond this point, and there are large insect-like monsters all the way to the temple."

"Large insects?" asked Skylka, pausing to catch her breath.

Valerie nodded. "They're like spiders but with a wasp's face, and they're about the size of a small dog."

Gary snorted. "Then I'll run all over them."

"We think they avoid this room due to the light," said Dalton. He raised his stun baton. "I can form a bright light with this and also shoot out a bright beam from my hand."

"Wish we could bring these red crystals with us," said Valerie.

Evot formed her humanoid shell. "I suggest Dalton use his vibrating blade to cut out some that can be carried."

"That could work," said Valerie. "Maybe some handheld ones and one that could fit around the neck."

Dalton studied the crystals. "There are several here large enough for that, assuming the crystals don't explode."

"I can assist," said Evot.

Dalton pointed at a massive crystal on the other side of the room. "All right. You get something made for Gary and Skylka. I'll cover Valerie."

"Of course," said Evot. She flew over and morphed into her swarm mode, then landed on the crystal.

Evot formed two thick necklaces and wristbands. She also cut out four handheld rods. Dalton did the same.

Valerie slipped on the red crystal necklace and squeezed her hands through the two wristbands. Although Dalton made two rods, she only required one since she needed a free hand for her stun baton. She placed the second rod on her back.

Gary wasted no time in putting on his necklace and wristbands. He waved the rods around like he was an air-traffic controller. Skylka donned hers, and between everyone in the group, they were a red light factory.

Dalton surveyed them. "I think we're good to go. The next step is to reach a cave area before going to the temple.

We can rest there while Evot scans the last part of the trip to the portal."

"Your survival skills are most impressive," said Skylka, waving her red crystal rods around. "You act like this is all routine."

Dalton shrugged. "I've been in far worse situations. The main thing is to remain focused. We have a roughly thirty-minute trip ahead to a room with a hole in it, then it's another hour after that to get to the tunnel that slopes up and a place we can rest. I suspect we'll make better time since we know what to expect."

"So an hour and a half until we can rest," said Skylka, sighing. "I…I didn't realize how tired I was."

"We're not too far away. All right, let's move. I'll take point. Gary, you got the rear, and, Valerie, stay on Skylka."

Gary and Valerie nodded.

As they continued on, Dalton held his right arm out, lighting the way. Valerie liked his setup since if need be, he could still shield-bash with his left arm. She doubted any insect could bite through his armor. Her big concern was if the bugs jumped on the others, as they had no armor.

She surveyed the walls. The holes she had seen earlier made the walls look like they were diseased. Her skin crawled, as she sometimes saw the shadow of an antennae or leg waving about inside the hole. They were there, but the light kept them at bay.

After fifteen minutes, Dalton peered back. "Everyone okay?"

Gary rubbed his arm. "This place is messed up. I ain't seen a bug yet, but I can hear them."

"Same here," said Skylka, looking around. "How many did you two run into on your way to the fortress?"

"A lot," said Valerie. "Enough to not want to stick around."

Dalton nodded. "The light seems to be working. Let's move."

One of the insects dropped on Gary, bit him, then scurried away.

"Damn it!" he said.

"Go!" said Dalton.

The group ran.

Valerie grimaced. The bugs had taken a new approach. They could bear the light, at least long enough to get a tasty bite. That changed things, especially since the chittering noises rose to an almost deafening level. She focused on staying close to Skylka and had to knock away a few bugs that charged out of the holes.

Dalton kicked one away and aimed his stun baton light at another, which shrieked and ran.

Gary snorted and huffed as he swung wildly.

Valerie's heartbeat ramped up. Although they made good progress, there were more holes the closer they got to the temple. She realized that when she and Dalton had come this way, the creatures probably took some time to detect them. When they did, she and Dalton were in an area with fewer holes, which accounted for why the swarm appeared to come later. They came from the spot the group was in now, and the bugs were fully aware of them.

The ceiling moved as more and more creatures poked their heads about and ran between holes.

After a harrowing fifteen minutes, they reached the room with a large hole in the ground.

Dalton faced the oncoming bugs. "Valerie, get them across."

"Got it!" she said.

She motioned for Skylka to press against the wall, then Valerie got behind her and walked her over the narrow ledge. Gary had no problem getting across. His nimbleness, relative to his size, perplexed Valerie.

Dalton tossed a few creatures into the hole, then he jumped onto the ledge and hustled across.

The bugs darted across the ceiling.

Valerie gulped.

"Move!" said Dalton.

After a frantic forty-minute run, they arrived at the base of the sloped tunnel that led up to the temple. Several insects had fallen on Skylka and tried to bite her wooden form, but Valerie and Gary made quick work of them. Dalton got swarmed momentarily, but he shook them off and quickly tossed, kicked, and swatted them away. There were no more holes where they were at, but Valerie still sensed the creatures coming.

Dalton motioned at Skylka. "I need your red crystal necklace."

She gave it to him.

He pulverized it into a fine, glowing dust, then motioned for everyone to get behind him. After they complied, he tossed it into the air, where it hung.

"Ingenious," said Valerie. "The crystals hung in the air in the castle, so you figured it would as a dust cloud as well."

"That's the idea," said Dalton. "I thought about it on the way here, and I didn't know if it would work, but thankfully, it did. We should have probably tried it out back in the crystal room if I had thought of it then."

Gary shook his head. "I can't believe half the shit I'm seeing, but here we are."

Dalton nodded. "C'mon, there's a place we can rest ahead."

They reached the initial cave Dalton and Valerie had discovered after their fight with the three scouts.

Dalton had Gary and Skylka remove their red crystals. He placed the wrist ones on the ground and used the necklaces as a dust cloud inside the cave tunnel. Evot morphed into her humanoid form.

"Okay, everyone. Relax. Evot is going to scout ahead. We haven't been to the temple at the top from this location, so I'm not sure what to expect. We still have the bracelets if needed outside, but I don't think we'll see any more bugs."

Gary rubbed the wound on his forearm. "Nasty little shits."

Skylka nodded. "Yeah, but I don't think we need to worry about the guards following us through all that."

"Maybe, but there may be scouts guarding the portal now," said Valerie. "The Dagothians probably know where the underground network leads."

"Which is why Evot will let us know what we're facing," said Dalton. "Evot, come back if you get into trouble."

"Of course," she said. She morphed into her insect swarm and took off.

"She's quite helpful," said Skylka as she sat against a wall. "I…I'm going to close my eyes for a bit."

Gary sat opposite her. "Yeah, me too. I still can't believe I survived to be here. I came with two others. That red dude tore them apart and ate them while they were still alive."

Valerie shuddered. "That's disgusting."

"Yeah, and I was restrained. He even looked me in the eye while he did it. That fucker."

Dalton shook his head. "Per Skylka, he's an old one, but hopefully we don't need to worry about him now."

Valerie's mental image of Barguul chowing down made her nauseous, especially since she had a good view of him when Evot had scouted earlier. Barguul would most likely do everything in his power to get Gary and Skylka back. What form that would take, Valerie did not know, but she suspected they had not seen the last of the Dagothians.

Valerie leaned against the wall and crossed her arms. It was 6:35 a.m. Earth time, and she was tired. A quick nap was in order. Although she wanted to get out now, she understood Dalton's measured approach. He was cautious, and in this environment, that could be the difference between life and death.

She studied Dalton as he faced the entrance to the sloped tunnel. He protected it, which is what she expected. The more she got to know him, the better she liked him.

CHAPTER
SEVENTEEN

Todd squinted as he woke up from a good sleep. The SUV was more relaxing than he had expected. Even Rick's occasional snoring had not roused Todd. He was the first to handle his morning business. A cup of coffee danced in his mind, but there was work that needed to be done. It was 10:00 a.m., and he was not sure what Dalton's status was or when he would come back, but the portal area needed to be secured.

It would be a challenge to convince the Ogben Coven to help secure the area. He did not have a name in the nonhuman world, or at least not a good one, that carried gravitas with the Ogben Coven. Maybe they would listen to reason and understand it was in their best interests. The fact Dalton risked his and Valerie's lives to rescue Skylka should be all that was needed, but Todd needed to frame it in a way the coven would find acceptable.

After everyone was up, they assembled outside the SUV. "What's for breakfast?" asked Rick.

"I got some beef jerky sticks," said Brad. "Quite a few, actually."

Rick nodded.

"I have a better idea," said Todd. "Now that Rick is with us, I say we pick up breakfast, hit up the motel room for a shower and some coffee, then visit the Ogben Coven and ask for help."

"The Kaz Lodat might still be parked outside," said Brad.

Todd crooked a thumb at Rick. "I bet he's hoping they are."

Rick grinned. "I could use a morning workout."

Brad shrugged. "Count me in, then. I could go for some sausage biscuits."

"Then it's settled," said Todd. He glanced at Rick. "Just follow us in that thing you call a truck."

Rick laughed.

The drive back did not take long. Brad had already wolfed down two sausage sandwiches and several hash browns. He must have one of those eat-all-you-want-and-not-gain-anything metabolisms. It could also be a Wildborn thing.

When they arrived at the motel, the Kaz Lodat sedan was gone. Perhaps that was the group they took out the previous day, or they could have been the ones who went to the portal. Either way, Todd relaxed as they pulled in and parked. He did not want to spend any more time than necessary there, so his plan was to take a quick shower, drink a cup or two of coffee, eat breakfast, then head out.

Brad rushed to the room. It seemed he had other morning business to handle.

As Todd entered, he grinned at Rick. "I hope there's some breakfast left. Brad went wild."

"Well, there's a vending machine around the corner if need be," said Rick.

"I'm messing with ya. I got more than enough. C'mon," said Todd.

After an hour, everyone had cleaned up, eaten, and was ready to go.

Todd enjoyed their discussion about the plan. Rick had some experience with the Ogben Coven, although it was not good. There were two on his list who he took out long ago. Hopefully, that would not compromise anything, but it was in a different area much farther north and ten years before he left the slayer world.

"I'm riding with you this time," said Rick as they exited the room.

Todd locked up. "Not a problem. Let's move out."

After a half-hour drive, they arrived at the same trailhead used when they first met the Ogben Coven.

Todd remembered the last time they were there. He wished Dalton and Valerie were with them, but now it was up to Todd to make sure they had a secured area to come back to. He hopped out and made sure his SG-5 was ready to go.

"Evot, any signs of the Kaz Lodat or otherwise in the area?" he asked.

"I have seen no activity so far," said Evot. "It's also good to see you all again."

"We missed ya," said Brad.

"I am easy to miss," said Evot.

Brad laughed.

"All right," said Todd. "We're going to the same place we met High Priestess Kreelah. Feel free to join us if you want."

"I will do so," said Evot.

"Okay. Meet you there."

After Brad and Rick got their gear, Todd locked the SUV. Brad had his backpack, but Gizmo was out and roamed around. Rick wore his suit and looked like he was ready to scrap if need be.

They entered the woods and reached the site where they had their first encounter with the Ogben Coven. Todd recalled the forest coming alive. He was thankful to have survived that fight.

After a thirty-minute hike, they arrived at the clearing where High Priestess Kreelah had spoken with Dalton. Although everything was quiet, the hairs on Todd's arms rose. Rick peered around as if expecting an attack, while Brad acted like he recognized something but could not pinpoint the source.

"Evot, are you seeing anything from above?" asked Todd.

"Yes. The Ogben Coven has you surrounded, but I believe they are transformed," said Evot. She landed on Brad's shoulder.

"Okay, then, I'll get right to it," said Todd. He raised a hand and looked around. "I'm here to speak with High Priestess Kreelah. We bring news about Skylka."

His heartbeat ramped up as trees changed to humanoid forms. Several large animals walked into the clearing and transformed as well. Kreelah, flanked by Ranasa and others, appeared opposite the group.

"You may approach," said Kreelah.

The group complied.

"What news do you bring?"

Todd nodded. "We discovered where the creature came from. It arrived through a portal from the Kaz Lodat homeworld."

The crowd on the fringes of the clearing murmured.

"I see," said Kreelah.

Todd cleared his throat. "Dalton, Valerie, and Evot went through and discovered Skylka was a prisoner in a fortress. Last we spoke, they were on their way to free her."

"This is good news," said Kreelah, raising her staff.

The crowd's voices rose.

Todd sighed. "Yeah, that's the good news. The bad news is the portal is now a hot spot with the Kaz Lodat poking around. We fought them there earlier. The Faith Militia has been active as well."

"We've encountered both," said Ranasa. She eyed Rick. "Executioner, I take it."

"That's me," said Rick.

"You're quite bold to appear here, given your past. Others might not know it…but I do."

"I've changed," said Rick. "I help those who leave the Faith Militia and freely offer my aid to nonhumans, although I understand why most refuse it."

Ranasa shrugged. "I'm not worried about it. Your actions have been pure since you left, but most won't be as forgiving as us."

"I…I know," said Rick, looking down.

Todd shared his regret. Some of those they had killed did not deserve it, and it haunted both their pasts.

"I, too, have a bad history, but all we can do is try to walk the right path," he said.

Kreelah studied him. "Yes, and if you're with Dalton, that's a good first step." She glanced at Rick. "And for you too."

Rick nodded.

"We do have a problem, though…" said Todd.

Everyone focused on him.

Todd gestured at Rick. "While he's tough and we held our own, we can't hope to secure an open area like that without help. If Dalton does bring Skylka back, they're going to be walking into a Kaz Lodat kill zone. I'll do my best to prevent that…but we need your help."

"We don't use guns like the Kaz Lodat," said Kreelah.

Ranasa tapped her bow on her back. "We have ways of defense, though."

Kreelah eyed her. "Yes…but those are not as effective as the Kaz Lodat weapons."

Brad nodded. "Maybe not, but with tactics, you have the advantage of surprise. You have trees that can blend in, and I know you have shapers. They should easily handle guns. We're not asking for much, but if you have any value on Skylka's life, you'll aid us. If not and we fail, then all is lost."

"We can help," said Ranasa, staring at Kreelah.

She sighed. "Fine. Take half the defenders and secure the portal." She focused on Brad. "You can talk to technology, yes?"

"Sure can."

"Then we need your help. We captured a Kaz Lodat sedan and the demons within, but they won't talk with us. They had a laptop, phones, and other technology. Your assistance would be greatly appreciated in learning more about them."

Brad wrinkled his brow. "You want me to just check out what they know?"

Kreelah scowled. "We think they're responsible for the recent disappearances of two of our coven in the area. Although we sense our fallen members on the sedan, we have nothing concrete."

"Point me where you need me," said Brad.

Ranasa gestured at Todd and Rick. "I'll gather the defenders, and we can go to the portal."

"Works for me," said Todd. He glanced at Brad. "You okay here?"

"Yeah," said Brad. "Besides, Evot will keep us in contact, and I can come out after this."

Todd focused on Kreelah. "Sounds like we have a plan, then. I know I'm not Dalton, but we really appreciate this."

Kreelah smiled. "You did well in coming here. You'll have your aid, and we will have ours."

Todd slightly bowed to her, then motioned at Rick. "All right, let's go."

Todd thought getting their help would be much harder, but it went better than he expected. The Ogben Coven needing Brad's help was unexpected, but he could handle it. Ranasa seemed eager to fight the Kaz Lodat, and it made Todd wonder how many others were like her. The coven had captured a Kaz Lodat sedan and its crew, so maybe they were doing more than Todd was aware of. He hoped the portal could now be secured.

Brad's breathing increased as he followed Kreelah and her entourage down a dirt path. It was strange to be part of a team, yet here he was by himself. He understood he was needed for this, though. Dalton and Valerie and half of Evot risked their lives to rescue Skylka, while Todd got the Ogben Coven to help reinforce the portal area. All it cost was Brad spending some time scouring data for evidence, which he excelled at.

He walked among some powerful Daedroulds and Outsiders. It's what raised his blood pressure. Most Daedroulds had tried to kill him since he had been on this Earth, and he was not sure what the Ogben Coven's stance officially was. Outsiders always gave him a wide berth as well. However, the Ogben Coven tolerated him, maybe because he was with Dalton. All Brad carried with him was his SP-8 and Gizmo if things went bad.

How the coven caught a Kaz Lodat sedan with members inside remained a mystery. Then again, they were on the coven's turf. He was not aware of Ogben Coven justice, but he suspected it was probably brutal.

The sun filtering through the trees graced the trail. The warm temperature and sounds of the forest soothed him. He grew up in a concrete-and-steel jungle, with cities that extended underground, and environments like this did not really exist on his Earth.

After a thirty-minute hike, they reached a clearing where the sedan was parked.

Kreelah gestured at the car. "We stripped them of their clothes and devices, which we left inside. The keys are in the ignition in case you need to start it up."

Brad nodded. "I'll get to it."

She placed a hand on his arm. "I want to say we appreciate this. One of the young men killed was a friend of mine. I sense a trace of him on that car. Your ability is powerful, and although Wildborn in general are hunted, know that you are safe here."

"I appreciate it," said Brad, smiling.

He puffed his cheeks and walked over to the sedan. It was unlocked, and he did an initial survey of it. There were three cell phones, a laptop, a pager, a dashcam, and the car's internal system.

He took a few steps away. One thing he had learned was to keep some distance between himself and what he interacted with in case there were fail-safes. Although there should be none here, it was ingrained in him. He observed Kreelah and her group staring at him.

"Don't mind us," said Kreelah. "We're just curious."

"It's cool," said Brad, taking off his sunglasses.

He focused on the car and interacted with the cell phones. There had been several calls, but the pictures on instant messaging made his stomach churn. These Kaz Lodat members had found the two men, and they took pictures of their corpses being desecrated. He grimaced. As part of his job when doing searches, he hated finding some of the worst that humanity, or nonhumanity, had to offer.

He jumped to the dashcam and reviewed its temporary storage. It had looping on, so it overwrote as needed, but there was footage of them coming upon the men and subduing them. He hoped that was all there was, but to be thorough, he checked the laptop. The Kaz Lodat had a hidden forum where they discussed various topics. What they did to the two men was apparently a hot topic, and the comments made him sick.

He pulled out of the systems and took a moment to breathe. He squinted hard as if it would erase what he saw. Kreelah would want to see everything, so he figured the laptop would be the best way to do so. He could stream the dashcam footage as needed.

"Did you find anything?" asked Kreelah.

Brad sighed. "Yeah…but maybe I should show it to you first. Alone."

Kreelah raised her arm, and her group faded away into the forest.

Brad pulled out the laptop and placed it on the trunk.

Kreelah joined him.

"What I'm about to show you is from their dashcam footage. Are you ready?" asked Brad.

"I am," said Kreelah, gripping her staff.

Brad nodded. He flipped open the laptop and showed the video.

Her face dropped. "So they captured them. Where were they taken?"

He pulled up a map with the location, based on the GPS unit on their phones.

"They used GPS as a security measure, I'm thinking. Nonetheless, this is where they've been over the last two days, and they were there for some time while sending some images…"

Kreelah raised her head a bit. "We'll check the area out. What images are you referring to?"

Brad licked his lips. "This is from their cell phones."

Kreelah scowled at the pictures.

"Then there is this forum post," he said.

Kreelah gasped at the Kaz Lodat posing with the men's corpses while continuing to defile them.

"I'm…I'm sorry it wasn't better news," said Brad.

Kreelah closed her eyes and took a deep breath. She opened them and looked at Brad. "You did good, and I appreciate you showing this to me in confidence." She snapped her fingers.

Her group approached.

"Can you show the map again?" asked Kreelah.

Brad complied.

Kreelah pointed at the map and swung her gaze across her group. "Two things. One, our missing brothers are there. Two, prepare bio-bags for the Kaz Lodat. Go!"

Brad assumed from the women's startled expressions that a bio-bag was not something pleasant.

The women hustled off.

"Bio-bag…what's that?" asked Brad.

Kreelah nodded. "We bind the prisoner, then put them into a degradable organic bag that is buried. Their corpse feeds the forest."

Brad shuddered. "They're…still alive when buried, though?"

"They are."

That sounded like a nightmare to Brad, but then again, the Kaz Lodat were paying the price for their actions. This was Outsider justice.

"I hope I can count on your silence on this matter. It will be known they were murdered, but the how should remain quiet," said Kreelah.

Brad shook his hands in front of him. "No problem with that."

"I'll have someone escort you to the others at the portal. You can tell Ranasa that the Kaz Lodat killed her friends."

"Okay."

Brad wondered why the missing members had not been brought up before with Dalton, but maybe that was a trust thing. For whatever reason, she trusted them enough after learning Dalton and Valerie risked their lives. Ranasa would most likely be hell-bent on revenge for any Kaz Lodat member who came within view. Any Ogben Coven member present would be for that matter.

The Kaz Lodat members going into bio-bags sounded like a horrible fate. He could not fathom being bound in a bag and then buried. The thought gave him goose bumps. On the positive side, Kreelah trusted him enough to let him help and had even extended a warm embrace. His thoughts turned toward helping Todd and the others secure the area. There was no shortage of things to do.

CHAPTER
EIGHTEEN

Dalton smiled as Skylka and the others began to rouse. They had slept for almost eight hours. It was supposed to be a quick nap, but they looked like they needed the extra time to recharge. Evot scouted ahead while they slept and he formulated a plan. She was now in her humanoid form.

Skylka had curled up and rested her head on Gary's lap. Dalton did not think it was planned, but Gary barely moved when it had woken him up for a moment. Valerie had closed her eyes for a short while, then awoke and assisted Dalton in scouting the area.

"How long were we out?" asked Skylka, sitting up and rubbing her eyes.

"A solid eight hours or so," said Valerie, smiling. "It's 2:30 p.m. You're late sleepers."

"Whatever works. Best sleep I've had in a long time," said Gary as he stood.

Dalton nodded. "I'm sure you probably need to use the bathroom, and there's some side tunnels where you can handle that. When you get back, we'll go over what Valerie, Evot, and I discovered while scouting a way to the portal."

"Don't need to tell me twice!" said Gary as he hustled away.

Skylka went into another side tunnel.

After ten minutes, everyone had reassembled.

"All right," said Dalton. He motioned at Evot. "Display where we're at."

She extended her hand and showed a holographic map of the area.

Dalton pointed at a green dot. "That's us." He drew his finger along a sloping line. "As you can see, we're near the bottom of this long tunnel that leads up to a ruined temple. Thankfully, it's sealed at the top. I opened a small hole in the temple door for Evot to fly through so she could scan what's ahead."

The projection zoomed into the temple layout.

"Once we're inside, we need to go through a veritable maze of tunnels to reach the outside, where the portal sits on a platform that juts out from the mountain," said Dalton.

"And it's a clear path?" asked Skylka.

Valerie sighed. "I wish it was."

"What she said," said Dalton, crooking a thumb at Valerie. "However, that's not the main issue."

The projection focused on the portal area.

"Our good bud Barguul arrived with some friends around the time we reached this spot. I'd rather us attempt a run when you're refreshed as opposed to wiped out. He also placed some metal bell thing where the portal would be."

Skylka shuddered. "He's not going to let us leave."

Gary growled. "Then we steamroll that asshole!"

"Against that many?" asked Valerie. She pointed at the multitude of scouts and guards and other creatures. "He has a small army camped out there. He might even slip into our world."

"Everyone, relax," said Dalton, raising a hand. "I have a plan. We're going to get as close to the temple entrance as we can. I'll distract Barguul and the others and bring them into the temple via another entrance here." He pointed at the left side of the temple. "I'll escape over to where you three are on the other side, then I'll open a new portal to the existing one on the platform. We go through, then I portal us back to our world."

"You can open portals?" asked Gary.

"I can."

Gary tilted his head. "Okay…not strange at all. But what if only a portion breaks off to chase you?"

Dalton grinned. "Evot is going to use a hologram to portray you three entering this cave from the outside. The idea is for Barguul to feel like he's in control."

"I will be a good distraction," said Evot.

"I know you will," said Dalton. "Before we go through my portal to the one on the platform, Evot will merge back into me."

Skylka frowned. "I like the plan, but I don't think Barguul is that easy to fool. He struck me as highly intelligent. Brutal but smart."

"We'll see," said Dalton.

"I'm surprised they didn't find this cave," said Gary.

Dalton nodded. "I placed my projection cube on the outer entrance so it looks like it's part of the mountainside. I guarded the inner entrance at the top of the sloping tunnel after Evot went through the temple entrance above."

"Damn, you're efficient."

"I try," said Dalton. "Okay, I'll lead you three to the waiting point. Then I'll go do my distraction while Evot does hers. All you have to do is hunker down and wait. To that end, I've programmed my projection cube to display a large statue that will cover you. If anything gets close, they might smell you, but they won't see you."

Skylka laid a hand on his arm. "I appreciate all you're doing."

"Yeah, me too," said Gary.

"You can thank me when we're outta this hellhole. C'mon," said Dalton.

As he walked up the temple ramp with the others, he went over the plan in its entirety. It was risky, and a lot of unknown variables could be introduced. Some of the guard types he did not recognize. They might have unusual abilities. If the plan worked, then it would be as simple as connecting to the portal, hopping through the new one he created, then opening the other portal back to Earth.

His heartbeat ramped up. The worst case scenario was that the guards went after the others and there was a pitched fight. There was no place to retreat to, and Barguul could simply wait them out. Although Dalton was confident in his plan, he would not relax until everyone was safely back on Earth.

They reached the wall separating the tunnel from the temple.

It confounded Dalton that the temple had closed off the tunnel leading down to the underground network. He wondered if whatever was below caused that. The fact they even had a rock wall that could move was impressive. All that mattered now was it sat between them and escape.

He glanced at the others. "Is everyone ready?"

They nodded.

"Okay, stand back and to the side," he said.

He vibrated his hands and created the outline of a door. Once finished, he pushed the inner part forward enough that the others could slip in. He figured he would leave it that way, and if they had to retreat, he could close it after everyone escaped. Hopefully, it would not come to that.

After navigating a maze of dusty corridors, they reached the front hallway that ran across the dual entrances.

Dalton motioned for the others to go to the right side. Once they were in the corner, he placed his projection cube in front of them, then interacted with his forearm device. A projection of a stone column appeared. He made sure it appeared as part of the environment.

"Okay, get comfortable. This next part is going to be loud," he said.

He hustled over to the left entrance and entered camouflage mode. Looking out, he counted about forty or so guards around Barguul and ten scouts flying overhead.

A platform with logs of some sort underneath it made it obvious how the guards and Barguul had gotten there so fast. The scouts must have flown them up via the platform.

The metal bell structure where the portal opened presented a problem. He was not sure if the Earth side was secured. They could be rushing from one fight into another. He needed to rely on Todd and Brad for securing the other side, and he hoped they had been successful.

It was a waiting game now. Evot flew into position to use her hologram. He would reassess the situation after determining how many fell for the ruse. Hopefully, the scouts would go. If not, it would be a much tougher fight, and he was not sure everyone would make it out alive.

Todd surveyed the group at the portal area. Ranasa had tree shifters lurking at the edges of the clearing. They blended in seamlessly with the rest of the forest. The others roamed around in animal form. Brad had arrived, and he was with Rick in a makeshift treetop. The tree shifter had crafted a hollow branch large enough for them to crouch in. The top was removable, and Todd put that on his list of things to experience sometime.

Ranasa stood next to him, while Evot patrolled the skies. Todd loved the support from the Ogben Coven, and he was now more confident that he and the others could hold the area. Maybe no one would assault it, but he doubted that would last long. It was 2:30 p.m., and he felt like he had a good handle on things. Hopefully, when the portal opened later that night, they could get a status report from Dalton.

Evot reported in. "There are multiple sedans arriving in a nearby parking lot. Also, a group of slayers have congregated where the Kaz Lodat killed the two from earlier."

"Great, a posse's formed," said Todd. "And now it looks like the Kaz Lodat aren't playing around anymore. They aim to secure the portal."

"What's the plan?" asked Brad over comms.

Todd rubbed his chin. "I have an idea…but you're not going to like it."

"I'm not?" asked Brad.

Todd grinned. He imagined Brad furrowing his eyebrows. Over the next ten minutes, Todd unveiled his plan to keep the Kaz Lodat and slayers busy. Although Brad was worried initially, he agreed to do it. Now he and Rick were being carried by the tree shifter over to the area between the slayers in the east and the Kaz Lodat in the west.

Evot provided a visual, so Todd was able to keep track of both groups and where Brad and Rick were. Once they were in position, they updated Todd.

"Okay, doing my thing," said Brad.

Todd offered his inner forearm screen to Ranasa, who scooted in to get a closer look. He did not mind that. The slayers' cell phones all began to ring at once.

Ranasa giggled. "That's an interesting strategy."

"Just wait," said Todd, grinning.

"Over there!" said a Kaz Lodat member.

The Kaz Lodat grouped up and marched toward the slayers. The Kaz Lodat's phones chirped.

"It's coming from there!" shouted a slayer.

Todd watched in amazement as the two groups met. Evot had highlighted them with different colors, which made it look like a battlefield drawing.

"Demon scum!" said a slayer.

"Slayers!" said a Kaz Lodat member.

Gunfire erupted between them.

"That's our cue to leave," said Brad.

The tree shifter set them on the ground, then morphed into his human form. One of the slayers on the fringes caught sight of them and went to shoot. Rick threw a small knife that cut the guy's hand, making him drop the gun. The precision of the knife throw impressed Todd.

They ran as fast as they could, as the forest had become a war zone. Even from where Todd stood, he could hear the noise in the distance. Maybe they would wear themselves out and call it a day.

"There is a Kaz Lodat group headed your way from the south. They parked in another area," said Evot over comms.

Todd sighed. They would need to fight. "How many?"

"Sixteen."

Todd grimaced. "Great. Brad, Rick, you catch that?"

"Sure did," said Rick. "Action time."

Todd glanced at Ranasa. "Your coven ready for this?"

She nodded. "Based on Evot's aerial view, I'll have some of the tree shifters in their path. They can blend in and hide, and once the Kaz Lodat have passed, the shifters can provide a rear attack. I'll have some of the animal shifters take the sides so they can flank." She motioned at two young women nearby. "My friends, Kala and Selda, can manipulate an area in a bubble, like Sima."

"Shapers," said Todd.

"Yes. They will be here and provide a focal point for firing," she said. She laid a hand on his arm. "Just make sure you're behind them."

"Is that concern?" he asked, smiling.

She grinned at him. "Maybe. Let's get into position."

"Yes, ma'am," said Todd.

Rick and Brad joined up with Todd.

"Think we're safer here behind the bubbles," said Brad.

Rick nodded.

Todd studied his inner forearm screen. "The Kaz Lodat just passed the first tree shifters."

Kala moved to the right in front of the group and extended her hands in a T-pattern. A thin bubble formed around her. Selda got the other side.

Todd had seen the bubble in action earlier and had been impressed. His eyes narrowed as the Kaz Lodat came almost within viewing distance. One of the tree shifters had broken off and headed back to their sedans to ensure there was no escape. Todd scanned the forest, gripping his SG-5.

"Now!" said Ranasa.

The forest came alive as the sounds of animals growling and snarling filled the air. Trees creaking and groaning accompanied the sounds. Todd's heartbeat shot up when the Kaz Lodat members who did not get sacked rushed forward into the clearing.

Brad and Gizmo peeked out to the side behind Kala and stunned two members.

The Kaz Lodat opened fire.

Todd marveled again at the bubble shields' strength. They held against the firepower of multiple weapons. When the Kaz Lodat tried to get into better positions, he took advantage of the small lull. Rick disappeared off to the side, only to reappear next to a demon and knock him out. Todd stunned two demons who tried to shoot Rick.

"We got six in the forest, and I count five down here, so there's five left," said Ranasa.

"There's another problem," said Evot. "The Faith Militia has the Kaz Lodat on the run, but the sounds from this fight have changed the slayers' course. They're coming."

Todd sighed. "Great. Okay, let's get these last five Kaz Lodat, then re-form against the Faith Militia."

He focused on the five remaining demons. Rick pulled one into the forest, while a wereleopard got another. Brad and Gizmo stunned another two, so Todd aimed at the last one who tried to flee. A stun shot later, and he was down.

"Re-form!" said Todd, circling his hand in the air.

Kala and Selda turned around and moved behind Todd, while the tree and animal shifters went off to the side through the forest.

Rick moved up next to Todd and Brad. "You never mentioned it would be this fun!"

Todd shook his head. Only Rick would find this enjoyable. Maybe a few others would too. The Kaz Lodat who were taken down walked into a trap. Todd had no illusions the slayers would be a tougher fight, especially since they apparently handled the other Kaz Lodat group with ease.

He peeked behind and saw several shifters limping out of the forest. The Kaz Lodat did not go down as easily as it appeared from his perspective. Ranasa ordered some of the other coven members to escort them away from the area. They were down almost a good third of their force, but Todd was still confident they had enough.

Hopefully the oncoming Faith Militia would be dealt with in a similar manner, then the area could finally be secured for when Dalton came through. Todd looked forward to communicating with Dalton later that night when the portal naturally opened. That all assumed everything was okay on his side. Todd snapped his head in the direction the Faith Militia would come from.

"Incoming!" said Ranasa.

CHAPTER
NINETEEN

Dalton clenched his fists several times as he waited for the signal from Evot. The next few steps had a lot of uncertainty to them. One possibility was she could cause a distraction and Barguul and his guards stayed put. Another was they did go to investigate, and when he drew the others away, Skylka and the rest of the group would be detected. It would then become a firefight at the temple entrance.

"I'm in position by the cave we were at earlier," said Evot.

"All right. Go!" he said.

He watched via his ARI as Evot hovered inside the cave and projected the group standing outside. She made Skylka shriek and point up at the platform where Barguul was. Dalton peeked out. Of the forty guards, twenty boarded the makeshift platform while the scouts grabbed the poles underneath it, then flew into the air. Other scouts headed directly toward Evot.

Dalton had hoped for it to thin more, but with no scouts and the portal-guarding force cut in half, he would take what he could get. After the scouts and guards were on their way, he formed his RSG and aimed at the nearest guard.

Zap!

The guard crumpled.

The others burst into action and rushed toward the left temple entrance where Dalton stood. Barguul followed them but ordered six guards to stay by the metal bell at the portal.

Dalton's RSG only had twenty-five charges, and he used the heavy stun, which required three charges. That left twenty-two charges or about seven shots. With thirteen guards and Barguul charging toward him, he would not have enough to take them all down, and stun probably did not work on Barguul. The scouts from earlier had seemed annoyed by it, but Dalton was thankful the guards fell to it. He fired off the seven shots, leaving just Barguul and six guards who were almost at the temple entrance.

It was now time for the third part of the plan. Dalton ducked back into the corridor and activated his camouflage shielding. He ran into the maze of tunnels and waited until he heard several guards enter the temple. Thankfully, they stayed on the left side. Evot had flown back up the sloping tunnel and merged into his arm. The guards in the cave tore the place apart.

Dalton dashed over to the right side of the temple and met up with Valerie and the others. "All right. I'm going to open a portal to the one outside. It'll cut that metal bell thing in half, so we'll need to push that out of the way. Oh, there's also six guards we may have to deal with and Barguul, depending on how fast he can run back."

"Is that all?" asked Gary, laughing.

Dalton nodded and raised his right arm. It erupted into blue flames, and a portal opened next to him. Looking through the portal showed the inside of the bell structure.

"Go!" he said.

Gary morphed into his werebull form and charged through, slamming the metal bell out of the way. As he ran out, a guard stuck him in the side with a spear.

Valerie burst out and cut the spear in half, then kicked the guard away.

Skylka followed Valerie.

Dalton picked up his projection cube, then rushed through the portal, closing it behind him. Mayhem reigned on the platform. Gary used one of the guards as a battering ram, while Valerie took on three by herself. Dalton formed his nanoshield on his left arm, then used his right to open the portal back to Earth. The sounds of guns firing startled him.

"Go!" he said.

He slammed one guard who tried to attack Valerie from the back.

Valerie stunned two guards and kicked the third away, then she escorted Skylka through the portal. Gary tossed a defender over the side and followed Valerie.

Barguul jumped and landed between Dalton and the portal, then kicked Dalton away.

Dalton flew back from the impact. The kick would probably have shattered most humans on the spot. He tasted blood, and his chest ached.

"So…you can open portals," said Barguul in a deep, grizzly voice. "You're more valuable than Skylka. I may have use of your skills."

Dalton eyed the scouts returning with the guards on a platform, while other scouts hovered off the platform and surrounded him. The situation was not what he had planned, and now he had a small army between him and the portal.

"I don't know what you are, but I look forward to knowing you in great detail," said Barguul. "Your planet is rich in those with abilities. I think I may need to visit it."

"I'm not going to let that happen," said Dalton, coughing.

He went over his options. He could try to open a portal to the other one, but guards surrounded it. Plus, Barguul could reach back and hit him. Another option was to jump off the edge and then survive in this place until there was an opportunity to use the portal. Or he could attempt to fight over twenty guards, ten plus scouts, and Barguul. Dalton might be able to run past them, but one thing was clear: the portal needed closed before any of them could reach Earth.

A thick vine slithered through the portal and tossed a screaming guard off to the side.

"What is this?" asked Barguul as more vines burst through and grabbed anything within range.

"Run!" said Skylka through the portal.

Dalton was not sure how the vines were created or how they knew what to strike, but he charged toward the portal.

"Seize him!" said Barguul, batting away a vine that tried to grab his leg.

Dalton leapt toward Barguul and shield-bashed him in the face. As he crash-landed past Barguul, Dalton hopped up and ran as fast as he could. A guard speared him in the side, and another clubbed him over the head. He soldiered on, jumped through the portal, and landed on his back. His breathing went haphazard as Barguul reached through and grabbed his legs.

"I'm sealing the portal!" said Dalton. He used his left arm to anchor himself.

Skylka pulled the vines back.

Once the vines were clear, Dalton extended his right arm toward the portal and concentrated. The familiar blue flames erupted around his right forearm and hand.

The portal closed, severing Barguul's arm.

Dalton removed Barguul's hand from his leg. He took a moment to survey the situation. The silence was not what he had expected after hearing men crying out and guns firing earlier.

Todd, Brad, and Rick rushed over to him.

"What the fuck was that?" asked Rick, gesturing at Barguul's arm.

"It was Barguul, just your friendly neighborhood demonic old one," said Dalton, standing and reforming into his official outfit.

"You need to rest. You're hurt," said Evot.

He grimaced. "I'll be fine. I just need time to rest and heal up." He glanced at Todd. "I heard gunfire when I opened the portal."

Todd pointed at Skylka. "All her. She can control vines or something. Slayers in the forest stood no chance."

Dalton smiled at her. "I appreciate the help…on both sides."

"I figured you might need a distraction over there," said Skylka.

Gary shook his head. "I don't ever want to see another demon world again. Or a portal, for that matter."

"I wonder if Barguul was who the Kaz Lodat wanted to come over," said Brad.

"I don't know," said Dalton. "What I do know is I could really use some rest, food, and drink." He focused on Skylka. "Let's reconvene in a day or so after we're all rested up." He looked at Gary. "I'd like the Tanner Pack to be available as well."

"Whatever I can do to help, man," said Gary.

Dalton studied a Kaz Lodat corpse. "I guess we'll need to clean this up before we go."

"The Ogben Coven has it covered," said Skylka. "The corpses and those who are unconscious will be returned to their vehicles. This will serve as a warning to those who trespass on our territory, and now that I'm back, I will enforce that. You should get some rest. I'll deal with what's left out here."

Dalton nodded. "Sounds good to me."

Gary raised a finger. "I, uh…could use a ride out of here."

"You can come with us," said Dalton. "I'll drop you off at the Warehouse."

"Cool."

Dalton approached Valerie. "You did good getting Skylka through."

She smiled. "I had planned on going through with you."

"Situation changed fast," said Dalton. "Still, you performed well over there."

She nodded.

"Todd, we can use Barguul's arm and hand for evidence."

"Say no more," said Todd. "I'll pack it up, although I don't think we have a container that big. May just need to wrap it or something and get it on some ice."

Dalton nodded. "All right, then. Let's get out of here."

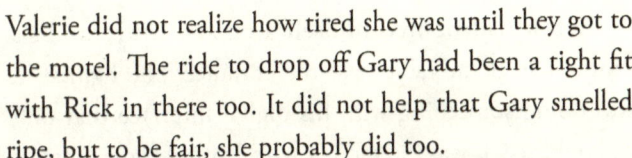

Valerie did not realize how tired she was until they got to the motel. The ride to drop off Gary had been a tight fit with Rick in there too. It did not help that Gary smelled ripe, but to be fair, she probably did too.

Barguul's arm and hand had also been placed in the back with some cloth coverings. It had an unpleasant smell, but thankfully, they had visited a store to get two large coolers and some ice to store it in. After arriving at the motel, Dalton got an extra room for Rick, and then Dalton crashed on his bed.

She had the other bed in the room, and when she lay down, her body told her it was time to sleep even though it was 4:00 p.m. Although she had napped occasionally on the demon world, they were not solid chunks of sleep. She did not mind sharing a room with Dalton. Brad had his own room, and she chuckled when Evot followed him. They would probably talk the night away. Todd and Rick had another room, and she guessed it would be like old times for them.

She went to the bathroom and washed up, then slipped out of her clothes and hopped into bed under the covers.

She did not care if Dalton saw her nude, and he probably did not either. She did ride him into a demon fortress after all. After a few breaths, she dozed off.

After a long rest, she opened her eyes at the sound of the coffee machine gurgling. The fresh aroma filled her nostrils. She yawned and stretched, then propped herself up on her elbow. The digital alarm clock showed it to be 2:40 a.m. She had not intended to sleep that long, but the bed was comfortable, and she felt safe.

Dalton had poured himself a cup of coffee and sat motionless at the table near the entrance. She figured he was doing something with his digital interface that only he could see or was interacting with Evot in some manner.

He coughed and peeked over at her. "You're up."

She nodded. "I didn't expect to sleep that long, but here we are."

"Here we are," he said, smiling. "I slept well too and only woke up an hour before you. I think Rick and Todd are passed out, and Brad is asleep."

Valerie grinned. "My sleep schedule is messed up now, but that's okay. I'll just stay up until later tonight. No naps."

"Same," said Dalton. He studied her. "So what did you think of our first case?"

She shrugged. "It was all right. Definitely more exciting than I expected."

"And the team? Did you like working with one? I know you're usually solo."

"I liked it," said Valerie. "It's nice to know someone has your back."

Dalton nodded. "Yeah. I couldn't imagine trying to do this by myself. I probably could have, but it would have been harder, and there would have been more casualties."

"Let's not test that theory."

They laughed.

"I'm hoping you stay on with the team after this," said Dalton.

"I plan to unless you're kicking me out."

He shook his head. "Not at all. Todd and Brad did some miracle work on this side, and we made a good duo back there."

She grinned. "I didn't plan on going to hell, but other than that, I agree. The money doesn't hurt either."

"After we check in with the Earth Ward, it should be directed to your account."

She scrutinized him. "And you're okay with not taking any?"

"The ancient vampires have me covered for basic expenses. I don't do this for the money."

The ancient vampires had a lot of power and wealth. If they covered Dalton, he would never be in need of money, but it sounded like he only wanted enough to live on and move around. With the Earth Ward providing resources, he could focus on being the best inspector he could be.

"So will we get a name? Or code names or something? Or are we junior inspectors or what?" she asked.

"I haven't thought of code names, but we'll be referred to as an inspector team. In that regard, you three would be my associates, but there are tracks if you want to move up the ranks. The Earth Ward actually requested that I teach some classes on being an inspector."

Valerie could see him doing that. He had a ton of experience and could relate to anyone. What she really liked about him was that he did not back down from his ideals even when there was an easier route. He adjusted based on the situation, and she appreciated his pragmatic approach.

"I'll take a cup of coffee," she said.

As he went to make her a cup, she hopped out of bed and into the bathroom. Her clothes lay on the ground nearby. She wrinkled her nose. They would definitely need cleaned. After washing up and getting dressed, she came out and sat next to Dalton, who had left her a cup of coffee on the table.

She smiled when she saw he had put some creamer and sugar in it, just the way she liked it. It made her wonder how much information he had on her. Apparently, her style of coffee was a data point.

"I was thinking of the Earth Ward and how they'll be perceived after all this. Do you think the Tanner Pack and the Ogben Coven will open relations now?" she asked.

"I do, actually," said Dalton. "I think there might be value in establishing a liaison in this area that can not only deal with them but also provide intel on various things."

"I'm sure the sheriff will love that."

Dalton grinned. "Oh, he wouldn't be aware of it. It would most likely be a rotating position where new agents are used."

"Sounds boring," she said.

"If they had already been established, they would have been a part of what we did."

She nodded. "Okay, so maybe not boring all the time."

They laughed.

"You know the Kaz Lodat are going to be gunning hard for you now," said Valerie. "Skylka said that Barguul mentioned other portals. I hope there isn't another here."

"If there is, then we deal with it. As for the Kaz Lodat, they're in a long line of groups I'm sure hate me, and that's okay. That means I'm doing my job."

She clinked coffee mugs with him. One thing she had learned from being an assassin was the more well-known you became, the more enemies you made. Friends were few, and being on Dalton's team would make her a whole new set of enemies. The difference this time was she had the backing of the Earth Ward and a team she had grown fond of after only one case.

"Another thing to consider," said Dalton, raising a finger. "We learned a lot from this case. Next go-around, we'll have better gear. Based on what I've seen so far of the team, I have a few ideas. Well, actually, Evot does. She tends to do that."

"I'm open to suggestions," said Valerie. "I think something that gives us visuals, sorta like what's in the goggles, would work. It also wouldn't hurt to have a tougher suit over the under one. Oh, and some holders for more gadgets."

"You've been thinking about this."

She shrugged. "More like 'I wish I had that' moments. Although I could breathe over on that hellhole, a filtration system of some type would have been nice. The bright-light pulse is a good idea, and I wouldn't mind having a few gadgets, such as smoke bombs and the like."

"We'll have plenty of time to go over all that," he said.

The thought of getting to use the Earth Ward research and development department for custom equipment made her mind race. Usually, she would have to procure things herself, and the more expensive items were not worth it for the cost. That did not seem like it would be an issue. She was sure Todd and Brad had ideas, and she looked forward to comparing notes with them.

"All right. Although I cleaned up, I really could use a shower," she said and downed the last of her coffee. She hopped up and strolled to the bathroom. Before she entered, she glanced back and smiled. "No peeking."

Dalton nodded.

She loved teasing him like that, and if he did not have super cells that would kill her, she might even have extended some feelers. However, he treated her with respect, not something she usually experienced with humans, although he was an evolved one. She enjoyed being able to truly be herself around him. Normally, she consciously held that back from others. For now, a hot shower had her name on it.

CHAPTER
TWENTY

B rad opened his eyes and sat up in bed. It took him a moment to realize he had a nightmare, a reoccurring one he wished would go away. In it, he was being chased by an exterminator, a corporate android with his termination as its main goal. When he was cornered, the android smiled and put its hand through his chest. He always died, then woke up in a panic. His rapid heartrate increased at a noise off to the side.

"Good morning," said Evot.

Brad normalized his breathing. "Hey."

"Are you all right?"

"I'm good." He motioned at the plate with food. "What's that?"

"Dalton picked up breakfast, and I made sure you had three sausage biscuits, two hash browns, a sausage burrito, and a cold orange juice in the refrigerator."

Brad nodded. "I…I appreciate that. You didn't need to do all that, though."

She smiled. "I wanted to."

He sat on the edge of the bed and accepted the plate. "Thank you. Breakfast in bed. Usually that has to be earned."

"How so?"

Brad laughed. "It's not important. What's everyone else up to?"

"Todd and Rick had their breakfast and are getting ready for the day. Dalton and Valerie woke up early and have been going over today's plans. They are ready to go."

"All right," said Brad. "I'll down these, shower, then be ready as well."

"Okay," she said.

A good breakfast and hot shower did him good. After getting dressed, he walked over to Dalton's room. Todd and Rick were already there, sitting on the edge of the back bed, and Valerie and Dalton sat in chairs around a table. Brad took a seat on the bed closest to the door. Evot joined him.

"Good, looks like we're all here," said Dalton. "It sounds like everyone is rested up. Now comes the fun part: wrapping up the case. Tomorrow, we'll go to the meeting with Kreelah and Jim. It's being held on neutral territory in a clearing. Kreelah said she'd contact me when everything is set."

"Sounds like fun," said Todd.

Dalton nodded. "I'm sure it will be. However, we have today, so I'm going to visit the sheriff and update him on events. Obviously, I'll keep the information quiet for the most part. Brad, I'll need you with me so that you and Evot can sort through any data they may have had on the event or its participants. That data can be erased."

Brad grinned. "No sweat."

"I also want to talk with the female deputy who is Wildborn. I think it will be good for her to see another of her kind."

"Whatever you need me to do," said Brad.

"Be careful with telling a Wildborn they're a nonhuman. Not everyone reacts well to that," said Valerie.

"I know, but she is an officer of the law, so she's had training, and I'm sure she's seen her fill of weird things." Dalton pulled out some hundred-dollar bills and handed one each to Todd, Rick, and Valerie. "The rest of you can hang. Here's some cash in case you want to do some shopping while Brad and I are out. Let's plan to eat out tonight, on the Earth Ward's tab, of course."

"Free dinner? Count me in!" said Rick.

Todd laughed. "Yeah, me too. Most expensive place they got."

Valerie smiled. "With the best liquor."

Dalton's gaze swept the room. "All right, stay safe." He nodded at Brad. "Let's go."

Brad found it odd that it would just be him and Dalton going. Brad understood why he was selected, but he expected at least Valerie and Todd to come.

Dalton and Brad entered the SUV and took off. Evot sat in the back in her humanoid form.

Dalton glanced over at Brad. "So your first case with me. Well, first voluntary case."

Brad laughed. "Yeah, that first one six months ago didn't count because *I* was the case."

"We've come a long way since then," said Dalton. "So what are your thoughts about the team?"

"I love it!" said Brad. "Cool toys, members, and cases. This is right up my alley. It also helps that I'm not being hunted, and if I were, I have a team to back me." He gazed out the window. "Back on my cyberpunk Earth, I never had a group. It was death to anyone who interacted with me. I was a pariah." He glanced at Dalton. "Here? I *get* to be on a team. Not only that, but I can use my skills."

"You are quite skillful," said Evot, leaning forward and peering at Brad.

"She speaks the truth," said Dalton.

Brad grinned. "I appreciate that. Assuming there's no issues, I'd like to continue on with the team."

"I think we can arrange that," said Dalton. He smiled big. "I'm sure you have a lot of ideas for new equipment and gear."

"Damn straight I do!" said Brad. He glanced at Evot. "We have a ton of planning to do."

"I look forward to it," she said.

After thirty minutes and some light conversation, they pulled into the sheriff's office.

"All right. Let's make this short. I don't want to be here longer than necessary," said Dalton. "Evot, scan the systems from here."

"Of course," she said.

Dalton and Brad exited the SUV and entered the station.

Dalton waved over the female deputy. "Deputy Holly Combs?"

She walked over. "Yes?"

"I have to update the sheriff before we leave town, but I wanted to talk with you outside after I'm done. Think you can spare five minutes or so at that time?"

Holly eyed him. "What's this about?"

"It's important," said Dalton. He looked around. "It's best discussed in private."

She shrugged. "I guess."

Sheriff Paul Anderson walked out. "Inspector Dalton! I was wondering when I'd see you again. You coulda called, but I'll always welcome a visit. Come on back."

As they followed the sheriff, Brad searched the local systems. There were reports of weapons being discharged and strange sightings of people in black sedans. Surprisingly, there were no dead body reports, but Skylka probably ensured there were no bodies to be found. He shuddered at the thought that she might have used bio-bags on some even though she said she would return them to their groups.

They entered Paul's office.

"So what's the good news?" asked Paul.

Dalton nodded. "It turns out there's no case here after all. However, as an inspector, I still had to investigate."

Paul studied him. "Nothing at all, huh? There's been some strange reports over the last few days."

"Like what?"

Paul grinned. "Well…you tell me what it might be, and I'll verify."

"It's okay," said Dalton. "There's nothing for us to report on, so we'll be leaving. I just wanted to come by and update you."

"You're not even gonna guess?" asked Paul.

"I think we're good," said Dalton.

"All right…" said Paul. "Tell me something…can you at least tell me *why* you came down here in the first place? Or give me some clue?"

Dalton sighed. "Supposedly, someone went missing, but they showed up alive recently."

"And who was this someone?"

"I can't say," said Dalton.

Paul shook his head. "Damn. Well, I'm thankful for that at least."

Brad figured Paul would hunt down any missing person reports after they left.

"No problem. Have a good day," said Dalton.

Dalton and Brad shook hands with Paul, then exited the office. Dalton gestured for Holly to follow them outside. After a minute, they reached a secluded area at the end of the parking lot.

"For the record…we do have cameras out here," said Holly.

"I understand," said Dalton. "This won't take long. Now…do you happen to heal fast?"

"What?"

"If you got an injury, have you noticed that you heal fast? Same with a cold or sore throat. Those don't stick around long, do they?"

She peeked back at the sheriff's office, then faced Dalton. "I just have a strong immune system."

"Not quite," said Dalton. "I'm going to be straight with you since your profile indicates you prefer that over beating around the bush. You're a Wildborn. You possess exotic energy that gives you a healing factor."

Holly wrinkled her brow. "A wild what? Are you being serious right now?"

"I am and for good reason. As you know, I'm with the Earth Ward. We deal with nonhumans…of which you are one. A Wildborn. I'm telling you this because while you may have gotten to this point in life, your type is generally hunted if not affiliated with the Earth Ward or another powerful group."

"Someone's hunting me? Or my family?"

Dalton shrugged. "They could be. You're in a unique position in that you have two large nonhuman groups in the area along with a sizable Faith Militia group."

She chuckled. "That's that dingbat group Derek's in."

"They kill nonhumans. If Derek discovered you were a Wildborn, he would send some slayers—what the Faith Militia calls their members—after you. They're humans, though, and generally, we call humans who know about nonhumans wisened."

Holly frowned. "He wouldn't…"

"He was outside our motel the other day, spying on us for them," said Dalton. He laid a hand on Brad's shoulder. "He verified it by checking his phone. Oh, this is Brad Washington. He's a Wildborn like you."

She scrutinized him. "You heal fast too?"

Brad smiled. "Nah. I talk to technology. That's how I read Derek's phone."

"You talk to technology," said Holly. She pulled out her cell. "All right, can you talk to this?"

Brad read her phone and found a text message. "Your husband, Mike, texted you at 8:42 a.m. and said, 'Hey, babe. Have a great day.'"

She checked her phone. "Wow, you got the time right, and your eyes…they went all blue or something."

"They usually do that when my ability is active. I can dim them, but it takes some effort."

"That's why you wore sunglasses in the office earlier."

He nodded.

Holly gazed at Dalton. "How did you know about my healing?"

His eyes glowed slightly. "I'm an evolved human, and I can see what someone is. I have an exotic energy in me, but it's different from what you and Brad have."

"This is a lot to take in," she said, looking down.

Dalton handed her a card. "This is for the Wild Haven Institute. It's in upstate New York, and it educates those new to the nonhuman and human world. I suggest you make the call and at least see what you're dealing with. If not for you, then for your family. On the back of the card is my personal number if you have questions."

He raised a finger. "And, yes, although we told Paul there was nothing here, there actually was. I won't go into details, but I would ask that you not mention any of this to Paul or your department. They don't need to become wisened."

She studied the card as she flipped it around in her hands. "I appreciate your being honest with me. I'm not sure I fully believe all of this, but I can't ignore what I've seen in the last five minutes either."

"I understand. From what I know, some Wildborn go crazy, but I'm banking that your no-nonsense approach to life will temper that," said Dalton. "Take your time, but don't wait too long. The sooner you're associated with the Earth Ward in any capacity, such as by taking classes at the Wild Haven Institute, the better."

"Okay." Holly smiled. "New York is a long flight."

"Not in a stealthed ship it's not."

Her smile faded. "Stealthed ship? Like an airplane?"

"Something like that," said Dalton. "Okay, our five minutes are up. Please make the call, and thank you for your time." He glanced at Brad. "Let's go."

As they walked away, Brad peered back. Holly studied the card. Her face indicated worry, but she seemed to handle it well. He understood it was a huge change in her perception of what was around her. He remembered learning about his ability, but he also recalled all the problems it brought.

After they got back into the SUV and took off, Brad glanced at Dalton. "You think she'll call them?"

"I do. Evot will let me know when."

Brad appreciated that Dalton looked out for Holly. He could have said nothing, but he went out of his way to help her. She might not believe yet, but he knew it would sink in, then become an itch that needed scratched. There would be a lot for her to learn, but by doing so, she would be protecting her family, and it would be safer for her to operate in a powder keg of a town with all its various groups.

Todd surveyed the clearing where everyone had gathered. The previous day had been good, and he enjoyed resting and hanging with his team. They had a good dinner, and everything almost seemed normal.

Today was a big day, and it was now 2:00 p.m. Everyone appeared ready for the meeting between the Ogben Coven and the Tanner Pack. High Priestess Kreelah came with Skylka and Ranasa, who stood off to the left. Todd was glad to see Ranasa, and she had smiled at him when they arrived. Jim brought Bog and Gary with him. They stood opposite the Ogben Coven. Bog was huge even without being transformed. Gary looked happy to be alive, and he had nodded at Dalton.

For the group's part, Dalton appeared relaxed, while Brad focused on Gizmo, which ran around the perimeter. Evot patrolled the sky and also was in her cat form on the ground. Valerie was her usual easygoing self, and Rick looked like he had a hard time believing he was there. That was understandable, as meetings like this were rare. Bog stared down Rick hard, and Todd suspected they had probably fought at some point.

Dalton raised his hands and cleared his throat. "I'm glad you all could attend this meeting. I know there's been an uneasy truce to some degree between both your groups, but I think it's in everyone's best interests to work together like we did on this last event."

Jim nodded. "To be fair, we didn't really do much other than give information and, of course, Gary helping you out on the demon world."

"He was a big help," said Skylka, smiling at Gary.

He winked at her.

Todd did not want to draw any conclusions, but he sensed chemistry between the two. It made him wonder what happened between them on the other side of the portal. Maybe a shared experience of being prisoners.

"Yes, Gary definitely helped," said Dalton. "The Kaz Lodat came in, expecting to commandeer the situation. We prevented that. As an Earth Ward representative, I want to open a dialogue between us. We'll have someone in town who you can contact for any Earth-Ward-related business, and I'll give you my personal contact information as well. I know there is no formal agreement between your groups, but I think now is the time."

Kreelah eyed Jim. "We're open to it."

"Yeah, same here," said Jim. "It's still hard to believe those demon bastards have a homeworld with some huge demon."

"Oh, they do," said Skylka. "Barguul was an ancient and powerful old one."

"He was an asshole," said Gary.

Everyone chuckled.

Todd liked Gary. He was down-to-earth and freely spoke his mind.

"Yes, he was," said Dalton. "Now, there are several things that will need to be discussed and hammered out. Once you both agree to a set of binding protocols, it can be formalized. Earth Ward can help arbitrate if necessary."

Jim grinned. "Be nice to not worry about what's allowed and what's not. It'll also make things a lot easier from a planning perspective."

Skylka nodded. "We plan to offer you a section of the forest for the Tanner Pack to operate in. In exchange, we'd like access to your supply network."

"I didn't know witches drank," said Jim, drawing his head back.

Ranasa laughed. "More than you know!"

Kreelah eyed her.

Ranasa looked away.

"Hell, that's not a problem," said Jim. "Plus, if those black-eyed demons come scurrying back, we can both put pressure on them."

"I agree," said Skylka. "It's also known you have some pull with the wisened in the local police department. That could be useful as well."

Dalton grinned. "It sounds like we have some things to discuss, then." He motioned at Evot, who swished her tail around his leg. "She'll record everything, and then we can produce documentation."

"That the hot chick from before? In your ride?" asked Jim. "I don't sense anything from her, like my crew outside the bar didn't."

Evot morphed into her human form. "Hello."

Valerie laughed as Jim, Gary, and Bog examined Evot.

She glanced at Dalton. "I'm a hot chick."

Dalton shook his head. "Yeah, you are. Let's focus on recording, shall we?"

"Of course," she said. She morphed back into her cat form.

Todd wrinkled his brow as he studied Brad. He was laser-focused on the other guys when they sized up Evot. Maybe Todd was seeing things that were not there, but Brad and Evot would actually be a good couple. With his ability to talk to technology, he would be able to interact with her in ways no one else could. Her ability to morph would probably help things too.

As everyone went over the details of the new agreement, Todd scrutinized the others. Valerie and Skylka talked, while Jim and Kreelah sat on the ground opposite each other and discussed various topics. Gary and Bog appeared to enjoy being out in the woods. Brad studied everyone, which Todd expected. Todd suspected Rick's silence was because he soaked everything in.

Dalton, as always, was the main person, and he sat between Jim and Kreelah. With Skylka and Ranasa in earshot and Bog and Gary nearby, it was a comfortable setting.

Ranasa walked over to Todd.

He grinned. "Hey."

She smiled. "Hey yourself."

"You're not doing any discussing?" asked Todd, gesturing at the others.

She shrugged. "That's not my role. I'm a defender."

He nodded. "I got ya."

"Do you?"

Todd's pulse quickened. In another place and time, he could see himself trying to gain her affection, but his focus was on making the best impression possible for the team. It would not hurt to maybe stay in contact. He did not know what the rules or regulations were for a witch to move around, but it was something he would look into.

Rick nudged him. "This is kinda wild."

"Yeah, and it's my first case too."

"You definitely earned whatever pay this is."

"And then some." Todd eyed Rick. "Maybe we could use some freelance help every now and then, or hell, you could just join the team."

"You got my number," said Rick. "As crazy as this was, I sorta enjoyed it."

"You would," said Todd as they slapped hands.

They laughed.

Todd glanced at Ranasa. "You think this new agreement between your coven and the pack will hold?"

"I do, actually," she said. "We've been operating on an as-needed basis, but this helps formalize things, and more importantly, it brings in a neutral third party, the Earth Ward. Dalton has shown that he works for the best interests of all, and despite whoever the Earth Ward might send down, he will be the face of the Earth Ward to Kreelah and Jim."

"I could see that," said Todd.

"You're part of a good team," said Ranasa.

"It looks like your defenders are a good team too."

She glanced off in the distance. "Yeah, but my team doesn't travel. New experiences will not be something common in my life." She sighed.

"You can take day trips or vacations, right?" he asked.

She shrugged. "I guess, but where would I go?"

Todd studied her. "You could come up and visit if you wanted. I'm not a socialite by any means, but I can show you around Louisville or wherever."

"You'd be willing to do that?"

He smiled. "Definitely."

Her smile made his heart thump faster. He could be playing with fire, but the thought of spending his whole life in one spot made his skin crawl. He grew up in a small town and understood the desire to go out and experience new things. As he got older, he enjoyed time in one spot. To be a part of Dalton's team meant he would be traveling a lot, and he was okay with that.

CHAPTER
TWENTY-ONE

It had been a day since Dalton had wrapped up the meeting between the Ogben Coven and the Tanner Pack. The team was back at Earth Ward headquarters. It was 1:00 p.m., and everyone seemed rested up. Dalton had already typed up his after-case report and sent it digitally, but those who assigned cases usually wanted an in-person update. He was fine with that.

As they approached Case Manager Dakris's office, Dalton went over the group's performance. Valerie was as advertised, and she was no stranger to unusual situations. She had adapted with ease, and when it came to fighting, her assassin instincts kicked in. It was no wonder she was as good as she was. He hoped she would stay on based on their previous discussion, but he would verify that after the meeting. She could have been appeasing him.

Brad had extended himself outside of his normal Earth Ward role. In addition to being a valuable asset, he had cleared any involvement of the team's presence in Southern

Ohio. Evot was happier with Brad around, and although she probably could not quantify why she was, he suspected she was intrigued by human relationships and had chosen Brad. That would be an interesting development to follow.

Todd's cool and calm manner made his leadership abilities shine. He had worked with the Ogben Coven and had gotten them to commit resources. No small feat for an ex-slayer who historically would have most likely tried to kill them. Dalton saw Todd as a second-in-command. His past did not bother Dalton, and if anything, it made him more qualified. Learning from your mistakes and adapting were good qualities to have.

The group paused outside Dakris's door.

"Great, this asshole again," said Valerie.

"Let's hope this is quick," said Brad.

Todd shrugged. "I'm sure Dakris doesn't want to see us either."

"Probably not," said Dalton. He knocked on the door.

"Come in," said a female voice.

They looked around at one another before entering.

Dalton's eyes narrowed. Director Kathy Sikowicz sat behind Dakris's desk. He was nowhere in sight.

"Please come in and sit," said Kathy.

They did so.

"Where's Dakris?" asked Dalton. He raised a hand. "Not that I'm complaining."

She smiled. "I figured. He's been reassigned. There have been complaints, and he made choices on cases that hinder them being resolved. Yours was not the only one."

Dalton nodded. "I see. I take it you received my after-case report?"

"Oh, I did!" said Kathy. "We're already getting someone ready to serve as liaison for the area, and…I can't believe you got the Ogben Coven and the Tanner Pack to talk to us."

"I think they always wanted to, but in order to save face, the offer had to come from us."

Kathy frowned. "But we did make the offer first, then made several others in fact."

"I talked to High Priestess Kreelah and Jim Duggan about that. Previous Earth Ward offers didn't have any meat on them," said Dalton.

"How so?"

"Well, we went down there and resolved the case. In addition, we rescued a Tanner Pack member and an Ogben Coven demigod. We removed a threat in the Kaz Lodat and also did some other adjustments digitally for them in regard to law enforcement information. Kreelah and Jim saw all this, and that is why they came to the agreement I sent. In essence, we had to prove ourselves to them first before they would come to the table."

Kathy's eyes narrowed. "I understand that. I guess maybe Dakris did more harm than we'll ever know. Sending the wrong person down there after they requested you is not only tone-deaf, but it showed a lack of respect for the Tanner Pack, which is something that put one of our agents in the hospital."

Dalton shook a finger at her. "Now you're getting it."

"Hopefully, the new liaison has some clue about the area," said Todd. "Otherwise, it's going to be a mess."

"I agree," said Kathy. "We'll make sure that they talk with Kreelah and Jim and whomever else you think we should."

Todd glanced at Dalton. "That should work."

Kathy grinned. "Your team performed well. I still can't believe this is your first mission with them." She studied Brad. "We're going to miss having you on other assignments, but I think you're where you should be."

"I like to think so," said Brad.

Kathy scrutinized Valerie. "And you're as fearless as the report mentioned. You jumped on a demon scout. I can't even fathom that."

Valerie laughed. "It was either that or be stranded up top. Killed two birds with one stone."

"I get it," said Kathy. She glanced at Todd. "And, of course, your contributions helped as well. You have the respect of the Ogben Coven. Not an easy feat for an ex-slayer."

He nodded.

"One last thing," said Dalton. "I would suggest setting up a monitoring station of some type near that portal area. Although I sealed it permanently, it's only the second time I've used that ability."

"You want to make sure it doesn't become unsealed. I get it," said Kathy. She tapped at a keyboard. "I've added a note."

Dalton nodded. "Anything else?"

She shook her head. "No, and I appreciate you coming in. I hope we can do more cases together in the future."

He stood and extended a hand. "Submit it through the normal process, and I'll take a look at it. If it comes from you, I'll give it a higher priority in terms of assessment."

She hopped up and returned his handshake. "Thank you." She shook hands with the rest of the team.

"Let's go," said Dalton.

After ten minutes, they were seated in the conference room where Dalton initially formed the group.

Dalton peered around the table. "Here we are. If you check your bank accounts, the contract money should be there." He glanced at Todd. "Have Rick send an invoice for his work, based on standard contractor market rates."

"He did it to help me out," said Todd. "I don't think he's expecting anything."

"Even so, he put his life at risk and deserves compensation. His payout won't impact the contract one," said Dalton.

Valerie whooped. "Money's there!"

"Sure is," said Brad. "That's a big step up from my normal pay."

Todd checked his phone. "Mine's there too."

"Good," said Dalton. "Now that that's out of the way, it's time for the big question: Who's staying on for the next case? I know I've already talked with each of you about this, but I want to make sure."

"You can count me in," said Brad. "I feel like for the first time in a long while, I have a purpose other than just trying to survive."

Dalton nodded.

"Well, this sure beats being a bouncer," said Todd. "I'm in too. Pay's good, work's interesting, and I sorta like you all."

The group laughed.

Everyone focused on Valerie.

She grinned. "No pressure, right?"

"I understand if you're having second thoughts," said Dalton. "I know you said you planned to stay on after our trip, but I wanted to verify it wasn't only to make me feel good. Not many would shrug off going to a demon homeworld."

She shrugged. "I still plan to be with the team, but there were lessons learned here, and I think we could be more efficient with better gear and equipment."

"Damn right," said Brad.

Dalton eased back into his chair. "Good. Then it's settled."

Evot walked in with three rectangular cardboard boxes, then placed one in front of Brad, Todd, and Valerie.

"Inside the boxes are your official cards, some swag, and some paperwork that needs filled out," said Dalton. "Essentially, everything needed to formalize your acceptance."

Valerie rifled through her box, while Todd studied his.

"Now, there is one last thing before we call it a day. Well, two, actually. The first deals with a base. As you may or may not know, the new regional Earth Ward headquarters is in Columbus, Ohio. The former base near there is abandoned or was until I claimed it. It has a parking garage, living quarters, conference rooms, communication ones, and the like. It's similar to a safe house in that regard but more expansive. I'll be staying there, and it's open to anyone who wants to as well."

"Rent-free?" asked Brad.

"Of course," said Dalton. "Oh, and there'll be some support staff for maintenance. It will also serve as a stopover for other inspectors and agents as needed."

"I'm in," said Brad, raising his hand.

"Yeah, me too," said Valerie. "If I'm going to stay somewhere for a while, may as well make it comfortable."

Todd cleared his throat. "I still plan to live at my house, but I can come up when we have cases or for whatever's needed."

"Excellent," said Dalton. "Evot will get you authentication cards, but the base does a bio-scan. Evot is also connected to it, so if you lose your card or whatever, you can talk to her directly."

"Evot's gonna spy on us!" said Valerie, eying her.

"I do not plan to," said Evot. "I only have access to the external parts of the base and, if Dalton allows it, internally in public spaces."

Valerie smiled. "I was teasing you."

"Of course," said Evot, nodding.

Dalton gestured at her. "Evot's right in that you don't need to worry about that. The only time I would turn on internal is if we had an infiltration in progress."

"Place sounds like it might be exciting," said Todd.

Brad nodded. "I'd settle for peaceful."

"All right," said Dalton. "Brad and Valerie can start moving in tomorrow. As for tonight, I wanted to bring you all to your first social event as a team."

"Where we going, chief?" asked Todd.

Dalton raised a finger. "To Lord Noskov's base in the Appalachian Mountains. There's a platform that sits on the side of a mountain, and he uses it not just as a landing pad for ships but also for cookouts. I wanted to introduce you all to them since they're close friends of mine. Evaran and the gang, as they're known, will be there too."

Valerie's eyes widened. "Ancient vampire base?"

Todd drew his head back. "*The* Evaran?"

Brad laughed. "I said that too." He focused on Valerie. "I think the ancient vampires want to clear the air with you."

"Sure…" said Valerie. "And we get to meet Evaran? That's crazy."

Dalton nodded. "I understand. We'll all be there, but if you get uncomfortable, I'll have Jake take you wherever you want to go."

"It's all right," said Valerie. "After this first case, I think I'm ready for whatever comes my way."

"Okay, then. We have a plan. Take a few hours to do what you need to do, then meet outside. Jake will be flying us out," said Dalton.

The others exited the room. It felt good to have a team again, although it was no Scoutspectre one. Dalton was okay with that, and the team had proven themselves already. Their first case had its ups and downs, but they persevered. He enjoyed their personalities, and Evot got along well with them.

It would probably be three weeks or so before the next case. He would need to spend some time determining which one would be a good fit for the team. If there were none, then they might do some of the smaller ones that still paid decently. He felt responsible for making sure the team was well cared for, and he vowed they would not have financial difficulties.

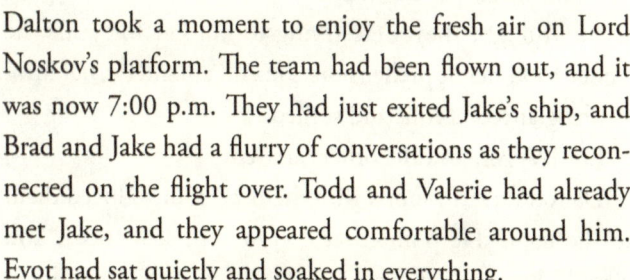

Dalton took a moment to enjoy the fresh air on Lord Noskov's platform. The team had been flown out, and it was now 7:00 p.m. They had just exited Jake's ship, and Brad and Jake had a flurry of conversations as they reconnected on the flight over. Todd and Valerie had already met Jake, and they appeared comfortable around him. Evot had sat quietly and soaked in everything.

The warm, light breeze stirred up memories of his original Earth. Burgers being grilled permeated the air with an odor he never tired of. Even the sounds of insects buzzing did not bother him. After being on a world made of basalt columns, sand, and lava, he was glad to be where he was.

He looked forward to seeing Lord Vygon, Lord Noskov, Mikhail, and Robert, Jake's father. This was where Dalton had first stayed when he arrived on this Earth six months ago. Since then, he had rented a place in Columbus, Ohio, to work from. He chose to live there to be within visiting distance of Dr. Snowden and Emily, Evaran's current traveling companions. Now Dalton would have a base to work from.

The sight of Lord Vygon and the others approaching relaxed him. He was glad to have a place to do these types of events. Lord Vygon and Mikhail wore their usual black armored suits, while Lord Noskov had on his black suit with a cape that had a red interior. All three had pale skin, but Lord Noskov's eyes were pure black, whereas the others' were not as much. Robert had on comfortable slacks and a short-sleeved button-down shirt.

Valerie's breathing increased.

Dalton figured she was still unsure of what to expect. If she thought they were trying to kill her for years, he understood her apprehension. He laid a hand on her arm.

She glanced at him and smiled.

Lord Vygon and the others arrived.

Dalton forearm shook with them, then introduced them to the team. He pointed at everyone in sequence. "You already know Brad Washington. Next to him are Todd Armani and Valerie Simmons. This is my new team, and we recently wrapped up our first case."

Lord Vygon stepped forward and extended a hand to Valerie. "We're sorry to hear about your sister. We want you to know that since you are the last Zikarian on the planet, we'll do everything in our power to protect you. Of course, joining Dalton's team might be hazardous."

Valerie smiled as she returned the handshake. "Thank you. It's been a wild ride so far."

"So we've read," said Lord Noskov.

Mikhail chuckled. "We're all vampires here, right?"

Valerie crooked a thumb at Todd. "Yep, and I brought dinner."

His eyes widened. "What?"

Everyone laughed.

Lord Vygon shook Todd's hand. "I think you're safe here. I read about your past, and I'm glad to see you're walking a different path now."

Todd nodded. "Me too."

Lord Vygon laid a hand on Brad's shoulder. "You've made a name for yourself due to your contributions to the Earth Ward."

"I try," said Brad, grinning.

Dalton pointed at another landing pad. "Evaran and the gang are here."

"I don't sense anything," said Valerie.

"Dalton's the only one who can since he's bonded to the *Torvatta*, which is stealthed at the moment, I'm guessing," said Brad.

As if on cue, the *Torvatta* decloaked.

Dalton smiled big when Evaran, Dr. Albert Snowden, Emily Snowden, and V in a holographic shell stepped out. Evaran had on his usual gray suit with armored pads. His pale skin contrasted with the suit, and his dirty-blond hair with a wave never moved. Dalton knew Evaran was old, but his human form appeared as someone in their mid-thirties. Dr. Snowden had on brown shorts and a button-up shirt, while Emily wore blue shorts and a T-shirt. V's holographic shell resembled an early twenties male.

The groups met up halfway to each other.

Dalton's and Evaran's eyes glowed when they forearm shook.

Evot and V high-fived.

Evaran looked around. "It is good to see you all, both new and old." He eyed Jake. "I am glad you could make it."

"Miss this event? No way!" said Jake.

"What he said," said Dalton. He introduced everyone.

Evaran extended a hand to Valerie. "Dalton suggested you may be interested in reconnecting with where you came from."

Valerie returned the handshake. "Maybe. We came to Earth for a reason, but perhaps it's changed since then." She wrinkled her brow. "How would you find out where I came from?"

He raised a finger. "I would travel back in time to your initial point of entry on the planet, then send a quantum beacon through before the portal dissipated. The *Torvatta* can then track it. Once that is done, we would visit there relative to this time. I can take video feeds if you wish to view them later."

"You can do that?" asked Todd, running a hand over his mouth.

"And then some," said Dr. Snowden, smiling.

Dr. Snowden and Emily shook everyone's hands.

V walked over to Todd and raised his hand for a high five.

Todd chuckled as he returned it.

V repeated that with the rest of the team.

"I'd like to see those feeds. Maybe not now but later," said Valerie.

Evaran nodded. "You can tell Dalton, and I will ensure it is done."

"I appreciate the option," said Valerie.

Evaran faced Dalton. "Your first case together was intriguing."

"Yeah, it was," said Dalton.

"A demon homeworld," said Emily, shaking her head. "And a portal to it here on Earth too!"

"It wasn't all it was cracked up to be," said Valerie.

Evaran half smiled. "It does not sound like it was."

Dalton motioned at the grill. "I'm sure Robert would like to introduce everyone to some good food and discussion." He waved a finger between Lord Vygon, Lord Noskov, and Evaran. "However, I'd like to talk with each of you."

Emily, Brad, and Jake sprinted to the grill. Valerie and Todd joined Dr. Snowden, Robert, and Mikhail and walked over. V and Evot formed cats and danced their way across the platform, which made the others laugh.

After they were alone, Dalton grimaced. "I wasn't expecting an alien world on this case."

"Especially a Kaz Lodat one," said Lord Noskov. "If an old one had crossed, we would be having some issues right now. Thankfully, the demons were still in the reconnaissance stage still."

"It's a good thing your portal abilities allow for permanent sealing, then," said Lord Vygon.

Evaran glanced at Dalton. "This is only the second use of that ability. Let us hope it holds."

Dalton sighed. "Yeah, definitely. I think there will be peace in that region, maybe the first in a long time, although the Faith Militia will always be a concern."

"You have done well so far," said Evaran. He peered back at the grill. "Your team seems competent, and they appear to have already bonded."

Dalton grinned. "Yeah. Hopefully not every case is as crazy as this one was. However, the more disturbing thought is that the timeline fractures we saw when I traveled with you allowed for the portal to be there in the first place. We know it opened once when the Kaz Lodat, or Dagothians, crossed over long ago. I don't think the recent opening was by accident."

Evaran rubbed his chin. "Yes. As they are part of the stable timeline, they will need dealt with as you come across them."

"You could just travel to the future and fix them all," said Lord Vygon, smiling.

"You know I cannot," said Evaran. He eyed Lord Vygon. "You are teasing me."

Dalton laughed along with Lord Vygon and Lord Noskov. Dalton loved Evaran's emotionless demeanor that lent itself to deadpan-like comedy at times.

"You will need to remain vigilant," said Evaran.

"I plan to," said Dalton. "We have a base now at least. It's within an hour of Dr. Snowden's house, so we may swing by every now and then."

"I look forward to it, and I suspect the others will to."

Lord Vygon gestured at Dalton. "You can host social events there. They have a nice platform that overlooks the nearby forest. It's not as isolated as this, but it works."

He nodded. "I think there's going to be a lot of cookouts in the future." He studied Lord Vygon and Evaran. "You two probably already know if there are."

"We couldn't say even if we did know," said Lord Vygon.

"Yeah, yeah, I know," said Dalton.

"Still, we are here if you need us," said Evaran.

Dalton grinned. "I know, but you all have your own things to do. I can handle these cases, especially now that I have a team."

He peered over at the grill. Everyone had split off into smaller groups. Todd, Dr. Snowden, and Robert laughed at something. Evot, V, Emily, Brad, and Jake discussed some topic. Dalton chuckled when Emily swatted Jake's arm. Mikhail and Valerie spoke off to the side, which intrigued Dalton. He wondered what they talked about, but she smiled and appeared more comfortable, so that was a good sign.

His gaze swept over Lord Vygon, Lord Noskov, and Evaran. Dalton was surrounded by the most powerful non-humans on the planet. That they trusted him to do what he did best made everything seem okay. He would try to do right by his team, and it felt good to introduce them to his close friends.

Their first case had been rougher than he expected, and he was not sure he would have been able to do it solo. Skylka or Gary could have died on the way out from the demon planet, or Dalton may not have even made it to the fortress. They all could have walked out of the portal and into a hailstorm of Kaz Lodat bullets. Although Dalton often studied his decisions in order to improve, creating a team was one he had no doubts on.

The Ogben Coven and the Tanner Pack would need to be monitored closely during the initial days of their agreement. The installment of an Earth Ward liaison would help with that. They would also have to monitor the portal area to make sure it was actually sealed. Local law enforcement would have questions as to where their data went, but that was to be expected wherever Earth Ward investigated.

He thought about Deputy Holly Combs. Hopefully, she would reach out for her family's sake. He would ask the liaison to keep an eye on her.

Evaran laid a hand on Dalton's shoulder. "You are deep in thought. Is everything okay?"

Dalton grinned. "It sure is. Let's get some burgers."

THE END

NOTE FROM THE AUTHOR

I hope you enjoyed *Otherworld*, Book 1 of *The Inspector Dalton Files* series! This book introduces the team Dalton will be solving cases with. He's been around for six months since *Transition*, *The Inspector Dalton Files* prequel and felt it was time to expand. Well, Evot did!

One of the big themes of the book was teambuilding. Brad, Valerie, and Todd got to show what they're made of. You may remember them from *Transition*. Things have changed since then, and now they have a team to rally around. I look forward to their journey as they become more experienced.

Another theme was to introduce a typical area with human and nonhuman factions. You have the Ogben Coven, the Daedrould, and various forest weretypes who are Outsiders. Then you have the Tanner Pack, a weregang made up of Outsiders. Between them is a town with a Faith Militia presence as well as wisened, humans who know of the nonhuman world.

And, as always, there is a case! In this scenario, it involved the Kaz Lodat, the demons of the Evaranverse. The case also introduced new concepts, such as holosketching, and more of Dalton's abilities, such as light pulsing.

As always, there are hooks to *The Evaran Chronicles*. Dalton summarizes his trip with Evaran in *The Time Cube, Book 11* of *The Evaran Chronicles*, and mentions some instances that occurred.

If you liked the book and have the time and inclination, a review would go a long way in helping out this indie author. If you do submit a review, I'll put in a word to Dalton should you find yourself on the Kaz Lodat homeworld! Want to be notified about new book releases? If so, you can sign up below.

WWW.ADAIRHART.COM/MAILINGLIST.ASPX

I will only send you emails about new book releases, major updates, and the occasional newsletter, usually once a month. I dislike getting spammed too, so I will use this sparingly to keep you in the loop.

ABOUT THE AUTHOR

I have been dreaming about fictional worlds since I was a kid. I devoured anything related to fantasy and science fiction. I developed a setting over the last twenty years and struggled to find a medium I could express it in. I discovered I enjoyed writing, and it is a passion of mine now. Exploring my setting through the written word has been an awesome journey.

I work in the information technology field and have my master's degree in it. It has helped me to shape some of the concepts I write about. I also enjoy keeping up on futurology and science in general.

I live in central Ohio and enjoy walking, reading, gaming, learning, listening to music, and trying to keep up on my never-ending list of TV shows and movies to watch. If you want to contact me, you can do so on my website at

WWW.ADAIRHART.COM

You can also reach me on

Facebook............................fb.com/AdairHart
Goodreads.....www.goodreads.com/AdairHart
Email..............Adair.Hart.Author@gmail.com

ACKNOWLEDGEMENTS

This was a great journey for me, but I wouldn't be here without the help of others. I would like to thank the following people in no particular order:

My editor, Miranda Miller. She continues to help me put my best foot forward, and I appreciate her guidance and help. With her assistance, I continue to grow and look forward to working more with her in the future.

My cover artist, Tom Edwards (tomedwardsconcepts@gmail.com), for an awesome cover. I wanted a team shot around a portal in the forest, and he made it look good.

My family and friends who helped encourage me along the way.

My proofreader, Alexa, for providing a professional service.

My formatter and interior designer, Colleen Sheehan (www.ampersandbookinteriors.com), for helping me make my pdf interiors shine.

BOOKS

You can see all books in *The Inspector Dalton Files*,
The Evaran Chronicles, and *The Earthborn* series at

WWW.ADAIRHART.COM/SERIES/ALLBOOKS.ASPX